Dolores J. Wilson

Barking Goats and the Redneck Mafia

Platinum Imprint
Medallion Press, Inc.
Printed in USA

Dolores J. Wilson

DEDICATION

To Marge Smith, aka, Elizabeth Sinclair, my valued critique partner and friend, who never hesitates to share her knowledge and her time.

Published 2006 by Medallion Press, Inc.

The MEDALLION PRESS LOGO
is a registered tradmark of Medallion Press, Inc.

Printed in the United States of America
Typeset in Times New Roman PS

Library of Congress Cataloging-in-Publication Data

Wilson, Dolores J.
Barking goats and the Redneck Mafia / Dolores J. Wilson.
p. cm.
ISBN 1-932815-63-5
1. Married women--Fiction. 2. Automobile repair shops--Fiction.
3. Georgia--Fiction. I. Title.
PS3623.I5784B37 2006
813'.6--dc22
2006012460

10 9 8 7 6 5 4 3 2 1
First Edition

ACKNOWLEDGEMENTS:

With special thanks to: My supercharged critique partners Vickie King, Heather Waters, Laura Barone, and Kat McMahon.

My husband, Richard, with love and appreciation for all you do.

Chapter 1

I never expected to spend my wedding night in a maternity ward.

"Mrs. Fortney, you'll have to calm down." Dr. Johns mumbled a few more words behind his mask, but I couldn't hear them because my mind was absorbing the *Mrs. Fortney* part.

I had acquired that name a mere three hours earlier in a wedding ceremony that would make any bride proud. Until then, I had been Roberta Byrd, Bertie to my friends. A life-long resident of Sweet Meadow, Georgia. Thirty-two years, to be exact. I'd worked in my father's garage and towing business, Byrd and Sons, since my early teens. A few months ago, Pop had turned the whole place over to me. Its newly painted sign proudly boasted *Bertie's Garage and Towing*.

Since then, my usually dysfunctional life was one pleasantry after another right up to the wedding. I was now Mrs. Arch Fortney. Bertie Fortney. At last, a name I could wear with honor as opposed to the one almost big mistake in my life where I would have married Lee Dew. I shudder each time I realize I could have been Bertie Dew.

Now, a few hours following my and Arch's "I do's," my teeth

chattered from the extremely cold delivery room inside Shafer County Hospital. Evidently, my screaming was a little disconcerting to Dr. Johns. He didn't understand this was my first birthing. I had no idea of the pain and agony one experienced to make the wonder of life happen. When I pressed my freshly manicured nails into the flesh of his arm, he ordered the nurse to remove me from the room.

"Out, Mrs. Fortney," the doctor demanded.

"Hey, hey, this can't happen without me." I exhaled an indignant huff. What was he thinking?

While I waited for the doctor to respond, I thanked God it wasn't me who was actually giving birth. It was my best friend in the whole wide world, Mary Lou Jarvis.

Today I married the love of my life, surrounded by my loved ones, and Mary Lou was my matron of honor. It was somewhere in the middle of the conga line she went into labor. Since we were old enough to dream of a husband and children, she and I vowed to be at each other's side when we gave birth.

So there I was, standing in the hallway with my back pressed against the door I'd just been shoved through. Banned from her delivery room because of over-wrought nerves. Running my hand over my beautiful, white satin wedding gown, I brushed away the wrinkles my slouching shoulders had caused. I was Mary Lou's best friend, and I was letting her down.

I'd cracked under the strain. While she showed nothing but the utmost decorum in her last stage of labor, I'd freaked out.

Determination stiffened my spine. I had to get back in there, beside my friend, cheering her on. Someone should knock me on my butt for being so self-absorbed.

I took two steps forward. My veil was caught in the door and sharply pulled me backward. In short order, I landed flat on my back-side. I wish God would quit taking everything I said so literally.

Just then, the door opened. "Bertie get in here. The baby's coming," Rex, Mary Lou's husband, called over my head. I scram-bled to my feet as quickly as the slipping crinolines, satin material, and highly waxed floor would let me. I swooshed into the delivery room and cocked a half-hearted smile at Dr. Johns. He shot me a full-hearted glare and stuck his head back under a sheet covering Mary Lou's spread legs.

Ten seconds later, he laid an alien on my friend's stomach. I glanced at Rex, who grinned wider than I'd ever seen, except for the time he won a trip to a Trekkie convention in Macon. Had all those sci-fi flicks he watched seeped into his wife's womb?

The doctor gave Rex a pair of scissors, and he cut the umbilical cord. I think he also cut the little fellow free from its mother planet, because, as the nurses wiped away the bloody, ashy covering, a baby boy appeared.

A nurse wrapped him in a paper blanket and stuck him in Mary Lou's arms. She pulled back the covering to look at her naked son.

"Ah, Mary Lou, he has your nose and your mouth and your chin," I said, amazed at how much the tiny person looked like his mom.

"Gee whiz, doesn't he have anything of mine?" Rex whined. Mary Lou stared at her baby. A mixture of fear and joy played across her face. She pulled the blanket further down to reveal his . . . lower parts. "Look, honey," she pointed, "he has your fixtures."

"Okay, we gotta weigh and measure him." A nurse plucked the

3

baby from Mary Lou's arms. She appeared to want to change the subject from Rex's fixtures.

Mary Lou looked up at me. "Thank you for being here with me."

I hugged my dearest friend. "I wouldn't have missed it for the world."

"Now go on your honeymoon." She fluttered her hand in a dismissive wave. "When you get back, bring your daughter over to play with Rex, the second."

My heart swelled to bursting. Mary Lou had a son, and I had a daughter. Petey. She was part of the wonderful package I'd gotten when I married Arch Fortney. His ten-year-old daughter had stolen my heart from the minute I met her. But over the last few months, we developed a mother-daughter relationship, with the extra added attraction of being friends.

I said goodbye to Mary Lou and Rex, aka Mommy and Daddy, and stole one quick glance at Little Rex, who wailed in protest to the sticking and prodding the nurses were doing to him.

Making my way to the waiting area, I found Arch sitting in his tux, leaning forward, resting his arms on his thighs. To the naked eye, he appeared to be in deep, prayerful thought. I knew he was sleeping. With my dress swooshing with every movement, I took a seat beside him. After a few seconds of me staring at his devilish profile, he woke up and smiled at me.

"It's a boy," I said.

"I know. Mary Lou and Rex's family have gone down to the nursery to wait to see him." He kissed my nose. "You look tired. Are you ready to go home?"

Home. My house was really a home now. "Yeah." He rose and

pulled me to my feet.

"Your mom put Petey to bed several hours ago. We'll go by and pick her up in the morning when we leave for our honeymoon."

There was never a spoken decision to take Petey with us on our honeymoon. It was just the most natural thing in the world to include her in the plans. Although we were supposed to leave immediately following the reception to go to Florida, one day's delay wouldn't hurt.

Arch and I headed to the house he'd grown up in. The house I rented after his father, Pete, was placed in a nursing home. The house where Pete's spirit had come to say goodbye the night he died several months ago. I'd been lucky enough to develop a relationship with Pete, the old goat. Although his presence is very strong throughout the house, it only serves to remind me how much I miss him.

But tonight, Arch and I would be home alone to consummate our marriage. Not that we hadn't already consummated it—many times and quite well, I might add—but on this night, Arch wouldn't have to slip out of bed and get home to Petey before she said her prayers. Yes, it would be a night to remember, if I could only stay awake.

The sun streaked ever so slightly through my bedroom window. Cuddled deep in the warm covers of my bed, a happy sensation inched its way from the tip of my toes to the top of my big hair. Yesterday I'd married the most wonderful man in the world.

The cold November air was nipping at the window, but I was

toasty and safe with Arch snuggled against my back. I reached behind me to run my hand along his body. He felt soft and squishy—like a pillow. I threw back the covers and sat up. The cold air assaulted my naked body. When had that happened? I shuffled through the covers like I thought I could have lost Arch in the rumpled mess.

Just then, I heard the front door open and footsteps running down the hall. Petey burst through the door. I snatched the tail end of a sheet and pulled it in front of me. It hid only a minuscule part of my body.

My newly-acquired daughter stopped and pointed. "Are you nekked?"

I gathered more material around me. Arch stepped into view behind her. He smiled widely, enjoying my "Bertie moment" as most people in Sweet Meadow referred to embarrassing happenings. I invented that recognition when I ran over a mattress, or was it when I got run over by an airplane? Or maybe—come to think of it, I'm not sure which mishap officially made my name synonymous with bad luck. I just knew I dragged it around like a dragon tail.

"Good morning, my dearest wife. Did you find my note?" Arch continued to smile like the cat that ate the canary. If he didn't stop enjoying my humiliation so much, canary would be exactly what he got for breakfast.

Petey jumped onto the bed. "Come on. Put your clothes on. We have a surprise for you."

I looked at Arch. "I told you that in the note." He plucked a piece of paper stuck to the back side of my arm and handed it to me. I read aloud, "I've gone to get Petey. Be dressed and ready to leave on our honeymoon. We have a surprise for you."

I pulled the sheet completely around me and made my way to the bathroom. Placing cool hands to my flaming face, I stared at my reflection in the mirror. My big hair, which Mary Lou had given me before my wedding, looked as if the mousse and hair spray had gone to war. My hair lost the battle.

Smudged mascara gave my eyes a lovely raccoon glow. Jeeze, I could have at least washed my face before going to bed. But, therein lay my problem. I didn't remember going to bed. My last conscious thought was riding from the hospital toward home with Arch at my side, and me filled with eagerness for our wedding night merriment.

Good Lord. I'd fallen asleep. Arch must have carried me to bed, heavy wedding dress and all. Bless his heart, he had to undress me. I glanced down at my naked body. He did that quite well and without waking me. Wonder what other talents he had I didn't know about?

A loud knock sounded against the bathroom door and reverberated through my throbbing head. "Please hurry. We're dying out here," Petey yelled.

"Okay, I'm coming." I showered and dressed in record time. My embarrassment at being caught naked was quickly replaced with anticipation for the surprise my husband and daughter had for me.

Petey shoved me down the hallway to the front room. "Open the door."

I did. There in my driveway sat a motor home. I'd never been in one, but I'd towed a few into local garages when they'd broken down.

This one wasn't big, but it wasn't small. It wasn't old, but it wasn't new. It was "A motor home?" My voice cracked.

"Yeah, we're going to travel all the way to Florida in it. We'll stay in campgrounds and have cookouts and do all kind of things. Isn't it terrific?" Petey was so delighted I couldn't very well dampen her joy, but the truth was I'd never really gotten the whole concept of RVing.

It looked like a lot of work, which I thought was what you wanted to get away from while on vacation. But who was I to question something I didn't know anything about, and something that brought so much happiness to Petey? It was part of being a mommy.

"It was ready to go after the reception last night," Arch said. "Your mom packed it with food and made sure we had everything we'll need. I loaded our suitcases this morning. Let's go." His enthusiasm matched his daughter's.

I marched to the home that would take me away from my home. The death march was playing somewhere in the back of my mind.

Petey climbed in first. I followed close behind. Arch slammed the door and made his way to the driver's seat. Petey dumped a box of crayons onto the dinette table and began coloring. I climbed into the passenger seat at the front.

Pivoting in my seat, I looked to the back of the compact coach. There seemed to be everything one would need to face the camping world. Refrigerator. Stove. Sink. A bed way in the back. Television. All the comforts of home. Maybe I'd been a little hasty in thinking this wasn't a good thing.

I looked back at Arch who was studying the instrument panel as if he was the pilot of a 747. "All systems go?" I asked.

"Huh? Oh, yeah. Just checking it out." He cranked the engine, and we were off.

"Where did you get this?"

"I borrowed it from another teacher at school." Arch pulled onto the main highway. "Jed and his wife and three kids use it all the time."

I looked around one more time. "What do they do, hang the kids on nails?"

"This is a fine coach, and it holds a lot more than you think. They gave me lessons." Arch reached across the aisle and took my hand. "Don't look so worried. This will be the experience of a lifetime."

That's what I was afraid of. We'd only known each other seven months. He knew so little about me, especially my lifetime experiences.

"I'm hungry." Petey had been coloring for about thirty minutes.

"Me, too." I leaned back in my seat and waited for Arch to pull into a drive-thru. After a few seconds, I realized he was staring at me; at least as much as he could and still keep his eyes on the road. I looked around at Petey. She was staring at me, too.

"What?"

"Well, we packed food so we could eat on the road." Arch smiled.

"Yeah, Grandma packed oatmeal. I like oatmeal." Petey started calling my mother Grandma the minute Arch and I decided to get married.

A knot twisted in the middle of my stomach. My mother didn't believe in instant anything. If she'd packed oatmeal, it would be the long-cooking kind. I didn't do long-cooking.

"That sounds good to me." Arch squeezed my hand and released it.

"You mean you want me to cook oatmeal in here? Now? Are

you at least going to stop?"

"Naw, Jed says his wife—actually he calls her his old lady—cooks while they're going down the road." My new husband twisted his face and snickered. It wasn't a pretty sight.

Balancing on unsteady legs, I walked back to the clean and orderly galley area. From under the sink, I pulled a pot which looked about the right size for oatmeal. Turning on the faucet, I waited for water to magically appear. It didn't. I pushed the lever open as wide as it would go.

Yippee! "We don't have any water." I'd been saved.

"Oh, you have to turn on the pump. See that white button on the wall behind the sink? Flip it on," Arch called over his shoulder.

I did as instructed. Click. Water spewed from the tap with so much force it knocked the pan into the sink and sprayed water all over the cabinet, onto the floor, all over me and Petey and I think some went as far as the driver's seat.

"Damn." I hurried to turn off the water.

Petey covered her mouth and giggled. "Mommy said a bad word."

"Everything okay back there?" Arch's inquiring mind wanted to know.

"Yeah, it'll just take a second to clean this up." First, I dried water from Petey's hair. "I'm sorry I said that. Sometimes I have a trash mouth, but I'll try to do better." Petey giggled again.

I wiped almost every inch of the kitchen. Then started on my oatmeal mission again. I set the filled pan onto the flame and stood next to the stove to make sure the pot didn't slide. Once the water started to boil, I poured in the carefully measured oats and stirred as directed on the box.

We were traveling smoothly and safely down the highway. Beautiful Georgia scenery whipped by the windows. Arch had turned on the radio, and Alan Jackson sang "It's Five O'clock Somewhere." Petey was putting away her crayons and water-spotted coloring book. I was cooking breakfast for my little family. All was right with the world.

Standing by the stove, looking out the front windshield, I saw a small car dart from a side street into our path. Arch used a tactical maneuver, swerving to the right and bumping over the curb. I'm not sure what he did next, because the pot of oatmeal slid from the stove, hit the floor with a thud, and erupted like a geyser. Gummy matter hit the roof, kitchen cabinets, the vinyl floor covering and, of course, my hair.

"That's gonna leave a mark." Petey wiped oats from the table.

"Damn." I covered my mouth. "Sorry, I've got to do something about my trash mouth."

Petey snickered.

Arch had gotten our tank under control and back on the road. "Everyone okay?"

"Yeah, I'll just be cleaning this up now." While I wiped down everything from ceiling to floor, my loving husband pulled into McDonald's and bought breakfast for us. That was all I wanted him to do to start with.

A few hours later, we were cruising southbound Interstate 75 singing "A Hundred Bottles of Beer on the Wall" when I realized I needed a pee break. "Can we stop at the next bathroom?"

"We don't have to stop," Petey said. "You can go while we're going down the road. Mr. Marshall showed us how to step on the pedal to flush it. Huh, Daddy?"

"He sure did, pumpkin." Arch looked at me. "That seemed to be the highlight of our demonstration for Petey. We are fully self-contained. We have our own water tanks and holding tanks and gas tanks. You just need to be careful not to waste the water." He winked at me. "You know, like throwing it all over the place."

I swatted him on the arm and then kissed him on the lips. He jerked back and shoved my head from in front of his face. "I can't see the road and kiss you at the same time. However, if you'll give me a minute, I'd be glad to pull over."

"Just for a kiss?" Petey stuck her tongue out and made a face. "Yuck."

"What'd you mean 'yuck'?" I grabbed her sweet little face and planted kisses all over her cheeks and forehead. We both laughed out loud.

Arch's cell phone rang. "Oh, hi, Jed." Arch drove the big piece of machinery with one hand and juggled his phone with the other. A man of many talents.

"No, I haven't seen it yet. Buddy, huh? Okay, I'll let you know." Arch was still talking into the phone, but I was scooting to the bathroom.

I made my way down the aisle to a small door—very small door—and opened it to peek inside. Sure enough, there was a toilet facing to the front of the coach and a small sink with a mirror over it. Compressed, but functional. I backed in, closed the door and pulled down my pants. After I plopped onto the seat, I pulled back a curtain covering a shoulder-high window. It was kind of cool speeding along the highway, watching towns go by and using the bathroom, all at the same time.

A tour bus loaded with sightseers cruised past us. A couple of them waved. I waved back. They didn't have a clue what I was doing.

Something moved near my feet. I looked down. Fear gripped my throat. Somehow I managed to open the door, jump from the bathroom in one leap, and scream at the top of my lungs, all in one movement.

"Mommy's nekked again, Daddy," Petey announced.

Before the chills had finished piggy-backing their way through every fiber in my body, and before I could get my pants up, Arch had already pulled to the narrow shoulder of I-75. He slammed the vehicle into park. Shutting off the engine, he strolled back to me.

"I take it you found Buddy."

"Well, if Buddy is a six-foot boa constrictor, he's in there." I pointed to the tiny door.

Arch had the nerve, or lack of good sense, to laugh at me. Pushing me aside, he opened the bathroom door, stuck his hand in and pulled out a tiny, green snake. Okay, so terror plays tricks with your mind.

"Just get the damn thing out of here."

"Trash mouth," he and Petey said at the same time.

She and I both gave her dad and Buddy a wide berth. Once outside, my knight in shining armor—or, in Arch's case, khaki shorts and a T-shirt—set my dragon free on the side of the road. He slithered down the embankment. The snake, not Arch. He came back inside and, in short order, we were under way again.

"Jed called as you were going in there to say his son had let his pet snake loose yesterday while they were cleaning the coach for us."

"But, you just let him go." I had a frog one time and my brother Bobby sat on it. It broke my heart. Now we'd just set an innocent child's pet free.

"Jed said to let it go. He'd been planning on putting it back into the woods anyway. Did you want to keep it in here until we get back home?"

I shuddered. "Uh, no." I shuddered again.

No wonder Jed called his wife his old lady. I bet she was young before they bought the RV. Was all this a test? Like an endurance thing all women had to take before they were truly wives? Was I passing or failing? Let's see. There was the water torture, the baptism by oatmeal, and then the reflex exam to see if I could run, scream, and pull up my pants all at the same time.

I leaned back against the passenger's seat and closed my eyes. Thank goodness our marriage couldn't be annulled. Or could it? I still didn't know what had gone on in our marriage bed the night before.

Late in the evening, we arrived at a campground near Perkin's Park, an amusement center north of Lake Okeechobee. There were no further incidents to report. Thank you very much. While Arch worked outside the motor home hooking up hoses and drain tubes, I made three bologna sandwiches and opened a bag of chips. After we'd eaten, Petey disassembled the dinette and turned it into a bed just like Jed had shown her. Arch opened closet doors and turned the hallway into a shower/dressing room. I placed a cutting board over the sink and turned it into counter space. We were like magicians, working our magic.

I tucked Petey into her bed. "Mommy?" She scooted over and patted a place next to her. I sat and pushed her hair back from her eye. "Do you think my other mommy can see me?"

A lump rose in my throat. "Of course she can, and I'm sure she's very proud of what she sees." Nola, Arch's first wife and Petey's mother, was killed in a car accident when her daughter was only three months old. I happened to have picked up Nola's car after the accident. The EMTs were loading her into the ambulance, and I heard her call for her baby. Many years later, I met Arch and learned I was one of the last people to see Nola alive.

Petey used the pad of her thumb to wipe a tear teetering at the edge of my eye. "Do you think she's happy you're my mommy now?"

"I hope so. I'll be the best mother I can. Maybe in some way she'll guide me so you grow up to be everything she'd ever want you to be." I needed all the help I could get. Even if it came from the spirit world.

"Know what I want to be when I grow up?" Petey's huge green eyes sparkled in the dim light of the coach.

Maybe she'd want to follow in my footsteps and some day I could pass the garage and towing business on to her. "What do you want to be, sweetheart?" Giddy expectation bubbled its way through me.

"I want to be a belly dancer."

Cough. Hack. Cough. "Oh . . . that's nice." My ego flattened like hours old coke. Out of necessity my mommy mode kicked in. "That's wonderful, dear. How did you come to that conclusion?"

"I think it would be fun to jump around and shake my booty. And wouldn't I look cute with a ruby in my bellybutton?"

"Oh, great. Okay, bedtime." I kissed her forehead and turned out the light.

In the bedroom, I changed into my lacy nightgown and slipped gently into bed next to my husband of one full day. "Petey wants to be a belly dancer when she grows up," I whispered into Arch's ear.

"That's nice," he mumbled into his pillow, so softly I could barely hear him. He shifted his position and began to snore loudly.

I eased his face back into his pillow. It muffled the buzz-saw noise coming from his nose. "That's better. Nighty night." Curling against his back, I inhaled his freshly-showered scent and knew I was in the most wonderful place in the world with Arch and Petey.

"Wake up, you two sleepy heads. It's time to go to the park." Petey jumped onto the bed and landed between her father and me. Perkin's Park had several employees dressed as characters from the famous television show *Perkin's Playhouse*. My darling daughter did not want to miss an opportunity to see any and all of them. "You promised we'd go early to see Buford Beaver."

"What time is it?" Raising my head I could see the red clock numbers glowing in the dark. "It's five o'clock." She pulled on the covers. I tugged back. "We have to hurry so we can be there first to see him."

Arch groaned and covered his head. "No self-respecting rodent is up at this time of the day."

"He's not a real rodent. He wears pants," Petey countered.

I pulled her against me to hug and stifle my daughter all at the same time. "I doubt Buford has his pants on at this time of the morning. He probably isn't awake yet. I need some more sleep." I stroked her hair. "You, too. Sleep. You are getting sleepy." I did my hypnotist impersonation.

She rose slightly. The light from the coach's dining area illuminated her sweet smile.

"Okay, but only thirty more minutes." She laid her head on my shoulder. It was my turn to groan.

Luckily, I went right back to sleep. After what seemed like only a few minutes, I opened my eyes and glanced at the clock. It was eight-fifteen. Petey lay sleeping on my arm which was filled with prickly needles. I couldn't move it if I tried.

"Hey, it's time to go." Petey sat straight up and the blood in my arm started to circulate again.

"We're late. I knew we'd be late." Petey scrambled off the bed.

Arch rolled to a sitting position and hung his legs over the edge of the bed. "Calm down, Miss Muffet. We're on vacation. We can't be late because we don't have a certain time to be anywhere. That includes seeing Buford Beaver. He'll be there all day. I assure you."

Petey was already getting dressed. So was I. It wasn't every day I got to see a walking, over-grown beaver with my daughter.

We were in the park only a few minutes when sure enough Buford Beaver strolled toward us. He waved his huge tan hands at Petey who giggled with delight. She and I hugged close to him while Arch took our picture.

"Say cheese," he said.

Arch finally got his picture, thanked Buford, and we started to leave. It was a happy family moment. Petey turned back to him. "Are you a self-respecting rodent?"

Jeeze. Isn't it amazing how quickly things can turn sour?

"Did you have your pants on at five o'clock this morning?" she asked.

Buford took two steps backward in mock surprise. He was about to step on a small child. I reached out to grab him, lost my footing and fell into the soft, over-sized rodent.

Buford Beaver and I both went down for the count. I scrambled to my feet and offered him a helping hand which he refused. By the time he got up, his tan hands were dirty, he had a bent tail, and one of his bucked teeth was broken.

"Are you okay?" I asked, unsure what I could do.

He held his hands up in a don't-touch-me motion. The last time I saw him he was limping away. Along with several spectators gathered around, Arch was doubled over with laughter. The little boy who I'd saved from being trampled pointed at me, and asked, "Hey, Dad, why'd that lady tackle Buford Beaver?"

"I don't know, son. Maybe she forgot to take her medicine like Grandma does sometimes." The man took the child's hand and strolled away. I wished I had big tan hands so I could hide my heated face. Or maybe I would use them to punch Arch so he'd quit laughing.

Chapter 2

The sun shone warm and bright on all the beautiful winter flowers decorating the grounds of Perkin's Park. Many hours and several rides following my unfortunate mishap with Buford Beaver, we had a chance to interact with another character, Dufus, an over-zealous Saint Bernard. Evidently, Buford hadn't warned him about me. Dufus was friendly and well . . . a dufus. He had a small pad of paper in his hand to do autographs, and for a short moment, I had an unexpected vision. He reminded me of Mildred Locke, the head waitress at the Chow Pal Diner.

Even Dufus' walk as he sauntered away brought Mildred to mind.

"Do you know who Dufus looks like?" Out of nowhere Arch asked this question. We must have had the same revelation at the same time.

"Mildred Locke?"

Arch closed his eyes and shook his head. When he reopened them he set me straight. "No, I was going to say a hound dog my dad got me when I was six. However, I'm curious why you thought of Mildred."

Dufus was strolling a little way ahead of us. "Well, she takes clod-hopper steps. Her tail wags to and fro. Of course, it isn't as long as Dufus'. Not quite anyway. Her hair is more gray, but she does have a lot of it covering her body."

Arch chewed thoughtfully on his bottom lip and watched the character disappear out of sight.

"I'm right, aren't I? Mildred Locke looks just like Dufus."

Arch didn't answer, but the smile tugging at the corners of his mouth told me I was right.

On the third day, Arch, Petey, and I had a chance to meet Darien the Dragon. I started to join Petey next to him so we could have our picture taken. DD shook his head and motioned for me to take the camera and to have Arch in the picture instead. At first I thought maybe Buford had spread the word about me. But, as the dragon limped away I had a sneaky suspicion the employees wore different costumes on different days. Surely I hadn't maimed him for life.

We arrived home on Wednesday evening in time to unpack and eat dinner. Before we left, Petey's teacher gave her several assignments my new daughter would have to complete before she returned to her class on Thursday. After she finished the last few pages of her reading assignment, I joined her on the sofa and asked her the questions at the end of the chapter.

"Who owned the boat?"

"Dotno," Petey answered.

"What do you mean 'you don't know'? You just read it."

"No, that's his name. Dotno." I flipped to the back of the book. Sure enough, she was right.

"Where were they going in the boat?"

"To the bottom of the sea?"

At this point, I became very intrigued with the story and asked a question not at the end of the chapter. "Why were they going to the bottom of the sea?"

"Because they just crashed into another boat, and they were sinking. Are we done now?" Petey's eyes twinkled. I reached across the kitchen table and tweaked her nose.

"You are such a smarty pants. If you're sure you know all the answers to these questions listed here," I pointed to the page, "then, yes, we are through. Go take your bath and get ready for bed. When you come out, I'll fix you a snack."

Petey traipsed off toward the only bathroom in our small house. Just before our wedding, Arch and I cleaned the spare bedroom where I had stored many of my unopened boxes since the day I'd moved into the house on Marblehead Drive. Petey helped me decorate so it could be her room after her dad and I married.

Arch was raised in the house and his mother had died there. His father, Pete, lived there until he could no longer take care of himself. Arch had moved his father into the Tall Pines Nursing Home a short distance down the road. On several occasions, Pete had escaped from the nursing home, pulled a key from a hiding place, and let himself into my home. I got to know him quite well on those little trips.

I never told anyone this, but the night Pete died, he came to me either in a vision or a dream or whatever that was that left me a scared mass quivering in my bed. He told me he'd tell my dearly departed Nana Byrd that I said hello. I think there might have been a puff of smoke, and he was gone. It still creeps me out a little, but also warms my heart to know he thought enough of me to say goodbye.

Arch, my wonderful husband, sat at the kitchen table putting the finishing touches on his lesson plan for his eighth grade science class from which he'd taken a three day hiatus for our honeymoon. I watched him from the living room. Happy butterflies wiggled and niggled inside me. The next morning Arch would be back at a job he loved. Last year, he'd been named Teacher of the Year, so he must also be good at it.

I knew for sure he was good at showing me and Petey how true and full of love his heart was. Rising from the sofa, I walked into the kitchen and placed my hands on his shoulders.

"I'm almost through here." Arch turned his head and rubbed his check against my hand.

"No hurry. I just couldn't keep my hands off you another minute."

As his lips grazed my fingers, I planted a kiss on top of his head. Leaving him to finish his work, I walked to the kitchen window facing the home of the craziest, yet best neighbor I have.

Rick and Barbie Jamison kept their lawn perfectly manicured and were always willing to lend a helping hand at a moment's notice. Rick is an accountant and Barbie is a . . . well, she's a fruitcake. Bless her heart. You've heard of people marching to a different drummer. Well, Barbie skips through life leaving everyone in her wake with nervous twitches. I'm proud to call her friend, which should tell you a little about my life.

Looking out the window, I could see the end of a beautiful

sunny day coming to a close. Pink and yellow light streaked across a slightly cloudy sky and dimmed with each passing minute. Barbie came out her front door and across her lawn toward my house.

A huge oak tree stands stately between our yards. Every evening about this time Barbie goes to that tree, climbs to a large branch and takes her place on an old tractor seat. That is her haven. On several occasions, I've joined her. It's quite relaxing to sit up there and watch the active neighborhood buzz by and not even know it's being watched.

Tonight, Barbie didn't make her usual stop at her tree, and for the first time I noticed she carried a container. Since she was walking to my front door, I hurried to open it. "Hi, Barbie." I gave her as much of a hug as I could without knocking from her hands what appeared to be a cake carrier.

"Come in. You did such a beautiful job decorating for our reception. I don't know how I'll ever repay you."

"Oh, I loved doing it. It was the most fun I've had in a long time. Here." Barbie shoved the plastic container at me.

"What'cha got?" I took it from her.

"I made you something to remind you of your honeymoon." Barbie giggled and jumped up and down. I thought she might wet her pants.

Setting the container on the end of the table not occupied by Arch, I hurried to look inside. There I found a cake in the shape of a . . . well, it was in the shape of a penis. A green penis. A green penis with a hole in the side of it. A piercing, perhaps? Confused and slightly embarrassed, I stared at it for a long time. I'm not sure what I thought it was going to do, but that's all I could do. Just stare.

Petey came up behind me. "What's that?" Her sweet voice startled me. I slammed the lid closed. Arch looked at me, a smile lining his lips. Poor man, he had no idea how embarrassed he was about to become. Barbie clapped her hands, giddy with excitement. Before I could object, Petey snatched the container open. I cringed. My face flamed. We all stared into the container.

"Cool," Petey cried. "A cake in the shape of Florida. Look," she pointed, "there's Lake Okeechobee. Can I have a piece for my snack?"

My heart dropped to my stomach and bounced about three times, like it was on a trampoline. I must have made a choking sound because everyone looked my way. I hustled to get plates to serve the green thing. Arch came up behind me and reached into the drawer to take out forks for us all. He leaned to whisper in my ear, "I know what part of our honeymoon that reminds you of. I'll remind you again in a little while."

I nudged him with my elbow. "I'll remind you to remind me."

I returned to work the next morning full of anticipation of what my day would hold. I'd worked for my father in our family business as a hired hand, more or less, until a few months before when Pop decided to retire and turn the business over to me. I returned from a short vacation and found he had given the building's exterior a make-over. He also changed the name from Byrd and Sons to Bertie's Towing and Garage. Each time I think of how I felt when I first saw the place with my family and friends standing in the parking lot, my heart melts and my eyes blur.

Pop still putters around the garage when the mood strikes him, or if we get slammed with business. Mostly he hangs out in the private office he had for thirty-five years, napping on the old sofa until Mom or I wake him up.

It felt good to be back at work. I never knew what my day would entail, but it always held the possibility of being unique. Loosely translated that means weird. Pop hadn't shown up yet, but Linc, the man who'd worked with us for several months, was washing the tow truck.

"Welcome back, Miss Bertie." He waved a wet soapy rag in the air and water splashed onto his coveralls. "Or should I call you Mrs. Fortney now?"

"Just make it Mrs. Bertie." I went inside the building and then stopped to watch him through the huge picture window. I like Linc. He's tall and lanky and always looks a little confused. He moved to Sweet Meadow from Atlanta where he worked for Craig Towing. Mr. Craig had a daughter he thought would make Linc a perfect wife. Linc didn't agree. So, lucky for us, they parted ways. Since he came to work with us, he'd been a loyal and trustworthy employee.

After he finished cleaning the truck, he came inside. "Got any jobs for me this morning?"

I moved behind the counter and shuffled through a few repair orders. Finding one, I handed him the paper. "You can start on the Dodge pickup. Here's the order Pop wrote up. Let me know what parts you need." Linc loped into the garage.

I picked up the phone to call Mary Lou, but when I put the receiver to my ear there was no dial tone. "Hello?"

"Bertie?" Millie Keats spoke in an unusually soft voice.

"Yeah, Millie."

"What's wrong with you? Don't I deserve a good morning?" Sarcasm abounded. That was the Millie we all knew and loved.

"Of course you do. Sorry. Good morning. Bertie's Towing and Garage. May I help you?" I can be pretty cynical when the need arises.

"I need a ride to the beauty parlor. My doo is a don't today." Millie could also be pretty funny.

"Would it do me any good to plead to your good nature and tell you I don't have time to take you? Today's my first day back from my honeymoon, and I'm really backed up."

"Well, send that little hottie that works for you." She referred to Linc. Through the window looking into the garage, I stole a glance at him curled under the hood of the pickup he was working on. Hottie? I didn't see it. The last time I sent Linc on a Millie run she scared the poor guy so badly he threatened to quit if hauling her carcass around was part of his job description.

"Okay, I'll be there in a few minutes. I'll drop you off, but you'll have to get someone else to pick you up. Is that a deal?"

"All right. All right. Jeeze, Bertie, you act like I got nothing better to do than spend my time finding someone to take me places." Millie hung up without a goodbye, kiss my foot, or drop dead.

I rubbed my eyes with my fists and took several deep breaths. Millie was a force to be reckoned with. She was demanding, self-centered, and old. I respect old people. Of course in Millie's case, I know what she's capable of. Therefore, I just plain feared her.

I told Linc where I was headed and jokingly asked if he'd rather go get Millie. He bolted upright and hit his head on the hood. "No.

I don't wanna go. Please." His voice cracked.

"Calm down. I'm just kidding." With shaking hands, Linc went back to work. Millie had evidently traumatized the poor guy. I should be ashamed of myself taking such pleasure in someone else's misery. An evil laugh threatened to erupt from inside me. I hurried on my way.

I collected Millie and drove her to the Curl Up and Dye hair salon located in the middle of Sweet Meadow. All the way there, she babbled about how good it felt to do her duty for women everywhere. "Even if the woman is that heathen Donna. At the end of the day, we are all sisters, and we must stick together."

I didn't really want to know what connection Millie had with Donna. The phrase "let sleeping dogs lie" seemed very appropriate where Donna was concerned. As Millie slid from the tow truck seat, two Garden Club ladies rushed to the door of the salon to greet her.

"I told Donna," Millie called to them. They all giggled like school girls.

As Millie headed to the door, I yelled, "Hey, you could at least give me a tip."

"Wear goulashes in muddy weather." She snorted and disappeared inside.

On my way back to the garage, I was traveling along highway 440 and had just passed the Stop and Flop Motel when a woman raced from a stand of trees next to the road. Even though she waved wildly, jumping up and down, and had twigs sprouting from her hair, I instantly recognized Donna Carson. Screeching my tow truck to a stop a good fifty feet away, I waited for her to catch up.

She yanked open the door and climbed in. Gasping for air, she clutched her chest and wheezed, "Go. Follow that car."

"Who do you think I . . . ?"

Donna smacked me on the shoulder, and I stomped the gas. "Which car?"

"The red truck turning left up there." Donna panted and pulled small pieces of trees from her hair.

"Oh, *that* car. Why didn't you say so? And why are we chasing it?"

"Udell's in there." Udell is Donna's husband and father of her three darling brats.

She stuck her leg over the transmission hump in the floorboard and tramped on top of my foot causing my vehicle to lunge forward like a cat with its tail on fire. And I would know about such things. I have two brothers.

As luck would have it, Chief of Police Bob Kramer cruised past us. If he tried to pull me over for speeding, I wasn't sure Donna would let me stop, and there'd be a high-speed police chase. I couldn't chance that, so I flipped on the wrecker's beacons. Chief Kramer would think I was hurrying to an accident and leave me alone. It was only a small lie because if I didn't get my truck under control, there was going to be a for-real accident.

"Stop it, Donna." I shoved her leg away and slowed down a little in time to make a turn onto Franklin Street. I only took up half of the on-coming lane, causing Martha Dandridge to swerve to the curb. "Why are we chasing Udell?" I demanded.

"He was at the motel with Joline Thomas. Millie called to tell me he was there. I was slipping through the woods to catch him when he came out of the room and got into his truck. I didn't have

28

time to get back to my car to go after him." She pointed ahead. "Hurry, he's getting away.

Udell's red truck was a good quarter mile ahead of us. I could have caught him, but I didn't want to watch Donna murder her husband. I didn't have time to go to court as a witness or to jail as an accomplice. I stayed at a safe distance, but gave the impression we were in hot pursuit.

Udell threw a piece of paper from his truck. It flew at us and wrapped around my antenna. I reached out the window and pulled it inside. Donna snatched it from my hand.

"You can stop now," she said.

I pulled to the side of the road.

"This paper gives me all the proof I need that Udell's been cheating on me. That good for nothing son of a shish kebob." She slumped back against the seat.

"What is it?" I'd be lying if I said I wasn't dying to know.

"It's the receipt for the motel room. He paid cash." Her voice quivered. Was Donna going to cry? I've known her all my life and have never seen her cry. "He is such an idiot."

Good. At least she wasn't crying.

"He registered under the name of Smith . . . Udell."

The Carsons had never been known for their intelligence. As a matter of fact, Udell's brother once stuck a hand gun down his pants and then practiced his quick draw.

You're way ahead of me, aren't you? That's right. Udell's brother's family is jewel-less.

At the end of the day, Linc pulled the huge overhead garage doors down and locked them for me. I'd already put the money into a tiny safe we'd used for years and was ready to leave when he did. Since he was on duty that night, Linc drove the wrecker to his house. I walked next door to my parents' home to get Pop's car keys. I drove his car on nights I wasn't on duty.

From the front door, I could hear Mom talking in the kitchen. I moved down the hall toward the sound of her voice. "Oh, sweetheart, she's here right now." Mom looked my way and shoved the phone in my face. "Say yes, Bertie."

"Yes."

She put the receiver back to her ear. "See, I told you. See you soon. Love ya." She hung up.

I snagged a cookie from a cooling rack. "What did I agree to?" I bit into the warm chocolate chip treat.

"Billy and Nancy are going on a second honeymoon, and they need someone to watch Brenda."

Ugh. "Mom, you know I'm not good at taking care of kids."

"Well, you better get good at it. You have one of your own now. Besides, Brenda and Petey are the same age. They'll be company for each other. Your brother never asks anything from you. It's the least you can do."

Billy and I were closer in age than we were to our older brother, Bobby. As a child, he was so rotten Billy and I had to join forces just to stay alive. Mom was right; he'd never asked me for a favor like this, and it wouldn't hurt me to watch my niece for a few days.

"How long will they be gone?" I reached for another cookie.

Mom smacked my hand. "Those are for the bake sale at the church tomorrow. They'll be gone four days. They'll be here Saturday." She handed me a cookie and smiled.

The morning was quiet. Too quiet. I watched as Linc pulled into the parking lot in front of the building. Jumping out of the driver's seat, he sprinted toward the entrance. He took a quick look behind him, flung open the door and stumbled in.

"Help me," he squawked, jumped over the counter, and slumped to the floor. He curled into a fetal position.

I stood dumbfounded behind the chest-high divider that doubled as my desk. "What's going on?" I looked down at him and stepped aside so he wouldn't drool on my shoe. "Is Millie Keats chasing you again?"

He looked up at me with more pleading in his eyes than I'd seen since the last time Donna caught her husband with another woman. Actually, Udell did more than plead; he begged Donna to spare his life and that of his hound dog, which Donna didn't like anyway.

But I digress.

Out front, two men on Harleys skidded to a stop next to the tow truck out of which Linc had just bailed. In short order, they sidled in. The first one's height didn't compute with his width. He was approximately five foot ten and easily tipped the scales at four hundred pounds. Evidently, his T-shirt also served as his lunch box, because there were enough food droppings on it to feed a tiny nation. The other man was tall and thin and clean. I liked clean in a man.

The big guy stepped to the counter. "I'm looking for Lincoln."

I quickly glanced down. Linc had his eyes squeezed shut and appeared to be praying. I looked back at Big Boy. "He isn't here right now." Surely God would forgive a little lie like that since it appeared to be so important to my trustworthy and dependable employee, even if he did happen to be sniveling at my feet. I knew there would be a good reason.

"Ma'am, I know he's here 'cause his wrecker's outside." The man hooked his thumb toward the window.

"Oh, I drove the truck this morning." Sometimes lying came so easily, it scared me.

"No, you didn't. I was at his house last night, and that truck was parked in his yard."

Linc wrapped his arms around my legs making it impossible for me to move without falling over.

"What do you want with Linc?" I asked.

"You tell him he can't hide forever. I'll find him and make him pay for what he did to my daughter."

Linc tightened his grip. I leaned my arms on the counter top, raised my feet off the ground, and did a scissor spread with my legs, breaking his hold on me. He moved away, and I lowered myself back to the floor. The two men watched with interest.

"Sorry." I grappled for a reasonable explanation for my actions. "Just doing some exercises." I lifted myself up a couple more times and then said, "Didn't want to cool down too quickly."

"You all through now?" the big guy asked.

I stretched my arms over my head and across my chest a few times. "Oh, yeah. All through, and ready to face the day."

"Good. Now, you pass that message along to Lincoln for me, ya hear?" He started backing away.

"Sure." I gave him thumbs up. "But whom shall I say left him the message?"

He pulled a small, spiral notebook from his back pocket. As he held out his hand, his quiet companion handed him a pen he pulled from his shirt pocket. The bigger man scribbled something and tore the sheet loose. He came only close enough to hand it to me. I looked at it. It contained one word. "Budda."

"Okay, Mr. Budda, I'll tell him you—eeoowww!!!"

With his fist, Linc had hit me soundly on top of my shoe, sending shards of pain radiating through my entire foot and out my toes. Without taking my eyes off Budda and his little buddy, I kicked Linc in the shin. "Leg cramp." I explained.

The man nodded. "The name's Bubba, ma'am."

"But you spelled it with d's." From the floor, I could tell Linc was raising his fist to give me another whack. I moved my foot a fraction of a second before he struck. He hit the concrete. I stomped my foot a couple of times and said to the two men, "Oooo, those leg cramps are dillies. Ever have one?"

The small guy stepped up. "Yeah, boy, I had one right—" With one hand, Budda turned the fellow and shoved him out the door.

He turned back to me. "Tell Lincoln the next time he sees blood it will be his."

Thankfully, the slamming door nearly drowned out the whimpering coming from the floor by my feet. Until the two men got onto their Harleys and disappeared out of sight, I pretended to shuffle through the papers on the counter.

"Okay, they're gone," I said to the quivering mass on the floor. "You can get up."

He did. I fisted my hands to my hips. "What's the big idea hitting my foot? That hurt."

"I didn't want you to say anything about his writing."

I wish I could say this was an unusual occurrence for me. But it wasn't. It's my world, and welcome to it.

"Linc, what are you talking about? Who are those guys?"

"That's Bubba Craig." Linc inhaled a ragged breath.

I glanced at the paper he had given me. "It says Budda here."

"He writes his letters backward. He's dizzy something or other."

"You mean he's dyslexic?"

"Yeah, and he gets downright mad at people who correct him."

I wiggled my toes hoping some of the feeling would come back. "Okay, so you didn't want me to point out he writes his name backward, but what does he want with you?"

"He's Broomhilda's father." Linc swiped at tears clinging to his long lashes.

"The man who fired you from your last job because you refused to marry his daughter?"

"I didn't exactly tell the truth about that. I didn't get fired. I ran away. It was the only way I could escape Broomhilda." He removed his ball cap and twisted it in his fists.

"Okay, so you didn't get fired. And quit calling her Broomhilda. She can't be all that bad."

Linc laid his hat aside and pulled his wallet from his back pocket and removed a folded newspaper clipping. He opened it and handed it to me. It was a photo of a woman in a witch's costume.

"So?" I handed it back.

He shoved it back at me. "Read it."

I sighed. I didn't really have time for this. I had work to do, but I looked at it again.

"It says, 'Judy Craig Elected President of Wrecker Association'." Linc had long ago confessed Broomhilda's real name was Judy. Now she was the president of something. What was he trying to tell me? Why was she dressed up like a witch?

"Was this taken at a Halloween costume party?" I handed it back.

"Don't you get it?" He took it and pointed at it. "She's not in costume. That's how she looks all the time."

I took another look and did an inward shudder. "Cripes, has she ever heard of plastic surgery?"

"What she really needs is a plastic surgeon to work on her disposition." His voice quivered. I thought he might cry.

I patted his shoulder. "There, there. Budda . . . Bubba can't make you marry his daughter."

"But you heard what he said. The next time I see blood, it'll be mine."

"You can't let that bully scare you." I took a hard gander at Linc's long, long legs. "For one thing, you can outrun him, if you have to. And when's the last time you saw blood? A long time, I bet. And it'll be a long time before you see it again." I tried to make light of the situation with a heartfelt laugh.

"I saw lots of blood this morning." His bottom lip trembled.

I stopped laughing. "Where?"

"In my bed."

"Okay, Linc, I'll bite. How did blood get in your bed?"

"Bubba came into my room while I was sleeping and put a raccoon head in bed with me." He slumped into a chair.

"Good heaven. What is that? The redneck's version of the Mafia?"

"Exactly. And Bubba is their godfather." At that, Linc burst into tears.

Chapter 3

*A*re you there, Bertie?"

"My dear, dear Pop. Where else would I be? Did you or did you not just watch me pull the wrecker out of the parking lot onto the highway to go to the bank and to pick up lunch?"

"Are you there, Bertie?"

"Let go of the button, Pop. Yes, I'm here." Screaming would do no good. He always started his radio dispatches that way, and I didn't foresee any chance it would ever change.

"Well, good. Kramer wants you to go to 811 Bonefish Drive. Says he's going to impound Booger Bailey's car for non-payment of traffic violations. What the hell kind of name is 'Booger'?"

I could picture my father scratching his sparsely covered head and furrowing his brows in deep concentration as if pondering the circle of life.

"I don't know what kind of name 'Booger' is. I've never met the gentleman." Hopefully I wouldn't have to today, either. I'd just hook up his car and be on my way. Oh, if only I lived in that perfect world.

A small group of people were gathered in front of a white house with a picket fence. In the front yard a goat grazed. It was either a goat or a very ugly dog. Chief Kramer's cruiser blocked the driveway.

I proudly made my way to the front of the crowd, right up next to the crime scene tape. Jeeze, why was that there? "Where's Chief Kramer?" I asked Deputy Carl Kelly.

"He's inside with Booger Bailey." Sweat beaded Carl's blanched face. He wrung his hands.

"Something wrong?" What a silly question. Crime scene tape should have given me a clue.

"Booger's holding the Chief hostage," Carl stammered.

"Oh, my goodness. What are you going to do?"

"I don't know. I failed Hostage 101 at the police academy." Carl was on the verge of hysteria.

As an avid watcher of cop shows, I knew what to do. "Get a bullhorn, and tell him he's surrounded and to come out with his hands up."

From out of nowhere a loud voice boomed. "Who's the cute little filly in the pink jumpsuit?" It rocked my teeth.

After I'd jumped three inches off the ground, I looked toward heaven. "You talking to me?"

Carl pointed toward the house. "No, *he's* talking to you. Booger has a bullhorn."

Why would Booger have a bullhorn?

"He took Chief Kramer's away from him." Carl answered my question even though I had not spoken it aloud. Still wringing his hands, he paced a few times.

"Where's Kramer?" Carl bellowed toward the house. "Is he okay?"

"Oh, sure. Just a little tied up right now." Booger laughed so loudly it sent chills through me.

"I'll send the chief out, if you send in the gal in the pink jumpsuit." He used the bullhorn again. "I'd rather talk to a woman than this old toad."

I grasped the sides of my coveralls and stretched them out from my thighs. Looking down at my clothes, I groaned. I didn't have to look around to know the crowd was staring at me. The sensation of their gazes bore into my flesh and caused the smell of fear to fill my nostrils. Slowly I glanced up at Carl and began backing into the crowd. Someone shoved me forward.

"You gotta go in, Bertie. We need the chief out here. He'll know how to defuse the situation, and he'll know how to get you out." Did Carl have tears in his eyes?

"I know how to get me out. By not going in the first place." Indignation shoved my fear aside. "You can't make me go in there." I glared at Carl.

"No, I can't, but I beg you, please, go."

A sniveling man always tears down my resistance. Besides, this was my chance to do something for the community. How bad could it be? "Okay, I'll go." I started walking up the path to the front door.

"Try to talk him out of his gun," Carl called to me.

I did an about face that would make any soldier proud and marched my pink covered butt right back to Carl. "Uh, gun? You never mentioned a gun. I think I'll pass."

"You can't pass. You already said you'd do it, and I don't want to have to bring you up on charges of breach of promise." Carl puffed out his chest and sucked in his stomach. I slugged Deputy Kelly in his bread basket and marched up to the steps.

"Mr. Bailey, I'm coming in," I shouted.

The door opened, a hand snaked out and yanked me into the house. I barely had time to look at Chief Kramer before he skedaddled out the door. The chief appeared to have his hands tied behind his back and tape over his mouth. The door slammed causing two pictures to crash to the floor. Glass flew in all directions. I was dancing and jumping out of the way.

"You having a spell?" asked the man with a gun in his left hand and a finger up his nose.

"No. I assume you're Booger." I could now tell Pop with great certainty how the man got this odd name. If I lived, that is.

He offered his hand for me to shake. "Yeah, that's me. Booger Bailey. Glad to meet you."

"I think I'll pass on shaking your hand there, Booger. Hope you understand, seeing as how you are holding me at gun point." I had other reasons for not wanting to touch the man's hand.

He looked at the gun. "This old thing? It ain't loaded."

Relief soothed some of my fear-stifled thoughts. "Then how did you overtake Kramer and tie him up?"

"I didn't tell him it wasn't loaded." He heehawed for a second.

"Okay, Buster. I'm a wrecker driver, and I'm here to impound your car. Anything over thirty minutes, and I get paid an extra sixty dollars an hour, so talk fast."

"Name's Booger, not Buster, and you're cheaper than a hooker." He raked his gaze over me. "But you're not my type."

"Hey, I didn't ask if I was your type, you old doo-doo head." I started toward the door. "I'm leaving."

He poked the gun in my stomach. "You aren't going anywhere. I gotta figure out how I can get out of here. I'm not going to jail. They have roaches there."

Among other things. "Get that gun away from me. Loaded or not, I don't want it pointed at me." Without a thought as to whether I could take this joker or not, I grabbed the barrel of the pistol and pointed it toward the ceiling. My brothers had taught me a thing or two about self-defense, so I chopped Booger's forearm a couple of times with my hand.

He screeched in pain, but continued to struggle to keep possession of the weapon. Filled with determination not to let that happen, I screamed to get my adrenaline flowing, held tight to the gun's barrel, and shoved Booger down. Before he let go of the gun on his way to the floor, he managed to pull the trigger. It discharged a round into the ceiling, raining chunks of plaster down around me.

Carl Kelly and Chief Kramer burst through the door. There I stood, plaster dust covering me, holding the gun by the barrel with it pointed toward the ceiling, my hand nowhere near the trigger.

"Now what have you done, Bertie?" Carl raced to me and took the weapon.

"Me?" I looked at Booger. "He lied to me." I kicked him. He yowled and grabbed his leg.

"So you tried to shoot him?" Chief Kramer asked.

"I didn't do it, you nincompoop. I was taking it away from him." I pointed to the massive man on the floor. "*He* shot the gun. I was just lucky to have gotten it pointed toward the ceiling before he pulled the trigger."

Carl stepped in front of me. "I ought to bring you up on charges of calling a law enforcement officer names."

"Go ahead, you King of Idiots. I'll weigh my name calling charges against your sending me, a private citizen, into a hostage situation in any court in the land." I thought about taking the gun away from Carl and shooting him. But I thought better of it. I didn't want to go to jail with the roaches either.

I left the men all standing there and walked out into the yard. The goat barked at me. After hooking up Booger Bailey's car, I drove to the impound yard. That was all I wanted to do in the first place.

Poor Linc was truly afraid of Bubba Craig. He tried to put up a brave front, but if the wind dared to blow a sudden gust, he jumped.

"Do you need to take some time off, Linc?" I asked. "I would understand."

"No, Mrs. Bertie. I need to be working to keep from thinking about the terrible things Bubba might do to me." He swiped sweat from his brow with a dirty rag. We were only a week from Christmas and it was forty degrees outside, yet my dear, shaken tow truck driver's cheeks glowed fiery red.

"As a matter of fact, since I don't have no family here and all your family is coming home for Christmas, I'd like to volunteer to work your call nights, too. Maybe I could just hang out here at the garage. You know, sleep in Mr. Byrd's old office. That way I'd be right here for any calls that come in. You'd have a lot of free time to enjoy the holidays with your loved ones. What do you say? Huh?"

"I'd say you are afraid to stay at your house because Bubba knows where you live." I crossed my arms over my chest and tapped my fingers on my elbows.

"Well, yeah, there's that, too."

I was going to have my niece visiting for four days and when her parents returned from their cruise, they were going to stay through Christmas day. It would be nice to be free to spend time with Petey and Brenda. Take them shopping. My evenings would be free to decorate the tree and finish wrapping gifts.

"Okay, Linc, you're welcome to stay here, but if it becomes too much for you to be on duty twenty-four hours for the next week, you have to promise to tell me so I can relieve you. Deal?"

"Deal, but it won't be too much."

Brenda arrived early Saturday morning. She and Petey met at the wedding and had taken to their roles of cousins from the start. As soon as her parents pulled out of the driveway, we three girls loaded into the car and drove to Ivey's department store for as much heavy shopping as Ivey's could provide. By noon I was worn out and starving.

"Let's go to the Chow Pal Diner and eat lunch. How 'bout it?" I asked.

"Oh, yes." Brenda seemed very excited about the suggestion. "I've always wanted to meet Mildred Locke."

"Okay." I was puzzled why my sweet niece wanted to meet the sixty-plus waitress who had a goofy grin eternally plastered on her face and a walk that would make any lumberjack proud. But I was too hungry to delve into the strange exclamation. "Come on, then. Let's go."

At the diner, we scrambled out of our coats and slid into the nearest empty booth.

Mildred had barely laid menus on the table when Brenda looked up with the face of an angel. "Are you Mildred Locke?"

"Why, yes, I am." Mildred's grin widened even more, though how it was possible, I'm not sure. "Do I know you?"

"No, but you used to date my father before he met my mother, who is a real woman."

I nearly choked. "Dear, that's not really a good thing to say."

Brenda stretched her arms onto the table and locked her fingers. "That's what Mommy says all the time. That Daddy was hanging out with a hussy until he met a real woman."

I placed my hand over her mouth, just enough to stifle my niece.

"I'm so sorry, Mildred. I don't know what to say." I glanced at Petey who seemed to be taking it all in stride. Luckily, since she was so young, she didn't know how embarrassing the things were going on around her.

"Is Bertie your aunt?" Mildred asked.

"Yes, ma'am." Brenda smiled her angelic smile.

"So your daddy would be Billy Byrd, right?"

Brenda nodded with pride.

"I see, well, honey, your father used to date my daughter. Her name is Mildred Locke, too. And you can tell your mommy we all thank her for taking him away. My daughter married the banker over in Shafer, and she has lots of money."

"Okey dokey, Mildred. I'll see that she passes that along." I fanned my flaming face with a menu. "Could we order, please?"

"Mildred Locke." Petey repeated the name in a very thoughtful way. Since this was the first sound she'd made since we all sat down, we looked at her with anticipation.

My daughter tilted her head and spoke with loud clarity. "Isn't she the lady you said reminds you of Dufus the Saint Bernard when we were at Perkins Park?"

"No," I snapped.

"Yes, it is. You said she looked like Dufus and even walked like him."

Oh, good Lord. Could it get more awkward? I quickly tried to suck that thought back into my brain because it had been my personal experience that He would answer my questions with great emphasis and not always in a good way.

"We'll have three burgers all the way with fries and chocolate shakes," I blurted as quickly as I could.

"Aunt Bertie, you can't be serious." Brenda clutched her fist to her chest.

"What's the matter, My Little Drama Queen?" She takes after her mother.

"I don't eat meat any more. I'm a vegetarian."

Mildred's eternal smile had turned to a hard grimace. I believe she could have chewed ten-penny nails into nickels.

"I'll have macaroni and cheese." Brenda handed back the menu.

Feeling we should try to show some kind of manners, I cocked a weary brow at my darling niece. "And?" I asked.

"And I'll have fries and a chocolate shake."

"I meant, thank you." I spoke through clenched teeth.

She bounced in her seat. "Oh, yeah, thanks. Bring it on." Unfortunately she got that from her father.

"How are things going in school, Brenda?"

"Ooh, I was picked the Star Student of my class last week. I beat Arnie Walden. He said he was glad I won because he loves me and wants me to have everything." I told you she was a Drama Queen.

Her gaze snapped to Petey who sat quietly, hanging on Brenda's every word. Or, maybe she was in shock.

"Who loves you?" Brenda asked Petey.

"My dad and mom." She nodded in my direction.

I loved it when she called me Mom. I smiled from ear to ear.

"I mean a guy." Brenda's voice carried a tad of indignation. "Do you have a man?"

"She's too young to have a *man,* as are you, Brenda Jean Byrd." I needed to protect my daughter from my brother's child. Evidently, she lived a worldlier existence than Petey. Maybe than me. No, wait. I had a man.

"Well, Arnie is definitely my man. He shares his chocolate pudding with me every day at lunch time." Brenda spoke with a grown-up air.

I stuck out my tongue with a not-so-grown-up air.

"I have a man." Petey spoke loud enough for the next three tables to hear.

"Good for you, sweetie." I whispered, and hoped the girls would follow my lead. "What's his name?"

"Randy," Petey announced. "Randy Carson."

My heart stopped for a full beat. "Please tell me you are kidding." Surely she couldn't have a thing for Donna's son. Good heavens, all three of her children were expected to be the youngest kids in the county jail.

"No, I'm not kidding, Mommy. The day before we started our Christmas break, our room mother brought in cupcakes, and Randy wanted me to take a lick of his. But he had a fever blister, and I don't love him that much."

I patted her hand. "Smart girl."

Our lunch arrived. Thankfully, Mildred's smile had returned. After she'd left, I steered the conversation away from "men." "When did you become a vegetarian?"

Brenda finished her bite of mac and cheese. "When I found out that hamburgers come from poor, unsuspecting cows."

"So what do you eat?"

She waved her hand toward her plate of macaroni and cheese.

"Well, surely you eat other things."

"Sometimes, but no meat." Brenda scooped another bite into her mouth. "Where does macaroni come from, Aunt Bertie?"

"It grows."

My niece gasped. I thought she must have pasta lodged in her throat.

"From crows?" Tears filled her eyes.

"No. I said it grows."

She finally exhaled. "I thought I'd never get to eat anything ever again." She started to take another spoonful, but stopped in mid-scoop. "You're sure you didn't say crows. There's no animal in macaroni, right?"

"That's right." I took a big chomp of my burger. "But the cheese comes from milk which comes from cows." I dipped a French fry into a pile of ketchup. "So you might want to consider not eating that." I loved torturing my brothers' kids.

"But the cow didn't have to die to give me cheese, now did he, Aunt Bertie?" And they loved torturing me.

"Petey." I stood on our front porch. "Brenda." I hollered the girls' names several times, but they didn't appear to be anywhere near by. Shading my eyes from the sun, I looked toward Novalee's home just a few houses down from mine.

"Petey. Brenda. Where are you?"

I heard it. Faint to start with, but growing steadily louder with each passing second. A girlish giggle. They were hiding in Barbie's tree. I closed my sweater tighter across my chest and braved the nippy afternoon air to head toward the big oak.

"Girls, I don't think Miss Barbie would appreciate your being in her tree. That's her special place. Come on now. Get down from there." I worked my way to the edge of my yard and stood directly under the sprawling branches. Sitting on the tractor seat attached to a huge limb, Barbie flutter her fingers in the form of a wave.

"Oh." I looked up at her. "I thought I heard the girls. Was that you giggling?" It wouldn't surprise me if Barbie had been laughing out loud, all alone. She certainly was very unpredictable. The truth of the matter is, she's a nut. Pure unadulterated nut. But I love her. Bless her heart.

"Wasn't me." She pointed up.

I looked. Four skinny legs hung from branches several feet above Barbie.

"Petey! What are you doing up there?" My heart pounded so loudly I could barely hear my own screeching.

"We tried to sit down there, but the seat was taken. I climbed up here lots of times when I came to visit Grandpa Pete." Of course she would have. She visited the house many times before I even knew it existed.

I glanced at Barbie who sat with her arms folded. "It's my tree. I wasn't giving up this comfortable seat to sit on an old hard branch. Do you think I'm crazy?"

"Oh, heavens no." Nuttier than a fruitcake? Yes.

I motioned to the girls. "I think you and Brenda should come on down."

My daughter started to twist to slide from the branch. Brenda threw her arms around Petey's neck and screamed at the top of her lungs.

"You're choking me." Petey tried to loosen my niece's hands. It did no good. The screaming became louder. Barbie was screaming, too.

I stood on tip-toes and tapped her on the leg to get her attention. "What is wrong with you?"

She quieted long enough to say, "I don't know." Then she started in again.

"Everybody," I yelled, "shut up." They paid no attention to me.

Petey tried to get free from the death grip Brenda had on her, and Brenda continued her screaming and begging for someone to save her. Barbie just squeezed her eyes shut and screamed over and over again. I couldn't get them to calm down enough to help them out of the tree. The way Petey was hanging from the high branch,

I feared that if and when Brenda did let her go, Petey would tumble to the ground, probably bringing Brenda with her. I couldn't let that happen.

"I'll be right back." They didn't hear a word I yelled.

Inside the house, I called 911 and told the dispatcher my problem. She assured me help would arrive momentarily. Thirty minutes later, help showed up. A truck with a cherry picker basket attached to a boom belonging to the local electric company backed into the yard. I couldn't understand how this was going to help get the girls down, since the bucket would only go as high as the lower branches. Dang, I could have done that with a ladder.

"Just step back, ma'am." The nice looking man escorted me from under the tree. He walked back. "Well now, I can get you down without the truck." He spoke in a very gentle tone.

The sound of flesh slapping against flesh rang through the air. "I don't want to get down, and don't you touch me again," Indignant Barbie shouted. "Next branch up."

Not looking worse for wear, the man climbed inside the basket and maneuvered the lift into place. Just able to reach his arms up through the branches, he could very easily lift Petey and Brenda down one at a time. However, they were scared spitless and were holding tight to each other.

"Come on, Brenda honey, you have to let go so the nice man can get you down." I'd moved back under the tree and was motioning to them.

"No," my frantic niece cried. "You come and get me, Aunt Bertie. Please. I'm scared."

"Mom, you got to hurry." Now Petey joined the pleading.

"She's choking me, and I have to go to the bathroom."

The man lowered the boom and climbed out. "Here, get in. You can get them down."

I would have looked over my shoulder to see if he was talking to someone behind me, but that would be useless. Of course he was talking to me, and I was going to be up a creek (or tree in this case) without a paddle. I climbed in and listened intently as he gave me a brief lesson on raising and lowering the cherry picker. The controls were a lot like those on my wrecker. Forward for down. Back for up. Left and right for . . . well, you get the idea. I could do this.

On my own, I moved the first lever back. Evidently the controls were a little more sensitive than on the wrecker because I shot rapidly upward, bonging my head on a branch.

"Damn." I rubbed the spot.

"Aunt Bertie!"

"Mommy has a trash mouth," Petey explained to Brenda. "You just have to live with it like Dad and I do."

Jeeze. I ran my fingers through my hair hoping I wouldn't find a gaping hole. Good. Nothing there. I lowered the boom, slowly this time. I needed to move to the left just a little and then I could raise high enough to take the girls in my arms. That would be just a slight lever movement to the left.

The bucket took off like a race horse on steroids. The contraption hit Barbie, who had just been hanging out enjoying the activities buzzing around her tree. She swayed a little before falling to the ground with a thud.

"Oh, my God. Barbie, are you okay?" I screamed. She didn't answer.

The electric man stooped beside her and felt her pulse. "She ain't dead." He shrugged. "Yet."

"Call 911. I'll get the girls down," I yelled to the electric man.

Slowly I raised the bucket, plucked the little darlings from their perch and efficiently lowered the boom to the ground. I got the hang of the control levers. It just took a little practice. Regrettably, I may have killed Barbie in the process.

Chapter 4

Mom arrived minutes before an unconscious Barbie was placed in the ambulance. Brenda and Petey left with Mom, and I rode to the hospital with my friend.

"I'm so sorry," I repeated over and over again.

One of the EMTs, Guy Weitzel, graduated from Sweet Meadow High with me. "Do you want me to give you something to settle your nerves?" he asked.

"No, I want you to wake her up." Fear and tears strangled my voice.

"We're trying, but you have to stay out of our way." Guy reached in front of me to grab a tube of some sort.

"Bertie." We all looked at Barbie. Her eyes were open and a slight smile wobbled across her lips.

"Are you okay?" I leaned closer and took her hand.

"Move, Bert." Guy shoved me out of the way. While he shined a light in Barbie's eyes, I closed mine and gave thanks I hadn't killed my petite neighbor.

Once inside the emergency room, I answered all the questions I could for the hospital staff. Barbie gave me her husband's work number, and I went to the phone to call Rick. I was thrilled he wasn't in his office, but his secretary would get in touch with him and send him to the hospital. I had a slight reprieve—not having to talk to him for a little while. He constantly tells Barbie not to play with me because I get her into trouble. I bet he was going to issue a big timeout for our friendship just as soon as he found out I almost killed her with the basket of an electrical truck.

It's funny how time passes at different speeds, depending on events. Waiting for the doctors to report back on Barbie's condition seemed an eternity. For Rick to arrive, that happened faster than a young girl can run to the water hose after she eats a jalapeno pepper because her brothers told her it was a big green jelly bean. I would know about things like that.

Rick raced down the corridor with his arms outstretched directly toward me. I raised my arms to cover my face and head so I wouldn't feel too much of the blow I thought Rick was about to administer. Instead, he wrapped his arms around me.

"Oh, Bertie, I'm so glad you're here. How is she? Where is she?"

"I . . . well . . . ah . . . sheeee . . . ah." Just like that, I'd lost my ability to talk, to put coherent words together.

Dr. Johns came through a set of double doors. "Mrs. Jamison is going to be just fine."

I sighed, releasing so much air from my lungs I became dizzy. Rick grabbed one arm, Dr. Johns the other.

"I'm fine." I pulled loose and introduced the two men.

"Your wife has a slight concussion. She's going to be fine, maybe just a little confused," Dr. Johns gently reassured Rick. "So if she says a few strange things, don't worry, that will go away in a day or two."

"Oh, good Lord, Rick, how will we ever know when she's back to normal?"

Christmas Eve arrived with Jill Frost nipping at our noses. Her big brother, Jack, was wreaking havoc a little farther north causing *my* two brothers, Billy and Bobby, to be late for dinner at Mom's and Pop's. While my mother fussed over the gravy, which she declared had taken on a life of its own, I stood lookout at the front window. It would be my job to warn everyone when the "Byrd Boys" arrived.

From my post, I could see next door to the side entrance of *Bertie's Garage and Towing*. For the past week, Linc had stayed there under the pretense of being an on-call driver. In actuality, he was hiding out from Bubba Craig and the Redneck Mafia. The blinds of the office were pulled, but a soft light glowed from inside. Every once in a while, I saw Linc's shadow slash in front of the illuminated windows. Once his head appeared so he could look through the bottom slat of the blind covering the side door window. I saw him peeking out, but only for a second. His shadow disappeared completely out of sight.

I slipped on my jacket and raised the hood over my head. After going out into the cold evening air, I walked down the steps and started toward the garage. The sky was dark except for a few bright stars. I stopped a few feet short of the garage door and glanced upward. There in the massive blackness, a star winked at me. Instantly, I thought of Arch's dad.

Pete, you old goat.

I often imagined the deceased man watched over me like God's right-hand man, protecting me from harm. The Lord knew I could use all the help I could get. Somehow, thinking of Pete always brought composure to my ever-jangled nerves. I closed my eyes and enjoyed the crisp air on my cheeks. I'd settle for something to quiet the rumbling in my hungry stomach.

A hand came from behind and closed over my mouth. It was warm and smelled like an old grease rag. I elbowed my captor's stomach, stomped down on his instep, and twisted from his grasp. I did my version of a boxer's shuffle, fist raised, bouncing from one foot to the other.

"Come on, buddy. Bring it on." I think I might have swiped my nose with my thumb. Who did I think I was? Mohammed Ali?

"Mrs. Bertie?" Linc's strained voice finally penetrated my adrenalin fog. I stopped my bobbing and weaving and then punched my driver in the arm.

"What the heck is wrong with you? Why'd you grab me like that? You got a death wish or something?" I sputtered.

"I'm sorry. I'm sorry." The small amount of light from the window allowed me to see the sincerity flashing across his face.

"Okay, I know you are, but what they heck did you grab me for?"

"I thought you were Bubba," Linc whispered.

I knew I'd put on a little weight lately, but . . . "Do I look like Bubba?" I squeaked.

"No, ma'am. I couldn't tell who you were sneaking around out here in the dark." He opened the door, and we stepped into the warm room.

"Okay, first of all, I wasn't sneaking, and why would you think I was Bubba?" I crossed the floor to the counter and shuffled through some of the work orders in the in-basket.

"He called about an hour ago. Said Judy was crying because she's alone on Christmas Eve and he's coming after me."

"Oh, good Lord. You can't let that bully intimidate you. He can't force you to go with him. You're younger than him and only a fourth his size. If nothing else, you can outrun him."

Linc took a few steps toward the other side of the room. When he got to the door, he bent at his waist and scurried under the window until he cleared it. Standing in the corner, out of the view of any openings, he turned to face me.

"He's mean, Mrs. Bertie. He hired me to take the place of a driver who just disappeared from the face of the earth. The man's wife came by several times after I started working there to see if anyone had heard from him. As far as I know, they never found the man."

Okay, it didn't sound good, but things like that didn't happen in a small, quiet, peaceful town like Sweet Meadow. Why would it start at my door? I shivered slightly and took a step out of range of the window in case I was about to be shown why that would happen.

"He wants me back there, and he won't stop until I marry Broomhilda."

"Linc," I snapped. "Now, you quit calling that poor lady that. She has a name. Use it." His childish behavior reminded me I had a daughter who would be wondering what happened to me. "I've got to go back to Pop's house. My brothers will be here soon. If Bubba shows up, call and they'll come right over." I walked to the door and opened it. After I'd taken a peek into the darkness and didn't see Bubba, possibly glowing in the dark, I stepped out.

Suddenly I was grabbed by both arms and lifted from my feet. My scream was over-powered by the donkey braying of my two brothers. They placed me back on the ground, but held tight to both my arms. When I got free, I'd clobber them, and they knew it.

Linc, who had never met Billy, but did know Bobby, rushed to our sides.

After surveying the situation, he turned and limped back inside. "Okay, you guys are on your own," he called over his shoulder. Quietly, the door closed. The lock clicked loudly.

I wiggled loose from my brothers' grasps. "Okay, you horses' behinds, let's get over there and tackle Mom's gravy."

Bobby lifted me over his shoulder and carried me like a sack of potatoes. "Dang, Ro-Bert-A, married life must be agreeing with you. You've put on weight since I was here for the wedding." He placed me on the bottom step leading to my parents' porch.

I turned and bounded up the stairs, two at a time. "Not so much that I can't beat you to the table." We burst through the door. Mom, who had just entered the dining room carrying a large platter, barely jumped out of our way. We scrambled past her and giggled our way into our chairs.

"Hey, hey, hey," Mom scolded. "You almost made me drop my turduckhen."

We three Byrd kids stopped in our tracks. "A who-what-hen?" Billy asked.

"Ah, it's one of your mother's hair-brain . . . I mean, superior

58

ideas." Pop took the tray from Mom and set it in front of him. "She saw it in the turkey bin down at Hines' meat market and thought we should have one."

"It's a hen inside a duck inside a turkey," Mom explained. She disappeared into the kitchen.

"I don't like duck." And I hadn't since one chased me back into my wrecker when I'd gone to repo a car for Joe's House of Parts, who also sells cars on the side.

"We had so much turkey at Thanksgiving, I've grown a wattle." Bobby chimed in.

"You've had that for years." His wife, Estelle, tapped his double chin.

My other brother, Billy, plopped a spoon of mashed potatoes onto his plate. Some stuck to his finger. He licked it off. "I only like the breast of the chicken."

Mom returned with a huge platter of sweet potatoes. She always cooked like she was single-handedly feeding the Sweet Meadow Baptist Church on Homecoming Day. "You know the rule here. Don't knock it 'til you tried it." After she set the plate in the only vacant spot on the table, Mom took her seat.

We all joined hands, and Pop said grace. Arch locked his fingers in mine. I stole a glance at him. He watched me through misty eyes. I cocked a questioning smile. He squeezed my hand and bowed his head and closed his eyes.

"Amen," Pop said.

"I have something I'd like to say." Arch spoke loud enough to be heard over the clattering of bowls and platters being passed. Everyone stopped. "Petey and I," he nodded toward his daughter sitting at a smaller table with her new cousins, "want to thank you for welcoming us into your hearts the way you all have. For the last couple of years, we've spent most holidays alone except for a visit to the nursing home to see my father."

The mention of Pete caused a twinge of disappointment in my chest. I wished I'd known him in his earlier years. He must have been a remarkable man. I looked at husband. I loved Arch with all my heart, and I'd bet Pete had a lot to do with the man his son had grown into.

"I just wanted to say thanks." Arch ended his speech.

My father stood. "Well, thanks, Arch. We think Bertie hit it pretty lucky, too." Pop began carving the funny looking bird in front of him.

"Yeah, thanks, brother-in-law, we appreciate your taking Ro-Bert-A off our hands. We were beginning to think we'd have to take care of her in her old age." Bobby grinned.

I threw a roll across the table. He caught it. "Stuff it," I instructed.

"Speaking of breasts." Those words came from Bobby's mouth right there at the dinner table. We looked at him, not knowing what to expect.

"Who was speaking of breasts?" I passed the green bean casserole to Pop.

"Billy was." Bobby pointed with his knife. "He said he only liked the breast of chicken, remember? Stick with me on this, Bertie."

The aroma of all the wonderful food Mom had cooked was wreaking havoc in my tummy. I'd skipped lunch in anticipation of the big meal. Since Bobby and Billy were late arriving, hunger pains started doing a war dance in my stomach about an hour ago. I wanted to eat, but I couldn't wait to hear what words of wisdom Bobby was going to lay on us.

"Okay. What about the chicken breasts?" I asked.

"Did you see what I bought Estelle for Christmas?" Bobby didn't wait for me to answer. He barreled right on through. "Show 'em, Estelle."

My dear sister-in-law puffed out her red sweater-covered chest. For the first time I noticed her once sagging thirty-eights were now, my guess would be, forty double d's.

"I bought her new boobs. Aren't they great?" I don't believe I ever saw Bobby prouder of anything. Estelle seemed quite proud of her present, too.

Mom flushed a bright fuchsia. Arch coughed. I just stared in disbelief.

"They're something, all right. You did good, boy." Pop went back to carving our Christmas turduckhen.

Billy's wife, Diane, cast a dirty look in her husband's direction and gulped a few swallows of her wine. "All I got was a robot vacuum cleaner."

Christmas morning came early at the Fortney home. The sun had barely opened its eyes when Arch and I heard the pitter patter of Petey's feet running down the hallway to the living room. "Come on," she yelled loud enough to shake shingles off the roof. "Santa's been here."

"Do you think she still believes in Santa Claus?" Arch pulled me into his arms.

"I don't know about her, but . . ." I snuggled closer, resting my head on his shoulder, "I do." The past few months had been so special, it felt like Christmas every day for me. "A few weeks ago, she asked if there really was a Santa Claus. I told her as long as she believed, he would continue to bring her presents on Christmas morning."

"Well, that explains it." Arch planted a kiss on my forehead and then sat and put his feet on the floor.

I reached out and stroked his bare back. "What are you talking about?"

"When we went shopping for your gift, she put her hand on a bicycle and said 'I believe.' Later, she touched several game cartridges for her Game Boy and said 'I believe.' I thought she had some kind of spiritual thing going on. I guess she was just re-emphasizing her wish list."

"Dad. Mom. I'm dying out here." Petey had caught a case of Drama Queen from her cousin, Brenda.

"Okay. We're on our way." I hurried out of bed and into my warm fuzzy robe and slippers.

While I passed Petey her presents and she tore paper from each neatly wrapped gift, Arch documented the whole wonderful experience on his new movie camera. I insisted he open it before we went to my parents' for Christmas Eve dinner. I wanted pictures of every minute of our first Christmas together.

If I were in the middle of an old movie, soft music would have played in the background, and cartoon hearts would burst above my head. But it wasn't a movie. It was real. Happiness filled every part of my heart and soul in a way I never imagined possible. For the first time in my life, I felt the electricity I saw my mom and dad exchange when they looked at each other. Even after forty-three years of marriage.

I was staring into space, deep in reverie when I realized Arch was watching me. His beautiful smile tugged at my heart. The glint in his eyes told me he understood what I was feeling and that we shared the joy of the moment.

Petey rang the bell attached to the handlebars of her new bicycle. Although it interrupted her dad's and my special moment, it was just part of the extraordinary package of being a family. I loved the feeling of all of it.

Before we married, she and Arch lived in an apartment on a busy street. A bicycle had been out of the question. Now that she was almost eleven and lived on a quiet street, not having a bicycle was unthinkable, according to Petey. Arch and I agreed. So did Santa Claus.

"Here." Arch handed me a large present wrapped a little haphazardly in red foil paper and curly white ribbon.

"I wrapped it." Petey beamed.

I tore into the package with the same enthusiasm she had used to open hers. It was a food processor. "Wow, thanks. Does it come with a chef?" I smiled at Arch.

"I don't know. Take it out and let's see." He turned the camera back on and pointed it at me.

I removed the small kitchen appliance from its Styrofoam haven. It was really stuck in there like it was holding to the safe place for dear life. I had a feeling it knew the unpredictable things that could happen when placed in my hands. Finally, it popped free. Inside the transparent bowl lay a small white box. I took it out.

"Hurry and open it." Petey laid aside her Mary-Kate and Ashley skirt and blouse Uncle Bobby and Aunt Estelle had given her, and bounced onto the sofa next to me.

I lifted the lid from the box and found a gold chain with a heart locket.

"Look inside the heart," my daughter urged.

I opened it. The left side of the locket held a picture of Arch. In the right side was a picture of me and Petey. Both were taken while the three of us were on our honeymoon. I didn't think it possible to be more blissfully happy than I'd been just moments before. But there it was. So much happiness it was bubbling at the back of my throat in the sound of sobs and filling my eyes with so much joy it spilled over and ran down my checks.

"Don't cry, Mommy." As Petey tried to mop up my tears, she looked at her dad. "I told you we shoulda got her a mixer."

On my first day back at work following the New Year, I let myself into the office of *Bertie's Garage and Towing*. The smell of fresh coffee filled my nostrils and assaulted my stomach. It probably wasn't a good idea for me to have eaten those two pieces of cheesecake for breakfast. Maybe it was the glass of orange juice I washed them down with.

"Linc? I'm here." I went around the counter and dropped my keys and wallet into a file drawer and shucked out of my coat. "Hello.

I'm here." The door to Pop's office was ajar so I peeked in. Linc's blankets were folded and lying neatly on the tattered sofa. He didn't appear to be inside the building. I opened the blinds and turned the "closed" sign around. Once I'd made my way into the garage, I pushed the buttons that opened the roll-up doors. They groaned and grunted, but finally cleared the entrances of the two work bays.

Back inside the office, I found Linc shuffling through the work orders in the basket.

"Good morning, Mrs. Bertie. Happy New Year." He smiled for the first time in days.

"Thanks, right back at you. You're in a good mood."

"Yep. It's been over a week since I last heard from Bubba. I gotta tell you, I'm feeling good about the whole situation. As a matter of fact, my New Year's resolution is to be a man. To stand up to that over-grown toad and tell him he better not mess with me any more."

"Wow. I'm proud of you." I had to reach up, but I patted tall Linc on the back.

"Thanks, that means a lot to me." Linc shoved his hands into his pockets and shrugged his shoulders so high his neck disappeared. He started for the door. "I'm going to go start the yard inventory. Page me, if you need me."

I'd grown very fond of Linc. He was kind and considerate like the brother I *wished* I had. My real brothers could be real pains. Each year, they and their families came home for the week between Christmas and New Year. And, for that week, Billy and Bobby reverted back to their childhood and took great pleasure in torturing the baby sister. By the time they packed up their presents and tons of food Mom prepared for them, and they pulled onto the highway headed home, I was exhausted. My nerves were like a basket of eggs being carried by a toddler. They were fragile and could crack at any minute, brought on by the practical jokes of the Byrd boys, or by my vivid imagination of things they might do to me. But I loved them. Bless their hearts.

Suddenly, the door opened, and a burst of chilly air swished in. Bubba Craig lifted Linc by the back of his collar. His feet barely touched the floor. Somewhere along the line, he lost his hat. Corkscrew brown curls danced in all directions. Bubba easily tossed him through the door. Linc staggered, but finally found his footing.

"What do you think you're doing?" I marched myself around the counter. With my hands fisted to my sides, I stood only inches from the big man's face. Had he ever heard of Big Red chewing gum? He certainly could use some.

"I'm tired of seeing my little girl cry. It tears me apart. And that's exactly what I'm going to do to Stretch there," he pointed at Linc, "if he doesn't haul his skinny butt back to Atlanta and make an honest woman of my sweet, delicate flower."

"You can't force him to marry Broom . . . Judy. If you don't get out of here," I shook my finger in his face, "I'm going to call the police and have you arrested."

"Little Lady, don't point your finger at me. I've broken prettier ones than yours. One with a French manicure."

I curled my pointer finger back into my fist and slipped both my hands behind my back. I didn't know what to think of this burly, obviously deranged man who knew about French manicures. Regardless, I refused to show the fear raging inside me. I walked to the phone. While I glared at Bubba, I lifted the receiver from its cradle and waited to see if he would leave. He turned to Linc.

"You have exactly two weeks to give your notice here and get moved back to Atlanta."

I couldn't believe my ears. Did this man have work ethics, but no morals? Or, was he just an A-class loony tune? My money rested on the latter.

He almost cleared the door when he turned back to Linc. "Two weeks. Do you understand? If you aren't there by then, I'll come back and move you to Atlanta myself. One body part at a time." He closed the door. I hung up the phone. Linc fainted.

By the time I got to his side, he'd come to. "Are you okay?" I stooped and tried to help him to his feet.

"I'm fine. So much for my New Year's resolution. I need to remember to breathe when he's around. Lack of oxygen makes me lightheaded."

"Really? Imagine that."

Linc regained his strength and composure. He worked hard and now he had two weeks to think things over and decide what to do about Bubba and his daughter, Broomhilda. I insisted Linc take off a day or two to reflect on his future. Pop would help me out at the garage. Reluctantly, Linc gathered his belongings from Pop's office and went home.

I ran to the bathroom and gave up my cheesecake and orange juice.

Later that afternoon, the phone rang. I answered it with my usual jovial tone. "Bertie's Garage and Towing."

"Is this Bertie Fortney?" a woman's voice asked.

"Yes, it is. How may I help you?"

"My twins, Art and Bart, are over at the elementary school. They'll need to be picked up at three o'clock sharp. Art'll need to be dropped at his piano lesson by three fifteen, and Bart has to be at his vocal coach's house by three-thirty. Don't be late. Art gets a little hyper when he's late being picked up from school." The woman finally took a breath.

"I'm sorry, but you have the wrong number. This is Bertie's Garage and Towing." I hung up the phone. My hand had barely left it when it rang again. Slowly, I picked it up, placed it to my ear. Softly, I whispered, "Hello?"

"I don't have the wrong number, and don't hang up on me again. This is Icie Bailey. You marched into my home, had some kind of confrontation with my husband who was then arrested. As if that wasn't enough, you impounded our only vehicle. We spent Christmas without our truck. Booger has to go to court next week, and it's all your fault."

Booger. Booger Bailey. How could this woman believe it was my fault her husband ended up in jail and their vehicle was taken away?

"Ma'am, I really can't help you. Chief Kramer is the one who ordered your pick-up impounded. So, call him, and he'll tell you what you need to do to get it back."

"I already know what I need to do to get it back . . . catch up the back payments because the finance company repoed it after it left our possession. I called this Kramer fellow, and he told me to call you."

I wondered what the penalty would be for beating the stuffing out of a police officer. "I'm sorry. I don't know why he told you to call me, but there is nothing I can do to help you."

"Don't you hang up," Mrs. Bailey bellowed. "I don't have anyone to go get the twins, and they have to be picked up and dropped off at their activities promptly, or Art will work himself into a tizzy that will take days to undo." She sounded like she was in a tizzy herself.

"Today is their first day back to school after Christmas vacation. They rode the bus there this morning, but they're expecting to be picked up. That Art, he won't like it if he . . . Get on out of there," her shrill voice demanded. She made a barking sound.

I pulled the receiver away from my ear and rubbed it, hoping the hearing loss wouldn't be permanent. I moved the phone to the other side of my head.

"What did you do that for? You deafened me."

"Oh, that darn goat is in the garbage." Stress squeaked Mrs. Bailey's voice.

"Did you just bark at the goat?" I was still rubbing my sore ear.

"Yeah, Booger taught the goat to bark. Now that's the only way I can get him to listen to me."

"I've never heard of such a thing." Although I could vouch for the fact that the goat barked. I heard him with my own ears, when they were both still working.

"That's how Booger taught the twins to listen to him, too. When he does his barking sound, they know he means business. Speaking of the twins, it's ten till three. Oh, no, Art's going to be in a terrible state. You better get on over there and get them two."

"Okay." Was I crazy or just plain nuts? "I'll go get them—"

"That's more like it," Mrs. Bailey's quick retort buzzed in my ears.

"You didn't let me finish. I'll get them *today*, but you have to find someone else to get them tomorrow."

"Well, I can't promise I can find anyone. Bye." Her voice faded.

"Wait," I yelled.

"What is it?" she asked me, but barked into the distance.

"How will I know them?"

"They look exactly alike." The line went dead.

Jeeze. All I could picture in my mind's eye was miniature Booger Bailey's.

I found the twins. They didn't look anything like their father. As a matter of fact, they didn't even look like each other. They were standing together. While one looked up and down the street, the other dug in his backpack. I pulled my truck next to the curb and rolled down the passenger window.

"Are you Art and Bart Bailey?" I asked.

They looked at each other and then back at me. "Yeah, who are you?" The one on the right spoke first.

"I'm Mrs. Fortney. Your mom sent me to pick you up." I leaned across the seat and lifted the door handle. "Hop in. You don't want to be late."

The redhead slid across the seat and the one with brown hair climbed in next to him. He slammed the door, and I pulled away from the curb. "Where to?"

"To Carter's Music Store on Franklin," the one next to me answered. "I hope you can step on it. I need to be there in just a few minutes. Mrs. Carter gets upset when I'm late. I don't like to be late. Being late is never a good thing. I was late once, and she made me play nothing but the scales for the whole hour. I didn't like that. Would you like that? I bet you wouldn't. I take it Mom didn't get us a new car. I didn't think she could all in one day. Turn right there." He pointed ahead.

I glanced at him. "I take it you're Art."

"That's right. How'd you know? Are you physic? I thought I was physic one time, but it turned out I'd heard Dad tell Mom we were going to Grandma's earlier that morning, but I forgot he had said that. So when we got into the car that night, I said we are going to Grandma's, aren't we? Mom said yes, how did I know? I told her I was physic, and Dad said that I'd heard it, but I didn't remember hearing it."

His voice continued to drone in my ears. Mrs. Bailey said he was hyper, but she didn't say it was with a capital "H." I knew where Carter's store was so I zoned out from the little chatterbox. He certainly didn't need me to carry on his conversation with. He was doing fine on his own.

Bart never said a word; he just continued to dig through his backpack. Art took a deep breath and I took advantage of his momentary lapse. "You've been digging through your bag since I picked you up. Did you lose something, Bart?" I glanced at the quiet boy.

"Pitch pipe." He continued to dig.

"He's always losing his pitch pipe. *Where's my pitch pipe* should be his middle name. My middle name is Ward. You know, like Beaver's dad. I don't know where Mom got it from. She has some weird ideas sometimes. She's not like Dad. He's the smartest person I know. I told him that one time, and he laughed until his sides hurt. I guess it was funny, but I'm not sure why. When he finally quit laughing, Dad asked Mom if I was the one she dropped on my head when I was little. I don't know why he asked that question, but she just said 'yes'."

I had a headache and Art's voice was grinding inside it, kicking the pain into overdrive. "That's all good—"

"I don't remember being dropped on my head. I think I would have remembered that. Would you know if you'd been dropped on your head?" He looked at me. "Your head is kinda shaped funny. Were you dropped on your head?"

I felt my head. "No. What's wrong with—?"

"Do you see that cat over there?" Art pointed to a black ball of fur sitting on a street corner. "That cat is there every afternoon when we come by here. I wonder what he's waiting on. Maybe his master walks by that corner on his way home from work, and the cat comes to meet him. I'll bet his owner works at the seafood factory at the end of town, and the cat knows he's coming long before he even sees him because of the smell. You know one time . . ."

I had to make him shut up. I was a mother. I should know how to handle a situation like this. I certainly couldn't simply tell him to shut up, although the thought was teetering at the back of my mind. I needed a sensible way to get this kid to be quiet. Just as I turned onto Franklin and was one block from the music store, I remembered something Icie Bailey had said about how Booger got his son's attention.

As loudly and as clearly as possible, I barked.

Chapter 5

What had I been reduced to? There I was barking at the ten-year-old Bailey twins like they were dogs. Or, goats, in their case.

I let Art out at Carter's and then drove the next few blocks in blissful silence to drop off Bart.

"Did you find your pitch pipe?" I asked.

He slid out of the truck. "No." He slammed the door and marched up the walkway to a large Victorian house.

I rolled down the window. "How about a 'thank you'?" I called to Bart.

"Yeah." He didn't turn around, just threw a dismissive wave into the air.

"Thank you, Mrs. Bertie," I said sarcastically aloud to . . . well, to myself. "That was very kind of you to pick my brother and me up and drop us at various places when it really wasn't your job to do so. You have no obligation to me or my family, but out of the goodness of your heart, or possibly your crazy mind, you did this. We can never repay you. Never in a million years."

I must have babbled on for three miles before I realized what I

73

was doing. Evidently, I caught a case of loose lips from Art. "My brother and I could have been standing on the street corner long after that cat had gone home. But you came and rescued us. How terribly thoughtful that was."

I felt like I was going around the bend of sanity. I needed help to quit talking. Suddenly, a sound rumbled at the back of my throat. I barked.

In complete quiet, I rode back to the garage.

A week and a half after my encounter with the Bailey twins and Linc's and my run-in with Bubba Craig where he'd issued his two-week warning for Linc to go back to Atlanta, he and I were in the storage yard doing inventory. We had to verify vehicle identification numbers on several unclaimed cars and make decisions on which ones should be junked. Pop was holding down the fort in the office.

Linc drove the golf cart, and I rode shotgun. As we cruised to the back of the lot, I broached a delicate subject. "Have you heard any more from Bubba?"

"No, nothing. I think he's a man of his word, so I won't hear from him until the two weeks have passed. Then there'll be heck to pay."

"What do you intend to do about him? Should we call Chief Kramer and tell him the situation?"

Linc stopped in front of a red Ford pick-up that had tangled with a semi. He walked around the cart and slipped on a heavy work glove. I followed close behind carrying a clip board to record the ID number as he read it to me.

"I'm just going to face the situation head-on. I can't spend the rest of my life hiding from him. I have to tell him I'm not going to marry Judy, and he has to face that. Killing me won't help his daughter's broken heart, and it certainly won't do me much good either."

"Well said." I pointed my pen toward the shattered windshield and twisted metal of the wrecked pick-up. Linc brushed away the shards of glass and read the ID number to me. I was jotting down the last few numbers when he sprinted past me, almost knocking me down.

"Come on," Linc bellowed like he had whistle lodged in this throat.

I had to run to catch up with him and the speeding golf cart. I'd barely jumped on when we hit a bump in the rutty ground and bounced my head against the hard plastic roof. "What are you doing?" I demanded.

"There's someone hiding behind one of the cars. It's the Mafia. They've come to get me." Linc made a sharp curve to the left and hit a bump, all at the same time. I slid from the seat and landed face first in the dirt. The rear wheel of the cart ran over my ankle. Pain of major proportion shot through my leg. I released one long, loud scream. Before I recaptured my breath, Linc had spun the golf cart and was trying to lift me back into the seat. Screams and obscenities flooded the air.

"Are you nuts? If you kill me, I can't sign your paychecks." I rubbed my ankle with one hand and held on for dear life with the other.

"I tell you, there is someone out there." Linc tried to look over his shoulder and nearly ran into the gate. He raced on past the office and onto the highway that runs in front of the garage. A van passed us. Until it was out of sight, its horn blared.

"Where are you going?" I shrieked.

"I gotta get you to the hospital. Look at your ankle." He pointed to my foot.

Black tire tracks marked my white sock. My ankle swelled with each passing minute. "I think it might be broken," I said.

"I know. I'm trying to get you to the hospital."

"But we're on a golf cart, for crying out loud." A semi came toward us in on-coming traffic. As it zoomed past us, the force of the wind pushed us off the road toward a water-logged ditch. Linc recovered and pulled back onto the highway.

"We're only about two more miles from the hospital. Just hang on. I'm hurrying." A man on a bicycle passed us.

"He's going faster than we are. Maybe he can give me a ride on his handlebars," I joked.

Linc shook his head. "That's a special racing bike. You'd be too much weight on the front."

I rolled my eyes so far back in my head it's a wonder they ever came back out. A few minutes and a couple of narrow misses later, we arrived at the emergency room. Skidding to a stop just outside the door, Linc bailed from the cart, rushed inside, and came back with a wheelchair. I was rolled in and, after a few minutes of questions, I was taken into a large room where the bays were divided by curtains.

Before I went into the examining room, I told Linc to go back to the garage and have Pop call Arch. He'd be leaving school soon.

"Yes, ma'am, I'll do that. I'll have Mr. Byrd go into the storage yard and see if there are feet prints where the Mafia was hiding."

"Yeah, you do that." I wished I could be a fly on the wall when Linc asked Pop to go out and see if the Mafia was hiding in the yard. What a hoot that would be. Should I be concerned for my employee's sanity? Naw, I had enough trouble hanging on to my own.

Once I was situated in my cubby hole, a nurse helped me slip into a hospital gown. She pulled off my shoe and sock. It was plain to see my jeans weren't going to go over my swollen ankle, so they were cut off. Were they my favorite pair? That would go without saying, wouldn't it?

"Dr. Johns is on call. He'll be in to see you soon." The nurse pulled the curtain closed on the right side of my stretcher/bed. In the process, she pulled it open on the left side. A man who must have been born when Washington was president lay in the next bed. He kept flicking his tongue out of his toothless mouth and winking at me.

I tried to ignore him, but every once in a while, he'd *psst* at me. I pushed the button for the nurse.

"Yes, Mrs. Fortney. What do you need?" a woman's voice came over the intercom just above my head.

I twisted to be able to shout into it. Pain stabbed from my toes to my knee. "I need someone to close my curtain, please."

"I'll get it," a gravelly voice sounded near my ear. I jumped and turned to see who was standing next to me. It was the old man. "I'll close it, nurse," he hollered into the metal plate on the wall.

"Thank you, Mr. Warren. Now get back in bed," the nurse said.

The man grabbed my sheet and started to get into my bed. "Hey, hey, hey." I snatched the cover away from him.

"Get in *your* bed, Mr. Warren," the nurse chimed.

"Dang." The man turned, his hospital gown gaping open exposing his backside. I should have closed my eyes, but I was too flabbergasted to do so. I just stared at his pale skin covered with dark ages spots. His butt cheeks looked like deflated soccer balls. Brrr! Once Mr. Warren was on his side of the room, he turned back to me, winked, and closed the curtain.

I melted back into my pillow, closed my eyes and violently shook my head, hoping to erase like an Etch-a-Sketch the disturbing image of Mr. Warren's backside. But that wasn't to happen. From the other side of the curtain, I heard Dr. Johns talking to someone. Apparently he was flipping through my chart.

"What's Bertie done now?" he asked.

I started to give him a piece of my mind, what little bit I had left, but since he was going to be in charge of relieving my pain, I decided to overlook his insensitive remark. I would withhold my strong desire to call him a doo doo head. But I thought it.

For the next couple of hours, I was twisted, turned, poked, x-rayed, and had to stand on one foot, lower myself over the toilet without actually touching the seat, and pee in a cup. Somehow I managed to get it all done without screaming aloud.

By the time Arch arrived, a nurse was wrapping my ankle in an Ace bandage. He hurried to my side.

"I'm sorry, sweetheart. I left school early to meet with the superintendent about the Science Fair." He kissed me lightly. "It wasn't until I got home that I got the message on the answering machine." He took my hand. "Are you okay?"

His nearness made my head spin. "I'm sure I'm going to be fine as soon as they give me something for the pain."

He glanced at the nurse. "Can you get the doctor to give her something?"

"He said he'd be in as soon as I finish wrapping her ankle." She secured the bandage. "I'll let him know I'm through." She disappeared around the curtain.

Arch squeezed my hand. "What am I going to do with you?"

"It wasn't my fault. Linc threw me off the golf cart and then he ran over me."

"I don't know what I'd do if something bad happened to you." My dear sweet husband put his arms around me and pulled my head against his chest, crushing my nose. He squeezed me so hard, I grunted.

"It's just a sprained ankle," I said.

"Today, it's a sprained ankle, but tomorrow . . . who knows." Did he choke back a sob?

I twisted to put my arms around him. "There. There." I patted his back. "It'll be all right. I've been through lots worse than this."

He pulled back enough to look into my eyes. "I love you, Bertie. I want us to grow old together. I want you waiting there in our little house when I sneak away from the nursing home and come visit you in the middle of the night. Promise me you'll stay alive until then."

"How could I refuse when you put it so eloquently?" I gave my wonderful husband the most passionate kiss I could, even though my leg throbbed painfully with each beat of my heart.

"Bertie?" A man's voice sounded behind us.

We separated and looked at Dr. Johns. "I see you've come to claim your prize."

"Yes, sir. How is she?" Arch moved away from my bed.

"Oh, she'll be fine." The doctor looked at me. "It's just a bad sprain. You'll need to stay off of it for a few days. I'd like to see you in my office the first of next week, so call and make an appointment. Thankfully, the fall didn't hurt the baby."

I sucked his words down the wrong pipe. They strangled me.

"Baby?" Arch asked.

"Yes, my guess is sometime near the end of summer Bertie will be delivering a bouncing baby." Dr. Johns chuckled. "Sorry, I had a vision of her actually bouncing the baby into the world." He mimed dribbling a basketball. When he realized I wasn't laughing, his expression went stone-like. "Where's your sense of humor?"

"I lost it somewhere between my sprained ankle and I'm pregnant. I never dreamed you could find something like that out by x-raying my ankle."

"Bertie, you're a hoot." Dr. Johns handed me a prescription. "We found that out when you peed in a cup. Have a good day, you two." He disappeared. Arch and I just stared at the swaying curtain. We were lost in dumbfounded silence.

On the way home from the emergency room, Arch and I went by the garage. Linc waited there for some word on how I faired from my run-in with the golf cart. Even though it was all just an unfortunate accident, I knew he'd be worried beyond belief.

We'd barely stopped when I saw a wave of people racing toward us. I didn't feel like actually getting out of the car, so I just rolled down the window.

"Are you okay?" Linc won the foot race, followed close behind by Petey, Mom, and Pop.

"I'm fine. It's just a sprained ankle." The pain killer I'd been given was very mild because of the ba . . . bab . . . because of my condition, but it relieved some of the agony.

Petey opened the car door and threw herself into my arms. "I'm so glad you didn't get killed."

"Well, so am I." I held her tight. "But there wasn't the slightest chance I could have been killed by just being run over by a golf cart."

She looked up at me. "I know that. I meant by the mean man who was hiding in the car out back." Fear darkened her eyes.

Suddenly, the meaning of her words impacted my thoughts. "You mean Linc really did see someone? The Redneck Mafia was out there?"

"You're half right." Pop stepped closer. "There was someone out there, but they weren't the Mafia." He heehawed.

I glanced at Linc who turned two shades of red. "Mr. Byrd don't believe me, but I know it was one of Bubba Craig's men in disguise."

"Oh, brother, I told you that man had nothing to do with that Craig fellow." Pop roared with laughter. He rested his hand on the car roof and leaned toward me. "Sid Winchell had a fight with Ethel, so he went to the Dew Drop Inn and drank his breakfast and lunch. By this afternoon, he had a snoot full and didn't want to go home. He was going to sleep it off in one of our cars. You two just happened along before he could get comfy in the back seat of a Chevy." Pop laughed so hard he had a coughing, wheezing spell.

Mom rubbed his back. "Come on, Tom, let's get you out of this cold night air." She leaned into the car and kissed me on the cheek. "Feel better, sweetheart." Arm in arm, she and Pop headed back to their house.

"I gotta get my books." Petey ran ahead of them.

I had big news for all of them, but I wanted it to be my and Arch's secret for a few days. I wanted to come out of the shock.

"I'm really sorry, Mrs. Bertie. I hope you'll be okay." Linc closed the car door.

"It was an accident, Linc. Please don't give it another thought. If I'd seen old Mr. Winchell climbing into a car, it probably would have scared me, too."

"Bertie has to stay off her feet for a couple of days." Arch rested his arms on the top of the steering wheel. "I'll call Mr. Byrd when I get home and let him know you'll be needing him at work tomorrow. And don't worry too much about it. You actually did us a favor. If she hadn't gone to the emergency room, we wouldn't know we're going to have a baby."

I heard Arch's words, but they didn't compute. Ugh. Yes, they did. I was pregnant and now I'd have to say the words out loud long before my brain could accept them. I wasn't ready.

"Please don't say anything to anyone, Linc," I pleaded. "We need to tell my parents and Petey before anyone else knows."

Arch put his hand on my shoulder. "I guess I jumped the gun. Sorry, I'm just so excited about the baby."

"Don't worry, Mr. Arch. Your secret is safe with me." Linc opened the back door for Petey who raced toward the car. Once she and her backpack were secured in the back seat, Linc closed the door, stepped back, and placed his finger to his lips.

"Mum's the word." He gave me a quick salute.

I half-heartedly returned the gesture. The glee in his eye told me Arch and I had better make the announcement as soon as possible, or Linc would burst.

When we arrived home, it was a little after nine. Petey ran ahead to unlock the door, and Arch helped me out of the car.

Barbie's front porch light came on, and she raced out her door and across our lawns in my direction. She threw her arms around me, nearly knocking me off my good foot. "I'm so excited for you."

I was still recovering from her tackle so my brain wasn't clacking on all cylinders. "Because I sprained my ankle?" It took so little to make my nutty neighbor happy.

"No, silly, because of the baby."

I felt like someone had hit me in the stomach. I looked at Arch. "When you're pregnant, are the words stamped on your face?" I ran my fingers over my forehead to see if I could feel letters imprinted there.

He looked as puzzled as I was. "How did you know that, Barbie?" he asked.

"Your mom called a few minutes ago to see if you'd made it home yet, and she told me."

Maybe the pain pills were stronger than I thought. Surely I was hallucinating. Things were happening too fast, and my spinning stomach couldn't keep up with it.

"I need to get inside. Thanks, Barbie. I'll see you tomorrow." *After I kill Linc.* Arch helped me into our house. I'd barely sat in the recliner when the phone rang.

Petey answered it. "What? I don't want a sister or a brother." She handed me the portable phone. "Mom, what is Grandma taking about?" Realization scowled her face. "Eeewww! You two did that?" She crinkled her nose and stuck out her tongue.

I felt like joining her. I placed the phone to my ear. Mom was already talking ninety miles an hour.

" . . . I had to hear it from your wrecker driver. Why didn't you tell me and Pop?"

"Mom. Mom. Catch your breath before you hyperventilate. It's a long story about why Linc found out before you did. I'm too tired to tell it tonight. I love you, and yes, you're going to be a grandma again. Just concentrate on that and not on how you found out. Good night, Mom. Okay. Sure, I understand. I'm going to hang up now." I clicked the off button. Glancing at Arch, I realized he found the whole situation highly amusing.

I pointed a threatening finger at him, or at least as threatening as it could be with my ankle bandaged. "This is all your fault."

Arch belly laughed. "I certainly hope so." He placed a light kiss on my forehead. "I'll be right back." He turned to Petey. "I'm going to fix Mom something to eat. You go get ready for bed." He kissed her, too. "When you get done, come back, and the three of us will have a talk about having a baby." He disappeared into the kitchen.

My sweet daughter gave me a hug. "I'm glad you're here. Dad and I have had a couple of *those* talks and he uses too many scientific terms. I need someone to translate for me." She skipped off down the hall.

Jeeze, where could I get a Mommy manual? I needed one quick.

Before Petey went to bed, Arch and I talked with her. She's the most perfect daughter I could ever ask for. Her dad had done a good job raising her to this point. I'm not sure I could have done so well.

However, he explained the facts of life to Petey with the precision of the science teacher he was. Her interpretation came close to putting seeds into, and watering, a Chia Pet. Hopefully, between her dad and me, we were able to make her understand the act of making a baby was a result of the overwhelming love the mother and father had for each other. Out of that love a new life was formed. When we finished our talk, she seemed a little less repulsed by the fact her dad and I had *done that.* And I was beginning to enjoy the fact that because of our love, the three of us were having a baby.

Mom stayed with me the next day so I could rest and keep my foot elevated. Having her wait on me and fix me chicken noodle soup almost made the whole incident worth it. Shortly after lunch, my best friend Mary Lou called.

"Is it true, Bertie?" Her whispered tone surprised me. "Are you pregnant?

Well, it looked like I would never get to announce the fact to anyone. Sweet Meadow should have been named Wildfire because that was how news spread in our quiet little town.

"Yes, Mary Lou, it's really true. Hard to believe, isn't it?" In about eight months her son would have a playmate. The two of them would be friends through their whole lives just like Mary Lou and me.

"It really is." She sounded almost disappointed. "I'll bet Arch is devastated, isn't he?"

"Devastated? Why would he be devastated?"

"Well." A disgusted huff came through the phone to my disbelieving ears. "What with you having an affair with your employee so soon after you and Arch tied the knot."

I bolted out of my comfy chair. "What are you talking about?"

"Millie called the insurance office today and said that Linc got you pregnant on a golf cart. I gotta tell you, my dear friend, I was never so shocked in all my life." She *tsk tsk tsked* a few times and then added, "Poor Arch."

Take deep breaths, Bertie. Breathe in. Breathe out. I felt woozy. Putting my head between my knees, I closed my eyes against the spinning world. Eventually, I got a grip on the situation.

"Mary Lou, honey, deary." I had to ease my way into the speech I needed to make. "Linc is not the father of my baby. Arch is. The only connection between me, Linc, and my pregnancy is the fact he knocked me off the golf cart and ran over me. He took me to the hospital on said golf cart. There the doctor determined I was pregnant."

"Well, that explains it," Mary Lou said. "Millie said that Linc had knocked you *up* on a golf cart. I guess she got confused. Jeeze, she's a trip, isn't she?"

"So are you," I yelled. "I have to go lie down. I'll talk to you later." I turned off the phone and slumped back into my chair. I had a headache as big as Mildred Locke's butt in a bathing suit. I don't know why that came to mind. It just proved how distressed I was.

Shortly after three, I awoke from a much-needed nap. Mom had everything spit-polished and shining. I'd just limped from the bathroom back to my recliner when Petey burst through the door. She raced past me and ran into her bedroom. The door slammed behind her. I hobbled back down the hallway. Before I knocked, I could hear her muffled sobs.

"Petey?" I tapped lightly and opened the door. She lay on her tummy with her head buried in her pillow. Her whole body shook from the forceful crying she was doing. I eased my way to the bed and rubbed her shoulder. "What is it, sweetheart?"

Through red-rimmed eyes she looked up at me. I helped her to a sitting position and pulled her close. "Talk to me," I coaxed.

"Randy Carson said now that you're going to have a baby you won't love me anymore." She sniffed. "He said I'll be treated like Cinderella, and I'll have to clean the ashes from the fireplace."

"Honey, we don't have a fireplace."

"That's what I told Randy, and he said I'd have to clean the toilets instead." She flung herself, face first, back into her pillow. "He said I'd have to do it so much my hands will turn blue like the water. I don't want to clean toilets for the rest of my life." My dead Drama Queen was piercing my heart.

"Sit up here and listen to me." I lifted her onto my lap. "No one is going to treat you like Cinderella. And as for not loving you, nothing could make me do that. There is no doubt I'll need your help when the baby gets here, but for things like holding and playing with him or her. Not cleaning the toilets. You'll be so busy teaching your little brother or sister everything you know about life you won't have time for things like cleaning toilets." I chuckled and squeezed her closer.

She pulled back and looked up with sadness dribbling down her cheeks. "You won't love me like you will your own baby."

I wiped away her tears and lifted her chin so I could look into her angelic face. "It's not *my* baby. It's our baby, mine, your dad's, and yours. No matter how many children we have, you'll always be the first in my heart. The first in my soul." I kissed her button nose. "And the first to call me Mommy." My throat hitched. "No one can ever take that away."

"Okay, but can I have a sister instead of a stinking brother?" Petey swiped the back of her hand across her nose.

"I don't have any control over that, but would a little brother be so bad?" I pushed a wisp of blond hair behind her ear.

"I'm afraid he would turn out to be as mean as Randy Carson." She pushed a piece of my hair behind my ear. The corners of my lips automatically pulled to a smile.

"Or maybe he'd turn out like my brothers, Uncle Billy and Uncle Bobby. How would that be?"

"You mean your brothers who gave you a box that exploded in your face when you opened it?" she asked.

I rubbed my eyebrows, thankful they'd grown back.

"You mean the brothers who tied a string around your tooth then tied it to a bicycle and took off, not pulling your loose tooth out, but dragging you a long way before you fell and knocked out the tooth next to the loose one?" Petey finally paused and cocked her brow. "You mean those brothers?"

My smile melted to a frown. "I see your point."

Chapter 6

I took only three days away from the garage to recuperate from my sprained ankle and to absorb the happy surprise that I was pregnant. I still hadn't actually gotten to tell anyone the good news. Everyone had already heard it through the kudzu vine.

I spent most of the morning filing, ordering parts, and cleaning the customer waiting area of the garage office. I straightened magazines and shoved chairs under the small dining table in the center of the floor. On the seat of one of the chairs was a KFC meal box. A sticky note attached to the top read "Lincoln."

Since one of my life's lessons had taught me not to open boxes carelessly, I plucked the broom from the corner and used the handle to flip open the top. When nothing exploded, I eased closer. Inside I found a long, white shoe string curled in a pile. I pulled it out, looked it over, and found nothing notable about it except for the fried chicken crumbs which clung to the limp string. I put it back into the box and closed the lid.

When Linc returned from a call, I told him about the package for him. He hesitated. I assured him it wouldn't explode. Slowly, he picked it up and opened it.

"Oh, no." Lanky Linc dropped the box and jumped about three feet backward.

"What in the world is wrong with you?" I limped around the counter. My driver shook so hard his cork-screw curls boinged from under his cap. I picked up the shoe string and tried to hand it to him. "Here, it won't bite."

"It's from the Redneck Mafia. That's what they use to kill their prey." He looked out the picture window on the front wall. "They're out there. Waiting for me." He sighed.

"It's . . . a . . . shoe . . . string." I spoke slowly so as not to lose him in my words. "Say it after me." I tapped his arm. "It's . . . a . . . shoe . . . string."

"It's a death string." His face turned white as milk.

"Linc, you have to calm down. You've gone way over the top with this Mafia thing." I sat and propped my foot in another chair. "I know Bubba threatened you, but what can he do? Really?"

Linc held up the shoe string. "He can strangle me with this."

"Good Lord, haven't they ever heard of piano wire?"

He jumped like he'd been shot. "Mrs. Bertie, please," he begged, "don't give them any ideas." He scooped up the box and tossed it and the shoe string into the trash can.

Linc was truly upset by the matter. "Okay, I won't give them any ideas, but you have to promise me you'll quit letting that bully intimidate you. I can't have you driving my equipment and being responsible for my customers when you are so easily shaken. Promise me you'll just ignore Bubba's attempts to scare you."

Linc removed his hat. "I can't let any of this put my livelihood in jeopardy. I need this job." He scratched his head. "I won't let anybody terrorize me again. I'll make you that promise."

I slapped him on the back. "Attaboy, now go pick up Millie Keats' prescription and take it to her." That should try out Linc's newly-found determination; Millie always struck fear in his heart.

Several days later, I was called to Shell Street to impound a vehicle belonging to Udell Carson's brother. He was arrested while driving his wife around in the car. Unfortunately, she was in the trunk, and it was against her will. When I arrived on the scene, Cheeter Carson, C.C. to his friends, was being loaded into an ambulance and Deedy, his wife, was in custody in the back of the squad car.

According to Deputy Kelly, Deedy took great exception to C.C.'s idea of a joke and was laying in wait with a tire iron when he opened the trunk. She got in one good surprise swing before the deputy could stop her.

I was instructed to take their car back to the yard and keep it impounded until I heard from the Chief that it was okay to release it.

Hours later a taxi stopped in front of the garage. A small, tow-headed boy bounded from the back seat. B.B. Carson, the five-year-old son of C.C. and Deedy, burst into the office while his father struggled to get out of the cab. A bandage was wrapped around C.C.'s head and covered his right eye. While he paid the driver, his son scooted a chair across the floor. Just as B.B.'s blond head appeared across the counter from me, his dad made it into the office.

"Bird Lady," the boy shouted, "my dad and me are here to get his car. You had no right to pound his car." With that, B.B. hammered his fist against the counter top. "You just took it from him and pounded it and pounded it." Bang. Bang. "You're going to be sorry you pounded Dad's car." Bang. Bang.

I reached out and captured the little tot's arm. "I didn't pound your dear ol' dad's car. I *impounded it*." He twisted out of my grasp and slammed his hand down again.

C.C. staggered in our direction.

"Control your son," I demanded.

He looked at me through his bloodshot, unbandaged eye. "Been there. Tried that. Ain't going back."

Bang. Bang. The little menace continued to thump the counter. Again I grabbed his wrist and held on for dear life. Linc entered the office.

"Get this twerp down, please," I instructed my bewildered-looking driver.

Linc quickly approached B.B., but the boy was having no part of being lifted down. I let go of his hand just a fraction of a second before Linc seized the kid's ankles and hung him upside down.

C.C. smiled a goofy grin. "Boy, you're in trouble now."

I thought he was talking to his son. I was wrong. B.B. reached up from his dangling position and latched onto Linc's private parts and squeezed with all his might.

"I tried to warn ya." C.C. doubled over with laughter. Linc howled with pain.

I grabbed my trusty broom and reared back. "You make him let go, now, or I'm going to make your good eye look like your other one," I yelled at C.C.

He complied with my request. Linc doubled over and waddled

into Pop's office. C.C. placed his little darling on a chair. "Don't move again, or I'll feed you to Booger Bailey's goat."

The boy looked up at me, his lip quivering. "You better not pound my daddy's car again, Bird Lady."

Before I could stop myself, I stuck out my tongue at him.

I pulled the tow truck next to the curb outside the Chow Pal Diner. I called our lunch order in and all I had to do was pick it up for Linc and me. Filled with many locals, the restaurant buzzed with chatter and the clamor of dishes. From the exposed cook surface, grilling burgers and onions sizzled, filling the air with an inviting aroma. Unfortunately, my stomach saw it as an interruption in its continuous undulating. I needed to grab my order and get out of there as fast as possible.

I waited at the register for the young pimply-faced boy to bag my food. From the corner of my eye, I saw someone approaching. Carrie Sue MacMillan.

I greeted her with a warm smile. "Hi, Carrie Sue."

She leaned closer. "When the divorce is final, can I have back the toaster I gave you and Arch?" she whispered.

I should have been shocked, but versions of that question had burned their way into my ears for the past several days. "We aren't getting a divorce. Contrary to what you've heard, I haven't had an affair with my driver. Arch is the father of my baby." I forced a smile I was sure was nothing less than a smirk.

"I'm glad to hear that. I couldn't believe the woman who was always such a prude would have sex with someone other than her husband just days after they were married."

"I'm not a prude about sex." Shouldn't I have been more upset by the affair reference than by the word prude? And shouldn't I have said that just a little softer than I did?

Mildred Locke happened by. "I guess you've proven that, haven't you?" She balanced a tray loaded with plates of food. I thought about tripping her, but, of course, I didn't.

By this time, the noise had lowered to whispered tones. I didn't have to look around to know all eyes were on me. This was all Millie Keats' fault. I should have driven her through town strapped to the back of my tow truck with her using Chief Kramer's bullhorn to tell Sweet Meadow's citizens that Linc had not knocked me up on a golf cart.

Now my headache matched the unrest going on in my stomach. I snatched my food from the boy at the register. "It's Arch's baby," I snarled at him.

"Ookkaayy," he said.

He appeared to be the only person in the place who didn't know or care about my alleged infidelity. I whirled on my heel, tossed my chin into the air, and marched my purple coverall-clad behind out the door. The vicious rumor was beginning to yank on my nerves. Surely it would die before too long.

I almost reached my truck when County Commissioner "Jack" Bigham waved and rushed toward me.

"Mrs. Fortney. Bertie. I've wanted to talk to you." His apple cheeks flushed pink from the cool air.

"Mr. Bigham, have any good tips for me?"

He once tried to scare me by writing me odd letters, and always closed them with a tip of the day. He was a strange little duck, but once I got to know him, I even voted for him in the local election.

"No tips today," he chuckled. "I was wondering, though." He appeared to be searching for the right words. "Would you like to have dinner with me tonight?"

Those were nowhere near the words I thought he was searching for. "Is there a special reason I would do that?" I asked.

His build could only be described as small stature, but sometimes, to appear confident, he puffed out his chest like a rooster about to crow.

"Since you will soon be divorced, I thought maybe you'd be needing some male companionship." He winked. "It's okay with me if you are having another man's child. I'd be glad to raise it as my own." Was that a smile or a leer smeared on Jack's face?

I didn't like the horrible path our conversation was taking. "The only male I need is my husband. Everything you've heard is a big fat lie. My baby belongs to Arch, and we are never getting divorced. Never. Never. Never. Do you understand?"

I deflated Jack's swollen chest and slumped his shoulders in one fell swoop.

"I'm sorry, Jack, but surely you didn't believe that rumor, did you?" I gave him credit for being more insightful than that.

"You can't blame a guy for trying. I thought it was too good to be true." He shoved his hands into his jacket pockets.

"I'm flattered." I wasn't sure what else to say.

"Well, maybe I do have a tip for you. You might want to have a talk with Millie Keats. She's confused and very convincing." He nodded his goodbye and hurried on his way.

"Thanks," I called to him. "I intend to do that very thing." I'd better do it today. I didn't want to give her another day to fan the flames of the bonfire raging through Sweet Meadow.

I dropped off lunch at the garage, but my tummy voted against eating right then. Evidently hearing the word pregnant is the stimuli for morning sickness to start. What a misnomer. For the past couple of days, I suffered from morning, noon, and night sickness. Just being in the office with lunch in a bag in the corner made me nauseous.

"Linc, I'm going out for a while." He glanced at me over the top of his huge burger and nodded.

Out in the open air, I looked at the sky. The sun warmed my face and soothed my uneasy stomach. Such were the trials of having a baby. My heart swelled. I was having a baby. Arch's baby.

The time had come for me to have a little talk with Millie Keats. It would be a job to undo what she had done, but I had to start somewhere. My mission—to stifle Millie.

When I arrived at her front door, I found it open. Music blared from inside. I knocked, but she didn't hear me. Slowly opening the screen door, I eased into the house.

"Millie," I yelled. "Millie, it's me, Bertie." Still no sign of her. I made my way through her living room filled with gold velvet furniture, hand-crocheted doilies, and ceramic figurines. Closer to the dining room, I caught my first glimpse of Millie. One I hoped wouldn't scar my unborn child.

With her back to me, the eighty-plus-year-old woman danced to a disco tune. Dressed in black exercise tights and leotards with a pair of bright yellow throng panties over top, she gyrated her hips seductively toward an imaginary partner. With one foot firmly on the floor, she used her other like riding a scooter to turn her swaying body to face me.

She screamed. "For God's sake, Bertie, are you trying to kill me?" She clutched her chest and slumped to a nearby chair.

"I'm sorry." I rushed to her. "Can I get you something?"

She pointed toward the CD player. I turned off the loud music.

"Are you all right?" I took a seat in a chair next to her.

"I guess so. What are you doing here?" She appeared to be okay.

"I came to talk to you about the rumor you started about Linc knocking me up on a golf cart. You know that isn't true; why would you say something like that?"

"How do I know it isn't true? All I know is that every time I've asked you to send that hottie to take me somewhere, you refused. Now I find out you were just keeping him for yourself." Millie rose, placed her hands on her hips, and sucked in her stomach. "But wait until he gets a look at the firm, luscious body I'm working on just for him. You won't stand a chance."

I rose and ran out the front door. Behind me, Millie hollered, "I need a ride to my Garden Club meeting at four."

I stopped dead in my tracks. Turning to face her, I placed my fists on my hips. "The only ride I'll ever give you again is to the moon. You have moved past being a fruitcake to being a vicious old woman."

Wow. That hurt my soul. I should have more compassion for someone who had lived so many years. She had earned her right to senility. I felt bad for the sharp, hurtful words I spewed in a moment of frustration.

Once inside the truck, I glanced back at the porch. Hurt plainly showed on Millie's face, leaving me feeling like gum stuck to the bottom of a shoe. I forced a smile and waved at her. "I'll pick you up at four." I drove away.

Only I could go to reprimand someone for wreaking havoc in my life and come away feeling crummy and agreeing to do something for that person I didn't want to do. If I hurried, I'd have time to eat my cold lunch and be back to Millie's by four.

Petey needed new panties and pajamas. Saturday morning was designated as a mother-daughter shopping day. So, we were off to Panties R Us where Donna Carson had recently been made Panty-Bin Manager.

My daughter picked out a nightgown with a hippie-flower print and a pair of pajamas jazzed up with Dufus the St. Bernard. I gathered cotton panties colored to co-ordinate with several of her favorite outfits. Why? I wasn't sure, since hopefully no one except Petey would know whether her drawers matched her blouse, but it seemed important to her.

At the counter, Donna smiled widely. "Hey, Bertie. How's things going?" She took the items from Petey and me and punched buttons on the cash register.

Excitement surged through me. I finally found someone I could tell about the baby.

"Things couldn't be better." Surely I was radiating. Pride

surrounded me. "I'm preg—"

"I hear you're going to have a brother or sister." Donna interrupted, and directed her statement to Petey who nodded with enthusiasm.

Foiled again.

"I hope it's a sister. I don't want no brother." Petey twitched her nose like she smelled something bad.

"Okay then, I'll help you pray for a baby sister." Donna glanced back at me. "Congratulations. Tell Arch the same for me."

I nodded.

"By the way, Bertie, I planned to call you later in the afternoon. I'm going to Bridgemont for a managers' meeting. Isn't that where your brother Bobby and his family are?"

He lived not too far over the Georgia line in Tennessee. Bridgemont was only a ten-minute drive from his town.

"Yeah, he does."

"I'd like to get his phone number so I can call when I hit town. Maybe I'll get a chance to visit with him and Estelle." While Donna finished ringing up my purchase, I scribbled Bobby's phone number on a piece of paper. As she handed me my change, I handed her the information she wanted.

Petey and I rounded out our day together with a milkshake. We toasted to many more mother-daughter days and voted to see who had the best milk mustache.

Sunday morning arrived with a deluge pounding against our bedroom window. Climbing out of bed didn't sound like much fun, so I pulled the covers over my head and hoped that, at least for another hour or so, the world could rotate without my help.

One loud, annoying ring shrilled from the phone. I peeked out from my hiding place to see the clock. Seven-thirty. From the kitchen, I heard Arch talking, and I smelled coffee. Let me interpret my thoughts at that point. Arch and coffee equals a good thing. Seven-thirty phone call on Sunday morning equals bad thing.

My wonderful, handsome husband magically appeared at the side of the bed.

"I brought you coffee." After setting a mug of the steaming brew on the nightstand, he handed me the phone. "Bobby wants to talk to you."

"Me?" I pointed to myself. Arch nodded. Bobby never called me. Especially early Sunday morning. Like I've already said—a bad thing.

"Hello?"

"Ro-Bert-A, what in hell is wrong with you?" my brother bellowed.

At first I was stunned. My brother loved me, but his words spewed venom. My brain zinged and buzzed like it had short-circuited. Why was Bobby attacking me? Had I broken a commandment, like murder or adult . . . ?

"It's Arch's baby, you idiot." The brutal rumor had now crossed state lines. "How could you believe such a thing? You know I love Arch. I'd never sleep with another man."

"Oh, my goodness." Bobby's voice choked. "Estelle," he yelled a little too loud for my tender ears, "Bertie's having a baby. Isn't that wonderful news?"

My sister-in-law hollered from the background, "Congratulations."

"Oh, yeah," Bobby said to his wife, "I forgot to tell you it's Arch's baby. Although I would have assumed that went without saying."

"Woohoo!" Estelle cheered. "Give Arch a big hug for me."

Confused is the only word I could think of to describe what I felt. "You mean you didn't know about the baby?" I asked.

"No, how long have you known? Why haven't you called us?"

I rubbed my temple near my right eye. Dang, that annoying twitch had returned. "If you didn't call because you'd heard about the baby, then why?"

"Oh, yeah, that." He lost some of his initial harshness. "I just wanted to let you know when I see you again, I'm going to kill you."

"I think Arch will frown upon that unless you wait until after the baby is born." I rose to a sitting position. "Just so I know, what have I done that's worth dying for?"

"You gave Donna Carson my phone number and now she wants to stay here at our house while she's in town for a meeting."

"I had no idea that was her intent. She just said she wanted to visit with you while she's in town. You, of course, told her no, didn't you?"

"Would you refuse Donna anything?" He emitted a nervous giggle.

I didn't have to think very long about that. For as long as I could remember, Donna's nickname had been "The Vindictive." The sad truth was I was afraid of her, too. "No, I wouldn't have told her no either."

A quick glance at the clock and I knew my lazy time had come to an end. "Sorry. I never thought about her asking to stay with you. That wasn't what she said she wanted your number for." Taking a sip of hot coffee, I put my feet into my slippers and stood.

"I guess I'll forgive you since you're making me an uncle again." Estelle said something inaudible in the background. "I got to run, Bert. I'm singing in the choir this morning. We have a new choir director, and he hates it when anyone is late. He points you out with his baton. Love ya. Bye."

A choir director who hated for members to be late and who pointed you out if you were. Sounded like Homer King. Our old director made a quick disappearance after he dared to grab my behind. I heard he moved to Tennessee. Could Handy Homer now oversee the music at Bobby's church? Naw, that would be too weird.

As I dressed for church, I reflected on the fact I finally got to tell someone about the baby, and what did I do? I drew attention to the rumor of my infidelity. Sadness burned behind my eyes causing them to mist. A happy time of my life was overshadowed by untruths. Tears ran down my cheeks and dripped off my jaw line. They left two matched spots on my mint green silk blouse. I'd have to change.

I pulled the garment over my head and got my earring caught in the material. With care, I worked to get it free, but the more I tried the more tangled it became. By this time, waterworks flooded my face. Mascara ran rampant. I couldn't stop crying.

Arch came to my rescue. "Here, honey, let me help."

He set me free from my captor. "Why are you crying?" Using his thumb, he wiped away my tears.

"Everyone thinks I'm carrying Linc's baby. I thought the rumor would die, but it hasn't. Everywhere I go, people stare and point and even verbally condemn me." Burying my face against his white dress shirt, I sobbed and sobbed. Arch held me. He stroked my hair and whispered sweet things in my ear.

"No one believes that story. They are just having a good time with you. Not one person has said that to me. Here." He moved to the sink and wet a wash cloth. "Wipe your face." He handed me the cloth. "We're going to be late for church. Finish getting dressed."

We both looked at the front of his shirt, soiled with make-up and tears. "You'll have to change. I'm sorry."

"Don't worry about it. It's worth it if I helped you to feel better."

"You have," I lied. As long as everyone continued with their flight from reality about my baby's father, nothing would make me feel better.

Once we shed ourselves of tear-stained clothes, Arch and I, along with Petey, made it to Sweet Meadow Baptist Church seconds before the doors closed. Thankfully, we were counted as present by the Garden Club ladies whose mission in life was to keep track of who did or did not attend Sunday morning worship. We took our usual seats next to Rex and Mary Lou. She and I sat together in church since we were in elementary school. Our marriages hadn't changed that.

"Are you okay?" my best friend whispered.

I nodded, not daring to speak for fear I burst into sobs again.

"I'll be back in a minute." Arch squeezed my hand and gave me a peck on the cheek. Rising, he made his way down the aisle next to the beautiful stained-glass windows, all the way through the door leading behind the pulpit and choir loft. The bathrooms were back there, too.

I started to tell Mary Lou about the sadness I'd been feeling, but the organ began to play, and Reverend Miller approached the pulpit. I'd talk to her later. Maybe she could help me work through some of the dog doo doo I felt like I stepped in.

"Good morning, my fellow Parishioners. What a beautiful, damp morning the Lord hath given us." Reverend Miller's announcement brought many amens from the congregation. "Before we begin, Arch Fortney has a few words he'd like to say." The Reverend greeted my husband with a handshake.

After a few awkward moments of Arch adjusting the microphone and me sliding down in my seat, he cleared his throat. "Good morning."

"Good morning," sang all the curious people seated around me.

"I know most of you are aware that my wife, Bertie," he nodded in my direction just in case there was one person among them who hadn't already turned to look at me, "is having a baby."

What was he doing? I motioned for him to come back to his seat. He shook his head. If I slid further down, I'd be on the floor.

"Bertie and I have heard the rumors running wild in our town." As he spoke, I held my breath. "As a matter of fact, my wife has actually been accosted by people who have known her all her life. People who watched her grow up right here in this church and know the true person she is."

While some emitted obligatory amens, others snickered. Some just coughed.

My face flamed. I squeezed my eyes shut.

"I want to set the record straight so Bertie and our daughter Petey and I can move on with the joy that comes from bringing a baby into this world. Bertie's baby is also my baby. Not her wrecker driver's. That's a vicious tale started by a misguided elderly woman who misconstrued the details of an accident Bertie had."

He became quiet. I dared to peek out at him. His kind expression melted the terror in my heart. How brave my hero was to stand up there and defend me in front of some of the most judgmental people God ever put on Earth.

The muscles in the corners of my mouth had just started to form a gratuitous smile when a commotion erupted from the Garden Club's line of blue-haired women. Millie Keats stood.

"That's not true," she said. She pointed her bony finger to her chest. "I haven't screwed anything in a long time." She motioned in my direction. "Bertie's the one who has all the explaining to do. She's the one who got knocked up on a golf cart."

Laughter exploded through the congregation.

"Excuse me." Arch tried to get their attention. "Excuse me." Finally, they quieted.

"She was knocked *off* a golf cart, Mrs. Keats," Arch said. "Knocked off. Can you understand that?"

"Well, of course I can. Why didn't she say so?"

Lord, let me wake up and find this is all a dream, I prayed. *I promise I'll never complain about my old recurring nightmare where I am here in front of these people with no clothes on.*

Somehow I made it through the worship service without spontaneously combusting. When it was over, several people rushed up to Arch and I. Handshakes and hugs abounded.

"No one believed that story, Bertie." Ethel Winchell locked her hand onto my arm. "We were just having a little fun."

"That's right," Helen Weidemeyer corroborated. "We get a big kick out of egging Millie on. Will you forgive us?"

"Of course." I smiled. "I'll forgive you."

Forgetting will be a whole different situation.

Chapter 7

When I was a child, Alma Taylor ran the Taylor School for Southern Ladies. City Council partially funded the institute. Mothers enrolled their darlings in the school in hopes they would learn manners and how to meld into society and maybe catch a man in ten easy lessons. Also, if a girl had broken a law, written or parental, she was sentenced to attend classes at the Southern Ladies' School. The city paid for the legally imposed attendance. Those girls were kept in separate classes from the upstanding ones. Stories ran rampant of the torture one endured at the hands of Mrs. Taylor.

When Mary Lou and I were sixteen, Mona Baines moved to town. A rough tough thug of a girl who intimidated everyone in her way. She was quite a fascinating character, and I understood how someone as impressionable as Mary Lou could get caught up in the shenanigans of Mona. It wasn't the fact I was smarter than Mary Lou that kept me out of harm's way where Mona was concerned. It was that I feared Pop's retribution more than Mona's. So, for a few short months, Mary Lou and I parted company. Even Rex refused to associate with Mary Lou as long as she hung around with Mona.

I watched from the sidelines as Mona and Mary Lou bullied

their way through the halls of our high school. Mona mostly. Mary Lou was a follower.

One fateful Saturday afternoon, when my dear friend tried to leave Ivey's Department store with a new tube of Rider's Red lipstick in her pocket, she was arrested for shoplifting. Of course, Mona had allowed Mary Lou to do the actual stealing, so Mona got off Scot free. My friend faced a sentence of a month of classes at Mrs. Taylor's Southern Ladies' School.

Mrs. Taylor had two sons. Elton and Grant. Elton was married and lived next door to the school. Grant had just returned to his mother's home following a two-year stint in the Navy. He was good looking, smooth talking, and a skunk from the word go. But to Mary Lou, he was the best thing since she discovered chocolate milkshakes. Soon she was lost in a lover's bliss. On the last day of her mandatory classes, Grant and Mary Lou eloped.

Her husband managed to keep his pants on around other women for a whole six weeks. After that, rumors of his infidelity flooded directly to Mary Lou's broken heart. She had taken an after-school job at an insurance company. One day, she left work a few minutes early to meet with a divorce lawyer. Chief of Police Kramer stopped her in the parking lot to tell her Grant's Jeep had been hit by a dump truck. He died.

Rex and I were at Mary Lou's side immediately. Her walk on the wild side took a toll on our dear friend. She needed a lot of support. I'd like to think I gave it to her selflessly, but the truth is I was glad to have her back in my life. It took several months before things were back like they should be. But time helped heal her wounds and restored her shaken confidence to make better decisions. Eventually,

Mary Lou and I were best friends again.

Mona married a dairy farmer in Florida. I guess you could say she moved on to heavily fertilized, greener pastures. About two years later, Mrs. Taylor closed the door on the Taylor School for Southern Ladies. Nowadays you can find her at the E.T. Donut Shop run by her son Elton.

As for Mary Lou, now that she's married to Rex, her life coasts along on a smooth highway. Something like my life had been during the past week. No speed bumps. No stray animals. No speeding tickets. Until . . .

By eight-thirty on a chilly Thursday morning, Linc hadn't shown up for work. Although it was unusual for him not to be there at eight, I didn't start to worry until Elton Taylor, Mary Lou's ex-brother-in-law, phoned from the E.T. Donut Shop.

Elton had learned to speak with a sing-song voice from watching his mother teach Southern Lady classes. Not because he attended, but because he had secret peep-hole from the kitchen into the parlor where his mom taught etiquette. When the girls were in the kitchen learning to entertain, he was peeking from the parlor. Perverted, yes, but he learned to make a delicious donut from watching those cooking lessons which is his livelihood today.

"Good morn, my lotus of the lube job," Elton sang.

"Hey, Elton. What's up?"

"Where's my little buddy this morning? I made him his usual two glazed donuts without the holes, but he's a no show."

"I'm not sure where Linc is. I haven't heard from him either." I flipped through my Rolodex. "I guess I'd better give him a call and find out." I started to hang up, but pulled the phone back to my ear.

"Those donuts without holes sound pretty good. Save 'em for me. I'll be by to get them in a few."

"Of course, Countess of Carburetors." We hung up. First I tried to call Linc on the radio in the tow truck, but no answer. I dialed his home number, but still no answer. He hadn't missed a day or even been late since he started working for me.

Luckily, there were only two wrecker calls, and they could wait until Linc and my truck arrived. But, when would that be? I called Pop to come mind the store while I rode around to see if I could spot my tow truck and Linc. Before I could get out the office door, however, they both arrived. A deputy drove my truck, and Deputy Carl Kelly helped a disheveled Linc from a squad car.

"What happened?" I raced across the parking lot.

"He's going to be okay." Carl led Linc into the office. I followed close on his heels.

Once Linc was seated, the deputy started for the door. "I'm out of here. I have to get back to the crime scene."

"Crime scene?" The words burned my throat. "For cripe's sake, what happened?"

Carl nodded in Linc's direction. "I'll let him fill you in on the details. Gotta run."

Pop handed Linc a cup of coffee and a couple of wet towels. "You got some green dirt on your face there, fellow."

He wiped at it, smearing it more than removing it. Now his face glowed yellow. The shocked expression told me not to push for answers. Let him sip his coffee and then he'd be better able to talk.

"Pop, you can go on home now." I rubbed his shoulder.

Pop pulled up a chair and plopped into it. "I ain't going nowhere 'til I hear the details."

Linc peeked over the top of this coffee cup. Lowering it, he sighed.

"I got a call around eleven o'clock last night. The man said he was stuck in a ditch at the entrance of Gilbert's Cemetery. He said he had cash and asked me to hurry." Linc took another drink from his mug. "I hurried out there and found an SUV parked by the side of the road. Didn't look stuck to me, but I stopped anyway and got out to check it out. Two men grabbed me. They dragged me into the cemetery and into a tomb. It was cold, dark, and stunk. The men bound my hands and feet and blind-folded me."

"Who were the men?" I asked.

"I don't know. They had pantyhose over their heads and plastic gloves on."

"How did you get free?" I was horrified by the whole situation. Over the years, I'd made many night calls to the cemetery. I could have been abducted like Linc.

"I heard the lawns keeper mowing the grass in the cemetery. Luckily he stopped to get a snort of booze he had hidden in the tomb. He slid the stone over."

"What did he do?"

"He screamed," Linc said.

"What would you have done, Bertie?" Pop asked in a tone edged with sarcasm. "Maybe danced around the tomb?"

"I'd've probably taken a drink from my bottle and went back to cutting grass." I had inherited Pop's sarcastic gene.

For the next couple of hours, when I wasn't fighting a major battle with morning sickness, my mind was trying to wrap around what happened to Linc. Kidnapping was a serious offense. During the act, my tow truck wasn't stolen or harmed. My driver wasn't robbed or beaten. It was all a direct act against Linc. Could Bubba Craig be responsible for stuffing my driver into a cold, dank tomb? Was it part of the Redneck Mafia scare tactic?

Surely not. Linc would have recognized Bubba who was short and very round, and his sidekick who was tall and thin.

Shortly after lunch, I needed to get out of the office and away from the combined smell of oil and gas. My stomach thought a holeless donut would help calm its rolling. I stopped by the E.T. Donut Shop.

"Good afternoon, Duchess of the Drive Shaft," Elton Taylor called from behind the counter. "Did you ever find my little buddy?"

"He was just running late," I lied. Linc could tell him tomorrow, if he wanted Elton to know. But for today, I would enjoy Linc's holeless donuts.

I'd been stuck under a car hood for about an hour and welcomed the sound of the phone ringing so loudly it hurt my ears. "Bertie's Garage and Towing."

"Hi, Bertie," Chief Kramer said. I could hear voices and passing traffic in the background, so I knew he was calling from his cell phone. "A car has run off the road into the marsh area about three miles down Crystal Springs Lane. How long before you can get here?"

"Ten minutes." I was already Go-Joing the grease off my hands. I hung up and woke Pop from his nap in his office. "I gotta run. Be back shortly." I was out the door and on my way to Crystal Springs.

Sure enough a car had spun around and backed into the swamp. Only the hood and front of the vehicle were not submerged. Dang. I didn't want to wade through the black murky water to hook the winch to the undercarriage.

While I was scratching my head and prolonging the inevitable, a young, thin teenager walked up beside me. She was soaking wet and had mud streaking her long legs sticking from a pair of Daisy Dukes.

"How much is this going to cost me?" Her meek voice bordered on tears.

Although I felt sorry for her predicament, I was going to have to brave the dark muddy bog and possible quicksand to get her car out. I quoted her a price higher than a regular tow, hoping she would not want me to do it.

From out of nowhere, a teenage male appeared. "That's outrageous. My girlfriend can't afford that kind of money."

That's what I was hoping for.

As I turned to face the young man, a very angry cotton-mouthed moccasin raced up the embankment, its head raised, charging toward the three of us. "Run," I yelled, and did just that. Without warning, someone jumpeded, straddled my back, and clutched their arms around my throat.

Hissing and spitting and sputtering were heard. It was coming from me. I staggered to stay upright. Daisy Duke screamed in my ear. I made it to Chief Kramer's squad car, spun to sling my baggage off my back, and jumped onto the hood.

The girl's boyfriend stood in the same spot we left him in, staring at us. "What is wrong with you two? It's just a snake."

"It was chasing us." My voice shivered from my throat.

"He'd only have taken one bite and realized how rotten you are for charging such out-of-sight prices. Come on. I scared him away." The guy motioned for us to come back to where we had started.

I glanced through the windshield at Chief Kramer who sat staring at me like I had two heads. "What?" I snarled. He shooed me off his hood. I went reluctantly.

"You want to save some money on this call?" I asked Brave Boy.

"How?" His glare bored a hole in me.

I stretched some of the cable from the winch and handed him the hook. "Go down there, get on the hood and reach through the wheel opening and hook it on the axle."

Without a moment's hesitation, he rudely yanked the hook from me and traipsed down to the water's edge. He climbed onto the hood and reached into the wheel well.

"Yeow!" He scrambled to a sitting position.

"What is it?" I bellowed, afraid of his answer.

"That damn moccasin tried to bite me."

"Don't worry." I felt smug. "He'd only take one bite and realize how rotten you are."

Did Brave Boy growl at me? I think he did.

Through some miracle, he got the car hooked up, and I pulled it out of its bath. After I took the car to the girl's house, I didn't charge them anything. I just wanted to go home.

PG doesn't really stand for pregnant. In my case it stands for Piggy Gal, because I could never seem to get full. I ate my three squares a day, and a few circle meals in between. Lunch was a big banana split from the Dairy Queen. So my afternoon snack consisted of a peanut butter and dill pickle sandwich flanked by a healthy, fresh spinach salad. I'd just tossed the empty containers into the trash and was wondering how old the powdered donuts were in the vending machine located in our waiting area. Could the mold peeking through the clear cellophane wrapper be detrimental to my baby's health?

Thankfully, the jangling phone distracted me before I was forced to make a decision.

"Bertie's Garage and Towing."

"Hey, Bertie, bring your wrecker out to Forsythe Park. I need you to impound a car for me," Deputy Kelly said.

Impounding a car at Forsythe Park could mean only one thing. Someone had been arrested for soliciting prostitution. I'd pick up the vehicle belonging to the arrestee and keep it safe until he or she was released on bail.

"Sure, Carl, I'll send Linc right to you."

"I think you might want to handle this one yourself." Carl appeared to be trying not to laugh.

"Don't yank my chain today, deputy. I haven't had enough carbs, and I'm feeling a little weak," I whined.

"Come on, Bertie. You're gonna love this one." By now Carl

was laughing out loud.

I rolled my eyes way back in my head. "Okay, I'll be right there."

Before I left, I dropped a few coins into the vending machine and pushed F-4. Donuts with a slight green tint dropped into the slot. I snagged them, told Linc I was leaving on a call, and headed to the tow truck.

On my ride to Forsthye Park, known locally as For-blithe Park, I pinched the mold from the powdered sugar donuts and scarfed one down.

A few minutes later, I arrived on the scene. The owner of the Mercedes I was there to impound was in custody in the back of a squad car.

"Okay, Carl, why was it important for you to drag me away from my lunch?"

He glanced at his watch. "A little late for lunch." He ran his tongue over his teeth. "Was that spinach so good you are saving it for later?"

With my tongue I found a piece of food lodged between my side teeth. I thanked the deputy and followed him to his car.

He pointed into the back seat. "Recognize him?"

I looked closely. My heart lodged in the back of my throat. When I was able to swallow without choking, a growl rumbled from deep inside me.

"Is that your warrior cry?" Carl inquired.

I grunted again.

Carl rolled down the back window of his squad car. "You have two minutes to tell this guy what's on your mind. I know you've been dying to."

Barry Mateson, King of Late Night television, stared wide-eyed at me from the back seat of the car with the same terror I saw in Linc's eyes when he was confronted by the Redneck Mafia.

"You remember me, don't you, *Marry Bateson*?" I meant to screw up his name. That's my story, and I'm sticking to it.

"It was done for the sake of laughter. Laughter is the best medicine, you know, Miss . . . "

"I didn't find it at all funny, you son of a baboon. You made me look like a fool in front the whole nation, not to mention here in my home town."

"Now, Bertie." Carl stood beside me. "You can't blame him for the town thinking that way. You've given us enough ammunition to last a lifetime." He brayed like a jackass. When I eyed the revolver on his hip, he placed his hand on it and took a few steps backward.

I glared back at Mateson. "You humiliated me, and you didn't even send me a case of Rice-a-Roni as a consolation prize." Drops of spittle flew from my mouth and landed on the car door. Mateson leaned back to avoid being splattered, but I didn't care. Because he had his hands cuffed behind him was of little importance to me. I could smack him without a twinge of remorse.

The arrogant lunatic had once pre-recorded my answers to questions regarding a life-threatening incident I had with a mattress. Once his late-night show went on air, he asked different questions, but played my original answers. He made me look like a fool in front of my family, friends, and people I didn't even know. Now I had him right where I wanted him. A captive audience.

As if he read my mind, Carl pointed a warning finger at me. "Don't hit him."

Dang.

"You have no right using my words in any capacity other than originally intended." I shook my finger in his face. "I should have sued you when it happened."

"You couldn't do that. You signed a release form at the time. It was there in black and white." He looked at Carl. "Speaking of suing, if you don't make her go away, I'm going to sue you for allowing harassment.

"Go on back to your work, Mattress Lady."

I tried to lunge through the open window to put my small hands around Mateson's thick, corded neck. Something stopped me mid-lunge. Carl had grabbed me around the waist and lifted me back to the ground. "Stop it," he yelled.

I stopped.

Barry Mateson's face had changed from red to purple. "That did it. You're crazy," he bellowed. "As soon as my attorney gets here, I'm having him press charges of attempted assault on me."

"Go ahead. I'd love to drag this whole incident into court, and what a field day the press would have with it all. I can see the headlines now, *Late-Night TV host assaulted by woman wrecker driver while he was in custody for soliciting prostitution.*" I crossed my arms over my chest and flashed the biggest, pearliest smile I could. "Bring it on, Big Boy, I think that sounds like lots of fun."

His purple coloring turned a light shade of green. I smiled all the way back to my truck. Once inside, I looked into the rearview mirror. "You told him, didn't you, Bertie?" I flashed myself the same smile I gave *Marry Bateson.*

It was then I saw the huge hunk of spinach stuck right there between my two front teeth. I dropped my head in embarrassment. There, all over the front of my coveralls, was a heavy dusting of powdered sugar. Humiliation abounded. He'd gotten me again.

By the time I dragged my tired body through the door that evening, Arch had dinner on the table. What a good Do Bee. While he did the dishes, I helped Petey with her homework. I think he got the best end of the deal. I couldn't stay focused, and once I even fell asleep in the middle of calling out her spelling words. Finally, it was time for all of us to retire for the evening. I wanted to do that for about a week and sleep nonstop.

In bed and cuddled in the curve of Arch's arm, I told him about my hectic day. The nightlight shining from the bathroom allowed me to study his strong profile. I felt safe and loved there at his side.

Once I related the details of Linc's abduction, the humiliation of reading Barry Mateson the riot act with spinach lodged in my teeth, my husband stroked my shoulder and cooed in my ear. But when I told him about the young girl who jumped onto my back as we tried to escape a charging water moccasin, his jaw tightened. He rose on his elbow, dropping my head onto the hard mattress.

"Ouch. What'd you do that for?" I shifted to my side and rubbed the back of my head.

"You're pregnant, Bertie. You can't be carrying people on your back. You'll hurt yourself and the baby."

"She didn't weigh much," I countered.

"Maybe not this time, but who knows about the next time?"

Arch was really upset.

"I don't tote people on my back on a daily basis." I guess that went without saying.

"My point is you can't be put in positions like that while you're pregnant. The garage is your business, and I stay out of it. But you and the baby are very much my concern. I want you to hire someone to take over your wrecker duties until after the baby is born. Do you hear me?"

"Yes, dear, I hear you. I'll see what I can do very soon."

"You will get someone, and do it tomorrow." Arch's sternness caught me a little off guard. I guess he saw it in my eyes. "Please," he added in a much softer voice.

"Okay, I'll start looking first thing in the morning."

He lowered his lips to mine. Our agreement was sealed with a sweet kiss.

Arch was right. I needed to hire another driver who could lift some of the load from Linc, because I physically couldn't be much help to him until after the baby arrived. I was growing in width, and it wasn't just me in harm's way any more. I had our baby to think about.

Early the next day, I placed an ad for an experienced tow truck driver. Two days later, I hired Yuma McPherson, a red-headed, burly fellow who recently moved to Sweet Meadow with his wife, Harry (short for Harriet, I hoped) and his pit bull, Snookums.

I liked to get to know someone I'd be working with on a daily basis. A little insight into what makes that person tick. "I assume you were born in Yuma, Arizona," I said.

"Why's that?" The man tilted his head to the side and gave me a long thoughtful look.

"Well, I just thought you might be named after the name of the town where you were born."

"Seems to me like I've heard of a place called Yuma, but, naw, I was named for the last words my daddy said before he passed away."

"Really?" He had my attention.

"Yeah." Yuma scratched his belly like he might have fleas. "Two days before I was born, Mom and Dad were in a bar in Fresno, California. My old man got into an argument with a biker. Before it was all over, the man shot my dad and as he grabbed his stomach and slumped to the floor he said, "Why you ma—"

Sure, I had other applications, but the pickins were slim, as my Nana Byrd used to say. I narrowed it down to Willie Wells, a man with a nervous twitch and six traffic accidents in the last year. And Millie Keats who applied in person wearing jeans and a T-shirt with a picture of a gun and the words "I Aim to Maim."

So, you can clearly see, Yuma was the best man for the job. Besides, he had experience with a wrecker company which specialized in big rigs. I checked him out in my little tow truck and felt assured he knew what he was doing. I also checked out his references and found he was trustworthy and dependable.

I showed him the paper trail we had to follow for each vehicle we towed in and which keys fit the office door, the storage yard gate, the lock-up shed for vehicles needing to be examined for evidence.

After pointing out which key was for the truck fuel tank, I turned over the key ring which Yuma proudly attached to his belt.

Feeling pretty satisfied I made the right decision, I left him on call for the night, and I headed home to my little family.

Around midnight, I was awakened from a sound sleep by the phone ringing.

"Hello?" My voice sounded gravelly in the quietness of my bedroom. Arch grunted and rolled onto his side.

"Okay, Bertie," Chief Kramer said. "What do you want first? The good news or the bad news?"

"Just spit it out." I know I was rude, but what did he expect? It was late, and I was tired.

"The good news is that Sweet Meadows' finest is on the job ridding the community of prostitution."

"I certainly hope so. Now, what's the bad news, and what does it have to do with me?"

"The bad news is we just arrested your driver for soliciting prostitution . . . in your truck."

"Holy cow." I sat up. Arch roused long enough for me to assure him I could handle the situation.

"Can one of you take my truck to the garage and park it in front of the building?" I asked the Chief.

"Yeah, we can do that, but you have to bring us a set of keys."

"Where are the keys I gave that idiot this afternoon?"

"They're attached to his belt." I knew by the snicker in Kramer's voice I wasn't going to like the answer to my next question.

"And where's his belt?"

"Well, the arresting officer could only catch one person. Your

123

driver. The prostitute got away and took this guy's belt with her."

"You mean to tell me, the keys to my business and my truck are in the hands of someone who sells her body?"

"This can't be good," Arch mumbled, and sat up.

I didn't wait for an answer. "Where are you?" I covered the receiver. "Go back to sleep, honey. I got it under control," I whispered to my husband. "I'll be right there," I said into the phone.

I took Kramer the keys. He and his deputy relayed my truck back to the shop.

Tomorrow I would have to run another ad for a new driver. I would also call the people who had assured me Yuma would be a trustworthy employee and give them a piece of my mind, if I had any left to give them.

Chapter 8

The next morning, it was back to the old drawing board. I had to start my search anew for a tow truck operator. Call me strange, but I preferred one whose hobby didn't involve hookers. Again, I called the Sweet Meadow News-Leader.

"Classifieds," a familiar voice answered at the local newspaper office.

"Carrie Sue? Is that you?" I asked.

"Hey, Bertie. How's married life? You call to place a single's ad?" She actually snorted on the other end of the line.

"No, I need to run another ad for a tow truck driver. The last one didn't work out."

"If the pay is right, I'll take the job." She cracked her gum.

"You? You can't drive a tow truck."

"If you can do it, how hard can it be?"

Was Carrie Sue pulling my leg or was she serious? I really couldn't tell. Come to think of it, years ago I had seen her handle a dump truck like a pro. She maneuvered the vehicle with great precision as she backed up to her ex-husband's beautifully land-scaped yard and dumped two tons of chicken manure onto Fletcher

MacMillan's azaleas.

"How 'bout it, Bert? Give me a chance?" She sounded like she meant it.

"What about your job with the newspaper? You've been there for a while. Are you sure you want to give all that up?"

"Jim Ed's been trying to fire me for a long time, but since I know enough about him to get him hung, he's afraid to. I guarantee he'd be thrilled." Carrie Sue moved the receiver away from her mouth. "Hey, boss," she yelled in the distance. "I'm quitting."

"Woohoo. Happy days are here again." Jim Ed Swain, Editor of the local paper, cheered in the background.

"I'll be right over, Bertie." Carrie Sue disconnected me into utter silence. I stared into space, wondering what I'd gotten myself into. Sometimes I had a tough time being in the same town with Carrie Sue, but now we'd be working together. Every day. Jeeze, I'd also have to teach her how to operate the tow truck.

"Wait a minute." I hung up the phone and headed toward the garage. "Linc?"

He slid out from under a car he was working on since he arrived that morning. Rising, he pulled an old rag from his back pocket and wiped grease from his hands.

"Yes, ma'am?"

"I'm going to be hiring another driver so I don't have to be operating the equipment until after my baby arrives. Would you have any objections to training someone for me?"

"I don't know, Mrs. Bertie. I've never been very good at learning anyone anything."

"You mean teaching anyone anything," I corrected.

"Yeah, that's what I said."

"You said . . . Never mind. I think you'd do a very good job."

Just then, the office door opened. I walked into the waiting area followed by Linc. Carrie Sue stood just inside the door.

"I'm here to start work as your new driver." She saluted me.

Linc shoved me aside and rushed toward Carrie Sue. "And I'm here to teach you how to do just that."

"Do you two know each other?" I'd never seen Linc react like . . . well, like a dog in heat. I shouldn't think such crude thoughts about him. Normally, he was so timid and blushed for no reason.

"I've seen him around town." Carrie Sue smiled up at him.

Linc grinned so wide if he had false teeth, they would have fallen out.

"Yeah, I've seen you, too." He motioned for her to follow him outside. "Come on." He held the door for Carrie Sue. "I'll show you how to operate my levers."

"Oh, that sounds like fun." Carrie Sue giggled.

I shuddered.

Late in the afternoon, I received a phone call from a lady who said her name was *Precious.*

"What can I do for you, Precious?" Hopefully she would just need her car jump-started or a tire changed. Something easy that Linc could show Carrie Sue how to do and begin her training.

"I need to talk to the owner."

Oh, darn, just a telemarketer. "I'm the owner but I'm not

interested in buying anything today." Before I could hang up, Precious bellowed into my ear in a voice edged with masculinity.

"I think I do have something you might be interested in. I have your man's belt."

This man/woman had Arch's belt? How could that be? And why? "Wait a minute. Are you the prostitute who stole my driver's keys?"

"You're slow, but you catch on. Now, I'd be ever so happy to give your keys back to you."

"Well, that's nice. I'll even be glad to come and pick them up. Where are you?"

"I'll meet you on the corner of 45th and Pearl," Precious said.

"How will I recognize you?"

"I'm six-foot-two and have legs that go all the way to my ears." She snickered in a hoarse voice. "Also, I'll be the only one with your keys. Bring forty dollars."

"Why?"

"You really are slow, aren't you? Bring forty dollars to pay for me for the keys. The one time in my life I didn't ask for the money up front, I did my job and then had to run before I got paid. Somebody's gonna pay me. Bring cash." She hung up.

Absolutely bum-fuddled, I told Linc I was going out. I didn't have the nerve to tell him where I was going. I didn't know if I'd ever be able to tell anyone my keys were being held for ransom, or that I was paying for services rendered and I hadn't received any services. Not that I would have wanted to, you understand. It was just the principal of the thing.

I moseyed over to the pink-light district of our fair town. (It was too small for a full-fledged red-light district. I paid the ransom and got my keys back. Precious' five o'clock shadow confirmed he was a man in drag, leaving me to wonder if Yuma's eyesight was really that bad, or if his wife's name really was Harry.

Then again, did I *really* want to know?

While on his lunch break, Arch called me at the garage.

"Hi, sweetheart." His voice made my heart go pitty-pat. "Would you like me to help you write the ad for the newspaper? There's no time like the present to start looking for someone to help you out."

Bless his little heart. He could be so thoughtful. "I wrote the ad, called it in, hired someone, and they are being trained as we speak."

"Oookay, then." Arch cleared his throat. "It's apparent you don't need me. I'll just be going back to my science class and whipping up a lethal concoction to have for lunch."

"Of course I need you. You're just so cute." I cackled. "I hired Carrie Sue MacMillan," I told Arch. "Linc's out there now showing her how to operate the wrecker to load and unload a vehicle."

I rose on tip-toes to see over a parked car to where the two of them stood. Linc had hooked up a vehicle and raised its front wheels off the ground. Carrie Sue clapped her hands, jumped up and down, then reached over and squeezed Linc's muscle. Did she not realize the truck was doing all the work?

"I'm not sure how it will work out, but I'll try her for a few days. What's the worst that can happen?"

Arch whistled. "Oh, sweetheart, you know better than to tempt the fates by asking a question like that."

"Oh, I'll be fine. Love ya." I listened for his "love ya" and then I hung up the phone.

Arch did make a good point about my uncanny ability to make the unthinkable happen just because I thought it. As a precaution, I made a finger cross and spun around three times in my own ritual to ward off evil things. All I succeeded in doing was making myself dizzy.

The rest of my day was spent trying not to listen to Carrie Sue and Linc coo over each other. I thought the day would never end.

Arch and Petey picked me up at five o'clock, and we headed toward our little home on Marblehead Drive. The brown winter grass was showing signs of spring green. Arch already prepared the flowerbeds, once maintained by his father Pete. Impatiens and petunias would soon be planted, adding color throughout the yard.

When I climbed out of the car, the waistband of my jeans pulled tightly around my belly, which was growing at an alarming speed. At the rate it was going, by the end of summer I would be bigger than my little house on Marblehead Drive.

Heading up the walkway, I unbuttoned my pants. "I guess it's time for me to get some maternity clothes."

Arch held the door open for me and smiled.

"What are maternity clothes?" Petey asked. "Can I have some, too?"

She already traipsed into the house ahead of us and deposited her backpack onto the sofa. Snagging a store-bought cupcake from the kitchen counter, she ripped it open.

"Maternity clothes are what mommies-to-be wear while they are pregnant," Arch told Petey. "The clothes fit loosely to allow room for the baby to grow in Mommy's tummy." He ruffled his daughter's hair. "Of course, if you keep eating all that junk food, we may have to buy you some maternity clothes, too."

Petey smiled up at him. Chocolate frosting blacked out several of her teeth. A mixture of laughter and happiness bubbled inside me like a fluttering butterfly. I rubbed my slightly bulging tummy. Was that what it felt like for the baby to move? It was so tiny, I couldn't be sure.

Arch stood behind me and slipped his arms around me. He locked his fingers on top of my hand. "I love you," he whispered against my ear.

I leaned against him. Sweet Meadow, Georgia equals heaven. Who would have thought it?

"Can I go with you to buy maternity clothes?" Petey swiped the back of her hand across her mouth.

"Sure, we'll go Saturday and make it a mother-daughter day." Reluctantly, I broke away from Arch's arms. He gave me a love tap on my backside.

"Petey, go brush the chocolate out of your teeth and start your homework. I'll have dinner ready in an hour or so."

She picked up her backpack and disappeared down the hall toward her bedroom. Arch plopped into the recliner for an activity he called *chilling out* before dinner. Others might call it napping and snoring loud enough to crack the ceiling plaster. For me, it sounded like trumpets in my own little heaven.

Arch and I crawled into bed a few minutes after eleven. Petey had been asleep for a couple of hours. My exhausted husband dozed off quickly. Unfortunately, indigestion stood between sleep and me. Around twelve-forty-five, I gave up chasing my elusive dream state and chose to head to the kitchen for a snack.

I barely finished slapping a glob of cold spaghetti between two slices of buttered bread when a loud clap of thunder vibrated the kitchen floor. Through the window I saw lightning veining the sky, followed by another boomer.

I stared out into the darkness for a few minutes and had almost finished my sandwich. Looking beyond the top of Barbie's house next door, and possibly as far away as downtown Sweet Meadow, I saw a humongous flash of light followed by a ball of fire that erupted into shooting sparks. I watched until the last embers died, and with it my kitchen light and all the streetlights. Must have been an exploding transformer I saw lighting the sky in the distance.

Rain began to beat against the pane. At first, slow, large drops fell, followed by a heavy downpour that sheeted across the glass. My stomach fluttered slightly. Placing my hand on my tummy, I waited for the movement to happen again. It did.

"Hello, my little butterfly," I whispered. "I'm your mommy." Happiness pulled my mouth into a wide smile. "I can't wait for you to meet your daddy and your big sister. I know you're going to love them."

The kitchen light flickered and finally stayed on. Even with chilly air filling the room, my body warmed with the knowledge I really felt my baby move.

"Your whole family already loves you, little one," I said. Before I turned off the light, I kissed the tips of my fingers and placed them on my belly. "Good night, Butterfly."

The next morning I watched about all I could of Linc and Carrie Sue prancing around each other in what I could only describe as a mating ritual. I took her with me to fuel the truck. She drove; I leaned against the door and hoped to steal a few minutes of zzz's I lost the night before.

Carrie Sue turned a corner, and I opened my eyes long enough to see exactly where we were.

"Stop." I shoved away from the door. Carrie Sue slammed on the brakes. I had to place my hands on the dash to keep from bouncing my head against the windshield.

"Oh, my God." Carrie Sue barely squeaked out the words, but I knew she witnessed the God-awful sight I just saw.

Parked in the middle of the road, I opened the truck door and slid from the seat. We were directly in front of the Keats' house. On her front porch, as if this were the most natural thing she'd ever done, Millie sat in a patio chair making obscene gestures at passing cars—totally nude.

"Millie." I ran up the walkway and climbed the few stairs to her porch. "What are you doing?" I tried to herd her inside. Each time I grabbed for her arm, she sidestepped me.

"You can't see me, Bertie." Millie placed her thumbs to her ears, wiggled her fingers, and stuck out her tongue. "I'm invisible."

"The only thing you are is a nitwit." I finally latched on to her arm and shoved her through the door. Several cars were stopped out front. All passengers stared in disbelief. I motioned for them to move along. "Show's over," I called to them.

Carrie Sue pulled the truck to the curb. I turned back to Millie. "Have you taken your medicine today?"

"You can't be talking to me, because you can't see me."

I didn't know where to look first. Her ash-colored skin held deep wrinkled creases all over her body except for her knees. They were smoother and more perfect than mine. Jeeze, my mind couldn't begin to wrap around why that was. Her body appeared flat and thin and her once-ample breasts were that way, too. They appeared to be in a race for her waist. The left one was winning.

"I can see you. You are standing before me with no clothes. Why?" I looked around for something to cover her with. The lace tablecloth on her dining room table would do. I snatched it up and wrapped it around her.

"I was abducted by aliens. They crashed right outside my house last night. Made a hellava explosion. The lights went out. The aliens came in and took me on their space ship. When the lights came back on, I was invisible." She started to remove her wrap, but I insisted she keep it on.

"What a hoot! I can run around naked and no one knows the difference."

"*Everyone* knows the difference, Millie. I can see you, all of you, as plain as day. Lightning hit a transformer last night. There

134

were no aliens." I shuddered. "Now, go put some clothes on."

"Dang. I liked letting it all hang out. You take all my fun away, Bertie." She stomped off to her bedroom like a child.

While I waited for her to put some clothes on, I studied the many pictures scattered on the mantel. Inside a silver engraved frame, I saw a faded picture of Michael Keats, Millie's only son. Long before I was even born, he was killed in a battle in Vietnam. Many times I listened to Millie talk about Mike as if he was the only young man who had died in a war.

Looking closer, I read the words etched into the metal. "Sweet Meadow's Hero. Mama's Little Boy."

Instantly I thought of Petey and the baby growing inside me. A crushing sadness forced tears to my eyes. Not until that moment had I realized the magnitude of Millie's pain from losing her son.

The next picture reminded me Mike hadn't been her only loss. She also outlived her beloved husband, John. I had to wonder if perhaps Millie's nuttiness was her way of dealing with the loneliness. How would I ever be able to handle everyday life without the ones I loved? I closed my eyes and prayed it would be a long time, if ever, before I had to find out.

A loud knock on the door yanked me from my painful trance. Deputy Carl Kelly waited on the front porch. I opened the screen and motioned for him to come in.

"Where's Mrs. Keats?" Carl removed his hat.

"She getting dres . . . uh, she's in the bathroom. She'll be right out. What are you doing here?"

"I got a report that Mrs. Keats was exposing herself to the passing traffic. That's the second time this week I've been called out here for that." The deputy slapped his hat against his leg and stared at the floor. "I'm going to have to take her in for a psychiatric evaluation."

"Carl." I grabbed him by his shirt front. "You can't take poor Millie in. You know she's harmless." At least I hoped she was.

He pulled free from my grasp. "Ah, Bertie, I'd rather be pistol whipped than run her in, but she hasn't left me any choice."

"You didn't see her without clothes, did you?" I asked.

"No, but others did, and they want something done about it," Carl barked.

"Something done about what?" Millie's voice caused Carl and me to jerk toward the hallway entrance. Thankfully, she was handsomely and fully dressed in a flowered day dress, support stockings, and sensible orthopedic shoes.

I turned back to Carl. "See. She's fine."

"But how long will she stay that way?" At least he wasn't yelling.

"Excuse me. Old woman entering the room." Millie walked in our direction. "Don't talk about me like I'm not here. I'm not invisible, you know."

I put my arm around her shoulder. "Sorry, honey. Do you know Deputy Kelly?"

Millie nodded.

"He's here because someone called in a complaint. They said you were flashing the passing traffic. He also said he's been here before for the same thing. You know it wouldn't be right to do that, don't you, Millie?" If she didn't go along with me, she would soon be headed to the county hospital. "So, tell him he doesn't have to worry about that, okay?"

Millie looked at me for a fleeting second and then turned to Carl. "I may have made a slight error in judgment, deputy. However, I've learned from my foolishness. I promise to walk the straight and narrow path of justice in a fully-clothed manner because I almost froze my tutu off." She cocked her head to the side then flashed a smile that could melt the hardest heart. Millie batted her eyes at Carl.

He made a choking sound and burst into laughter. "Okay, Mrs. Keats, I won't make you go with me today, but you better be on your best behavior. If I am called out here again, I'll have no choice but to take you in for evaluation. Do you understand?"

"No clothes, Millie goes." The elderly woman summed it up very well. "Got it."

Carrie Sue and I fueled the tow truck and headed back to the garage. The windows were rolled down, and lukewarm air swirled around us, making my hair dance around my face. As we passed a few long-time businesses along the way, I wondered what I might have been had I not followed in Pop's footsteps.

Zell Anne's School of Dance and One-Day Laundry had been a member of Sweet Meadow's Chamber of Commerce for at least thirty years. Carrie Sue, her sisters, Mary Lou, and I took dancing lessons when we were children. Much to Miss Zell Anne's dismay, I couldn't master the shuffle-ball-change step, the split, or back bend. Come to think of it, just putting on my leotard challenged me. Although the others hung in there until they were teenagers, I only lasted one year. So I scratched dance instructor and Rockette off my list of possible occupations.

The Chow Pal Diner? The best I could cook was Spaghetti-O's. Head chef was out of the question.

Carrie Sue stopped at a red light in front of Sweet Meadow Elementary School. Now, there's a job I thought about earlier in my life. Teacher. How wonderful it would be to guide little children, pump up their confidence, and mold their minds. A vision from the past flashed through my mind—first-grade teacher Mrs. Orr opening her lunch box and a happy green snake slithering out. My brother Bobby received three swats. Mrs. Orr took three days off.

I rubbed the armrest of my tow truck. I'd made the perfect decision. After all, look at all the interesting people I met pulling vehicles out of ditches, away from accident scenes, and into repair facilities.

The thought of some of them made me shiver.

"Bertie." Carrie Sue broke my reverie. "Isn't Linc the hottest guy you've met in a long time?"

Speaking of shivers. I literally shook in my seat. "Well . . . uh . . . I don't think I can legally think of my employee that way. I believe it could be sexual harassment." Or, just plain crazy.

"Surely being married didn't take away your ability to appreciate the opposite sex, did it?"

"Of course not." We arrived back at the garage and the object of our conversation was delivering a car to a customer. I'd grown quite fond of Linc, and, in a strange sort of way, he was kind of cute. Like a lost puppy. "So, are you falling for him?" I asked.

"I think so."

Carrie Sue hadn't had good luck where men were concerned,

not that I had either until Arch came into my life. But she deserved some happiness, and Linc seemed to feel the same about her.

"Well, I'm happy for you."

With the tow truck nosed right up to the big picture window of the office, she shut off the engine. Through the plate glass I saw Pop pick up the radio. A second later he keyed it, and his voice echoed through the cab of the truck.

"Bertie, are you there?"

I keyed mine up. "Yoohoo, Pop. Look out the window."

"Which window?"

"For crying out loud. The front one."

Finally he looked right at me, waved, and then punched the button on the radio again.

"Bertie, are you there?"

I banged my head against the passenger window. What was I going to do with Pop? Some days he was at the top of his game, whatever that was. But at other times he was a slice of bread short of a full sandwich. Although the doctor assured all of us everything was fine in his brain's power house, I couldn't help but worry about him. Especially when his technical responses seemed to be mal-functioning.

"Bertie, answer me," Pop shouted through the radio again.

I swiped a runaway tear from my cheek and went inside the office. I rounded the end of the counter and removed the mike from my father's hand.

"Have you taken your blood pressure medicine today?" I asked.

"Soy tin lee." He screwed up the word with a silly accent to make me laugh, but I felt sad. I didn't want there to be anything wrong with my wonderful father. I loved him and needed him to be around for a long time. And if it wasn't too much to ask, I hoped he'd have most of his faculties about him, at least long enough to see his grandchild I was carrying.

Tears bombarded my eyes, and I couldn't control them any longer. I threw myself into Pop's arms and sobbed.

"What's the matter, sweetheart?" Pop stroked my hair and held me tight.

"I worry about you, Pop. I mean . . . well, I was sitting right there in front of you and you act like you didn't even see me."

"Oh, Bertie, I know what's wrong with you. You forgot to take your sense-of-humor pill, because I was kidding around. I know how much it bugs you when I don't jump right into the crux of my dispatch. I saw you pull up, and I was chuckling my heart out in here. I had no idea I was distressing you. I'll tell you what. I won't tease you like that any more. At least until after my grandbaby arrives and you get your hormones under control."

He handed me a paper towel, and as I blew my noses I looked at Pop. How did he know what was really wrong with me? Evidently, the question registered in my eyes.

"Don't forget, young lady, I'm the father of three. If you think I'm nuts, be glad you didn't have to live through twenty-seven months of baby hormones with your mother. Talk about a train not clacking exactly on a track. Wow."

Okay, things weren't as bad as I thought where Pop was concerned. For that blessing, I'd say a special thank-you prayer that night.

Chapter 9

Carrie Sue drove a customer's car to their house, and I followed along in the tow truck to bring her back. She left a couple of minutes ahead of me. When I turned onto Bonefish Lane, there she was flailing her hands and dancing around in front of the gold Maxima she was supposed to deliver. I screeched to a halt, bailed out of my truck, and hurried to her.

She squealed so loudly I couldn't understand a word she said. Finally, she pointed to the ditch. Booger Bailey's barking goat lay perfect still. Dead just like the deer I hit a few years ago. At that time, blood covered the poor animal and the windshield of old Bessie, which also suffered from a crunched fender and hood.

Suddenly I realized the goat didn't have any blood on it, and there didn't appear to be any damage on the Maxima either.

"He started chasing the car like he thought he was some kind of dog," Carrie Sue sobbed. "I didn't mean to hurt him."

"You didn't."

We both jumped at Booger's booming voice. "You killed him. Don't you know the difference?"

Booger charged across his yard. About two feet from the dead goat, he stopped and clapped his hands.

The goat jumped to his feet and raced to Booger who rewarded his pet with a clump of grass and an ear scratching. "Good boy," he said.

Carrie Sue and I were dumbstruck. Had we just witnessed a miracle?

"What are you trying to do, you inconsiderate, son of a biscuit eater?" Carrie Sue sputtered.

Well, at least she quit crying.

Booger *woohooed* and jumped from one foot to the other.

"I trained him to do that. He chases a car, bumps his head against it, and then rolls over and plays dead. Pretty smart, isn't he?"

"You are a lunatic," I yelled at the crazy old coot. "Come on, Carrie Sue, let's get out of here before I do something he'll be sorry for."

I almost made it back to the truck when I heard Booger say, "Sic her." I turned just in time to see the goat running after me. I scrambled my way into the truck and slammed the door a half a second before the goat butted his head into the sheet metal. He staggered backward, shook his head and bleated several times like any self-respecting goat should.

"That's right, you silly thing," I called as I drove a way. "You're a goat. G-O-A-T. Gooooaaaattt!"

Back at the shop, I called the police.

"This is Bertie Fortney. I need to speak to one of the officers," I told the dispatcher. In no time, Deputy Carl Kelly came on the line.

"What'd you do now, Bertie?"

"I hate to disappoint you, but it wasn't me this time. Booger Bailey has trained his goat to chase cars, pretend like it got hit, then he plays dead," I whined into the receiver.

Silence assaulted my ear for about ten seconds. The line clicked. He hung up on me. I called right back.

"Mrs. Fortney, Deputy Kelly said that if you call again, he is going to bring you up on charges of misusing an emergency response number."

"Well, you can tell Carl that Booger Bailey is a hazard to the community. He's going to cause a serious accident." I started to hang up, but jerked the phone back to my ear. "And you can tell the good deputy he is a doo-doo head, and when he's ready to arrest me, he knows where I am, but he'd better bring back-up."

I remember when Mary Lou was pregnant, her hormones went crazy. She followed suit, so to speak. I wondered how a woman's body could change just because she was carrying a child inside her. Surely something of this nature could only bring happiness.

On Wednesday morning, when Arch asked if he could have whole-wheat toast instead of white, I slammed the bread in the toaster and snarled at him, "Would you like me to skip around and whistle a tune while I'm waiting for it to pop up? I wouldn't want to stand idly by on my shift. Or perhaps you'd just like to dock my pay." By this time, I'd slathered butter over a charred offering and slid his plate to the end of the bar.

Arch looked at me with a stymied stare, took a bite of his toast, and licked his lips. "Ummm, good," he said. "Really good." He downed his breakfast, hardly chewing at all, and chugged a whole cup of hot coffee.

"Gotta go." He kissed me in the vicinity of my lips and hit the door running.

I cried all the way to the garage. I just knew my marriage was over. Who would want to live with a raving lunatic like me?

Thursday morning Arch said he'd grab a bite in the cafeteria when the day-care kids, who were dropped off early, ate breakfast. I think he was simply trying to avoid a repeat of the toast turbulence of the day before.

Petey missed the bus, so I was going to drop her off on my way to work. I braided her two long pigtails and fastened them with stretch bands with balls that intertwined. I was admiring my handy work, and she was gathering the last of her books, when one of the stretch bands broke and fell to the floor by her feet.

As she casually bent to pick up the broken fastener, I began to cry. "Oh, look, it broke and now one of your pigtails is coming undone. You can't go to school like that." I was bawling my eyes out. She stared at me like I had a pigeon on my head.

"It's okay, Momma, I have another one." She ran down the hall and returned with a replacement. Quickly, she wound it around the end of her braid. "See? Good as new."

"I'm so glad. You are such a smart girl. Look how quickly you took control of the situation and fixed it all up." I dragged my long sleeve across my runny nose.

Petey took my hand and led me to a chair. "I want you to know that I understand what you are going through."

"You do?" Picture me puzzled.

"Yes, I discussed the way you've been acting with Randy Carson

144

yesterday while we were on the playground."

Oh, good Lord. I'd been analyzed by six graders swinging on monkey bars. What was my life coming to?

"And what is your diagnosis, Miss Freud?"

"Well, Randy said his mother was crazy too when she was expecting his little brother, Jude."

The Earth wobbled a little. I'd just been put on the same level as Donna Carson on the crazy scale. I cried harder.

Poor Petey. She was only trying to help, and I was probably damaging her psyche. She was going to grow up to be a serial killer or a White House intern. Either way it would all be my fault.

The dear child led me to the car, opened my door, and after helping me fasten my seatbelt, she got in on the passenger side. When I dropped her off at school, Randy Carson met her at the door. They really had a lot to discuss on the old playground today.

At work, Linc asked, "Would you like me to take Ethel Winchell's radiator out to be flushed?"

"No," I snapped. "I'll just go out, put my lips over the hole, blow into it and flush it out myself."

"That won't be necessary, Mrs. Bertie. I think the radiator place will do a sufficient job." He tipped his hat and headed into the garage. I swear I heard him mumble something about somebody being touched in the head, but I didn't inquire who. I already knew. After all, had I not already been analyzed by the team of Dr. See and Dr. Saw?

Friday my hormones were happy, happy, happy. No major toast incidents. No driving to work with tears streaming down my face. I was even having a good hair day. When I arrived at work, the

Sweet Meadow News-Leader was waiting for me along with a cup of coffee and one of those donuts without a hole. Linc had brought the offering to me in hopes I wouldn't try to behead him as I had the day before.

I decided to read the newspaper which only came out once a week. There on the front page, as big as life, was Deputy Carl Kelly's cruiser nose first into a ditch. I do declare it appeared to be in front of Booger Bailey's house. I was already cackling like a laying hen (pardon the pun) even before I read the caption beneath the picture. *Deputy has run-in with goat.* The story told of how the goat's owner taught it to act like a dog, and the deputy lost control of his vehicle when he swerved to miss the animal chasing the police car.

I had tears streaming down my face for a different reason now. I laughed so hard my side hurt. I couldn't wait to call Carl and tell him I told him so. Before I got the receiver to my ear, it dawned on me I had to see his face. A mere phone call wouldn't work at all.

I stuffed the rest of my donut into my mouth and called to Linc, "A'm goin oou for a wile. Ho don da for."

He stared at me from under the hood of Ethel's car. I hurriedly chewed and swallowed the donut and made my announcement a little plainer. "I'm going out for a while. Hold down the fort."

First he nodded his approval and then he shook his head in bewilderment. Poor guy, I may have to send him over to the playground for therapy.

At the sheriff's office, I found Carl behind a gray metal desk hunched over a stack of file folders. The back of his uniform was soaked with perspiration. Kind of early in the morning to have worked up that kind of sweat.

"How's it going, Barney Miller?" I sat on the corner of his desk and bounced my shoes against the hollow metal. It reverberated through the room. Another deputy glanced up from his desk and tried to hide his smile by lowering his head. Carl stopped my feet from swinging and glared up at me.

Hot dog, I loved it when I was right and got to say so.

"What'cha want, Bertie?" He wasn't at all happy to see me.

"Just stopped by to see how you're doing. How's Karen?" I dragged it out for a few seconds. "Hit any barking goats lately?"

He jumped up, sending his chair rolling several feet behind him. I grabbed his arm.

"You don't want to deprive me of saying I told you so, now do you?" He glared, but didn't pull away. "After all, I am with child and I need to find pleasure and contentment whenever possible. It's good for my baby."

He glanced at my swollen belly. "Okay, I guess you deserve to hear it."

I cupped my ear and motioned for him to say more.

"You tried to warn me Bailey had created a traffic hazard out there with his circus act."

"And?" I coaxed.

"You told me so." It pained him to say it, but it brought me so much pleasure.

I giggled. "Okay, that's all I came for. I'll be going back to work now. You have a good day, Deputy Kelly." I slid from his desk and turned my back to walk away. Behind me rose a clatter of major proportion. I spun just in time to see Carl hit the floor. He missed his chair and now lay sprawled at my feet.

"Not having a good week, huh, Carl?"

He fluttered his fingers to signal my dismissal. I offered a hand to help him up. He fluttered more insistently. The other officer came to help Carl, and I went on my way, whistling a merry tune.

When I walked into the office, Pop sprinted out the door. "Linc's on a call, and I've missed the first five minutes of *All My Children*," he called over his shoulder.

I offered an obligatory wave. Inside I went into his old office and made my way around his huge desk to the wooden office chair that had been Pop's since the early fifties. I used to sit in it and Billy and Bobby would roll me back and forth between them and then spin me around and around until I threw up.

Those were the days.

I backed my ever-growing body up to the seat, and as I sat down I grabbed the thick wooden arms and held tight so the chair wouldn't scoot out from under me. I planned to be extra careful for a few days so I wouldn't be paid back for laughing at Carl's mishap with his chair.

As the thought left my brain, I heard the crack of wood splitting, and the chair and I were propelled backward. I had just enough time to cradle my belly before I came to a crashing halt on my back. Now, had the chair gone all the way to the floor, I could have wiggled out of it and gotten to my feet. But that wasn't the case.

The back of the chair jammed into the Sheetrock behind me about six inches from the floor. Being surrounded by thick wooden arms and with my added weight, I couldn't roll to either side. I couldn't slide out because my head was mashed against the wall. Doing a sit-up was totally out of the question.

So, there I lay with my feet in the air, flat on my back. I thought of Humphrey, our gopher turtle. My brothers would lay him on his back and then laugh like crazy while they watched him struggle to flip. Billy and Bobby would get a real hoot if they saw me right then.

I stuck my feet into the air and pretended to be riding a bicycle hoping the movement would bounce the chair loose from the wall. I tried spreading my legs apart and then crossing them and repeating several times. At one point, as I opened my legs, I saw the Redneck Mafia Godfather, Bubba Craig staring down at me.

"Is that another type of exercise, little lady?" As he took my hand, his skinny buddy came around Bubba and lifted the back of my chair. Together they sat me up.

Dizziness overcame me. I slumped back causing the chair to sway, nearly knocking the little fellow over.

"Whoa, lady," Bubba said. "No wonder you're always exercising, what with all the weight you've put on. You're just a little rolly polly."

"It takes one to know one." I stuck my tongue out at the rotund man. I think standing on my head caused the oxygen to be cut off, rendering me incapable of using good judgment. Oh, who was I trying to kid? I'd have said that to the Mafia fellow, lack of oxygen or not.

"What can I do for you two?" I asked.

"We want you to fire Linc so he'll come back to Atlanta." Bubba smiled.

"I'm not firing him, and that's all there is to it. And I think it's time you face facts. Linc doesn't want to marry your daughter or move back to Atlanta. And you doing things like kidnapping him and putting him in a tomb are Federal offenses. So leave him alone, or I'll see to it you are arrested. Do you understand?"

"I don't have a clue what you're talking about. Do you, Conner?"

Conner stepped forward. "Not unless she's talking about the time . . ."

Bubba turned his little buddy around as easily as spinning a top. "You go start the car. I'll be right there."

"Consider this a warning—you better do what I say, or there will be hell to pay."

"You are without a doubt the biggest blowhard I've ever met. Now, get your mean-spirited self out of my office, and that's the last time I tell you without calling for back-up."

I hoped it wouldn't come to that, because I could only imagine what Deputy Kelly would say if I called him to come arrest the Godfather of the Redneck Mafia. Carl would have me committed for sure.

Saturday morning, I awoke a few minutes before seven. Arch nestled against my back with his arm around my expanded middle. I rubbed my tummy and our baby did what felt like a combination of sit-ups and the rumba. Just another reminder of how much my life had changed in less than a year.

Twelve months before, the wall across from the bed needed painting. I had adorned it with a Monet cut from a magazine and displayed it in a four-dollar frame from Wal-Mart. I had no stable man in my life expect for my father, who was also my boss. A husband was so far removed from my mind I couldn't spell matrimony if I tried. Children? Yeah, I wanted them and hoped to have a couple before I was collecting Social Security. But, a year ago, I couldn't see it happening.

I didn't have much luck with men. I proved that by almost marrying Lee Dew, an unfaithful sleazebag who got what he had coming to him when he left me to marry Carrie Sue's sister, Annie. She could open beer bottles with her teeth. They spawned a couple of kids who, for legal reasons, are not allowed to play with baseball bats.

Then there was Jeff House, the miller worker by day and male stripper by night. Oh, yeah, he came complete with a wife.

Somehow, I'd shaken free from the threat of bad last names and found the perfect husband and daughter, all in one package. Every day I thanked God for my many blessings. Arch, Petey, and the baby jitterbugging in my tummy. The little one was definitely going to be a dancer like his or her grandfather. My father, Pop Byrd, was famous all over Shafer County for his dancing ability. By the feel of it, his new grandchild might someday take Pop's place.

Now, hanging on the wall across from our bed was Arch's and my wedding picture. Next to it I placed one of Petey taken the day the three of us became a family. Her big grin made me smile. I constantly made jokes about our new baby giving me indigestion, but I knew the ache in my chest came from my heart filled to bursting with so much appreciation and love.

Last summer, Pop turned the business over to me, making me my own boss. I married the man of my dreams. Well, that wasn't exactly true, because Arch far exceeded any expectations I ever had of a husband. That should be apparent by the other men I dated. Arch was gentle, kind, considerate, and able to read my mind sometimes before I knew what I was thinking. That is scary on so many levels, given the unpredictable way my mind worked.

As much as I hated to, I crawled out of Arch's hug and was headed to answer the call of nature when Petey knocked on our bedroom door. When I opened it, she nodded toward the front door and whispered, "Miss Barbie's here. She said if you don't have dill pickles she can borrow, she's going to die." Petey leaned a little closer. "And you call me a drama queen." She rolled her eyes and returned to her room.

I found Barbie with her head stuck in my refrigerator.

"Good morning." I peeked around the door at her. "Having some kind of pickle disaster, are we?"

"I have the worse craving for dill pickles." My neighbor continued her search.

I grasped her shoulders and forced her to straighten. "Are you going to have a baby?"

She lowered her gaze to the floor. "Yes."

"That's wonderful. When did you find out?"

"Three weeks ago." She shrugged.

"Three weeks? Why didn't you tell me when you first found out?" Disappointment inched its way through me. I thought we had developed a close bond, and she would have told me her happy news as soon as she knew.

A tear trickled down her check. "I don't know how I'll be able to face people after what I've done."

My mind went blank. I didn't have the slightest idea what could be wrong, unless . . . "It's not Rick's baby?"

Horror froze Barbie's expression. "Of course it's Rick's. Whose

152

would it be?"

"I don't know. Let's start from the beginning. Why are you so unhappy about having a baby?" I led her to the kitchen table, and we sat down.

"I'm afraid to tell anyone because then they'll know what Rick and I did."

Dang, my eye twitch was back. It had been dormant for a while, but Barbie always managed to flare it up. "What are you talking about, you silly nilly?" That's what my mouth said, but my brain was screaming, "What are you babbling about, you idiot stick?" This was one of the few times it was good to have my mouth engaged before my brain was in gear.

"Well, now that I am with child," Barbie said softly.

I slid to the edge of my chair and took her hand, "Yes, with child. Okay, I understand that part."

"Well, with everyone knowing what Rick and I did, word will eventually get back to my mother. Then what?"

She looked at me like she thought I had the answers to her dilemma. For cripe's sake, I didn't even know what that was. "Then what? What?"

Her bottom lip quivered and the little info light bulb came on over my head. "Ooooooh, you think your mother doesn't know you've been having sex with your husband for the past . . . what . . . two or three years?"

Barbie nodded.

"Honey, I'm positive your mother knows exactly what you've been doing. How do you think you got here? Do you think they found you under a cabbage leaf?" Even as I said it, I could have bitten my tongue off. Of course she knew where babies came from. I shouldn't treat her as if she was an idiot. Although, I did have to admit my dear friend was crazy enough to have been found in a cuckoo's next.

Eventually, I think I laid her fears to rest. With Barbie, it's hard to tell. But it brought me happiness to have a friend to share the pregnancy experience with.

On Wednesday, we were so far ahead of schedule with our work load that I was reduced to reading a golf magazine. It had been in the customers' waiting room for over three years and, to make matters worse, no one in my family played golf. Once I read the article about how balls were manufactured, I two-pointed it into the trash can. Basketball was more our game.

Carrie Sue and Linc entered the office with a pizza from *Call McCall for the Best of All Pizza*

"Would you care for a slice?" Linc shoved the open box in my direction.

The intense aroma of pepperoni, onions, and anchovies assaulted my sensitive nostrils; my stomach lurched.

"Thanks, but I'll pass." I moved downwind of their lunch. "You two can handle this place for the rest of the afternoon. I think I'll go home."

They exchanged glances and giggled. I didn't want to know what transpired as they evidently read each others' minds. I waved and left.

I'd been home long enough to strip my bed and scour the bathroom. When the phone rang, I was in the process of emptying some un-identified mossy green substance from the refrigerator. It was Mary Lou. On the phone, not in the refrigerator.

"I called your garage and Linc said you'd taken the rest of the afternoon off," she said. "My mother-in-law is babysitting today. Wanna go shopping or something?

"Ah, I can't. I'm dejunking the frig-a-dater and I have sheets in the washer." I'd hardly seen my best friend in the past months. Mar-ried life kept each of us busy. "Why don't you come over here and hang out with me? We can at least catch up on things while I work."

In no time at all, Mary Lou was helping with the rest of my chores. She went to Petey's bedroom to gather her sheets to put into the washer. Mary Lou had been gone a while, and I went to check on her. She sat on the bed, her legs crossed in Indian fashion, read-ing Petey's diary.

"Give me that." I snatched it from Mary Lou. "You can't read that. It's an invasion of privacy."

She hurried off the bed and grabbed the book back. "I was just getting to the good part."

I deliberately allowed her time to read a little more and then I took it from her. "I have to put it back. Where did you find it?"

"It was stuffed in Petey's pillowcase. I was shaking the pil-low out and it fell to the floor. It is your motherly right to read your child's diary. Besides, from what I read, Petey is in some kind of trouble with a bully at school." Mary Lou reached, but I was able to keep it out of her hands.

I was dying to know what she'd read, but every nerve in my body screamed, "If Petey wanted you to know, she would have told you." I knew it was true, and it would probably cause her some kind of mental trauma if she found out someone had read her most private thoughts. But how much damage was being done to her by some bully at school? I weighed the odds and decided if Mary Lou told me what she read, it wouldn't be as if I actually snooped in Petey's diary. Maybe I could give her some advice in an off-handed way, and she'd never need to know anyone had seen it.

"What kind of trouble is Petey in?" I asked.

"Someone named Jessica takes Petey's snack money every afternoon and threatens her not to tell."

I didn't know if I was more disturbed by the threats made against Petey, or the fact she hadn't talked to me about them. I felt like going to the school and pulling Jessica out of the classroom and throttling her. How dare her threaten my daughter? Who was she, anyway, Bubba Craig's niece? A Redneck Mafia princess who got what she wanted by bullying people around?

I had a dilemma on my hands. I couldn't protect Petey if she didn't draw me into her confidence, and I certainly couldn't let her know I read her diary. Yet I couldn't allow her to suffer in silence.

Chapter 10

While Mary Lou and I finished cleaning my house, my mind weighed heavily with how I should handle Petey's predicament. Around four o'clock, Mary Lou went home. I still had an hour before I had to start dinner and Arch and Petey would be home.

I stretched out on the bed, and as I drifted off I kept going over different ways to approach Petey. What would her birth mother, Nola, have done in this situation? Surely after I rested I'd be able to decide my course of action. Hopefully, it would be a decision that wouldn't screw up our daughter for life.

I don't think I'd been asleep long when I heard footsteps. I opened my eyes and found the room surprisingly dark except for an aura of light at the foot of the bed.

A man stepped into the light. "It's me," he said.

It was Arch's dad, Pete. I didn't become as rattled as you would think seeing a vision of a dead man. He visited me before on the night he died in what I was sure was a dream. I lay very still so I wouldn't wake myself up.

"Hi, Pete. How are things where you are? Got your wings yet?"

He shrugged. "I'm working on it."

157

I meant it as a joke, but it appeared to be a serious thing with him.

"Is this a social visit, or you just stopped by to scare the heck out of me?"

"Nola wanted me to tell you you're doing a good job, and she thanks you for loving her child." He smiled and a warm shiver slowly moved through my body like it was on a Sunday stroll.

"Tell her thank you for me, okay?" I barely croaked out the words.

"I want to thank you for loving my child, too."

I closed my eyes against the heavy flood of tears and blubbered for at least a minute. When I looked again, it was daylight, my pillow was wet, and Pete was gone. My warm and fuzzy dream vanished with . . . a knock on the door.

I hurried to the front room. Along the way I straightened my hair and clothes and then flung open the door.

There stood Pete. Big as life. I screamed and slammed the door. Bracing against it, I wasn't sure how I could keep a ghost out, or why the fool continued to knock instead of materializing into the room. I could put up with Pete's visits in my dreams, but not during my waking hours.

"Hello the house," he yelled from my front porch.

"What do you want?"

"I'm looking for Arch Fortney. I'm his uncle."

Uncle. Pete had a brother I'd never met. I wracked my brain to remember the man's name. Earp? Doc Holiday? I couldn't come up with it. He had a case of angina at the time of our wedding, and he and his wife couldn't attend.

"Uncle who?" I asked.

"Uncle Wyatt. Arch's dad was my brother. Are you Bertie?"

Wyatt. Okay, I was pretty close. I eased the door open a crack and peeked out. He smiled and opened his arms for a hug. I could definitely see the family resemblance. It would probably be next Tuesday before my heart returned to a normal rate, but I swung the door aside and timidly hugged Pete's double.

I led the way back into the living room. "I'm sorry I screamed. You look so much like your brother, I thought you were him."

"Well, honey, his brother is dead." Behind me I heard a woman's voice. I spun around and almost knocked over a short elderly woman. Jeeze, where had she come from?

"I'm sorry," I stammered and tried to back away from her, but she wrapped her arms around me and squeezed with all her might.

"It is so nice to finally meet little Archie's new wife."

I looked down into a mass of steel gray curls. Trying to back out of the woman's clutch, I was amazed at how strong she was. Finally, she let go and I wobbled backward. "It's nice to meet you . . . too." I couldn't remember her name.

She was all of five feet tall and wore black-rimmed glasses swooped on the sides like cat eyes.

"Well, I can tell you, Hildy and I have been anxious to get over here and meet our favorite nephew's wife." Uncle Wyatt put this arm around Hildy. For some reason, the name did not compute with what Arch called her.

"Arch'll be very glad to see you." We sat in the living room. "He and Petey should be home any minute." *Please come home. Now.*

"How is Penelope Tam doing?"

It took a second to realize Hildy was talking about Petey.

"She's doing great," I said, but thought again about Jessica, the bully. Had she terrorized Petey again today?

"She is such a beautiful child. I'll bet she's grown a foot since we last saw her," Hildy said.

"Yes, she is growing into quite a little lady. Will you be staying in town for a few days, or just passing through?" I hoped I didn't sound ungracious, but I did want to know their intentions.

"Oh, we always spend two weeks here when we visit. I was unable to travel last year because of my vagina," Wyatt said.

"Angina, dear." Hildy cut her eyes to the right and then looked back at me. Only one eye came back; the other stayed cocked to the right. It was a strange sight. She tapped the side of her head with her open palm and her eye straightened out.

It was a disconcerting ordeal. I didn't know whether to comment or not.

"Excuse me, that dang thing's been doing that a lot lately."

I rubbed my temple. "Have you seen a doctor about it?"

"You see that spot right there?" Uncle Wyatt pointed to the back of Aunt Hildy's left hand. "That's the only part of her body that hasn't been treated by a doctor." A puff of indignant air whistled past his lips. I giggled, but suddenly realized it was inappropriate.

"I'm not sure what's keeping Arch. He's usually here by now." I was grasping for snippets of conversation. I wasn't sure what time Arch walked through the door because I didn't get home until he started dinner. He didn't even know I left work early and was waiting on him.

"Maybe he's got a gal on the side and had to stop by there first." Wyatt found himself to be very humorous. He laughed out loud.

I found him to be obnoxious with a capitol *O*.

"Don't pay any attention to him," Hildy said. "Maybe we could get settled in while we're waiting for Archie.

"Good idea. Go fetch the bags." Wyatt nudged her to stand. He put his feet on my sofa, boots and all.

My mind had trouble registering the whole scenario. They were going to "settle in" at our house. And while Wyatt sat with his feet propped on my furniture, tiny, elderly Hildy was to bring in their luggage.

"Excuse me." I took a deep breath and was about to tell that old goat what I thought of him, but thankfully *Little Archie* arrived to save the day.

"Wow. Uncle Wyatt. Aunt Mavis." Arch lifted his aunt and swung her around. He and Petey greeted our guests and were apparently thrilled to see them.

"You should have let us know you were coming so we could have prepared for you." It was then he looked around and I could tell by the look on his face he was surprised the house was not in the same shape it had been when he left for school that morning. Instead it was spotless from my afternoon of polishing the entire place.

His gaze snapped to me. As I walked past him, I whispered, "It's a fluke. Just roll with it."

"Well, we're glad you're here. Have you brought your luggage in yet?"

"Not yet, you can do that for Aunt Hildy," I said.

It was Arch's turn to whisper. "Her name is Mavis. Don't call her Hildy." He hurried out the door leaving me very confused. I told Petey to go to her room and gather some of her things. She would be sleeping on the sofa while Uncle Wyatt and Aunt Mavis/ Hildy were visiting. She did as instructed. When she returned, she had her diary tucked under her arm. Good. Maybe I'd broach the subject of the contents of the diary at bedtime.

In short order, Arch loaded our guests' bags into Petey's room. While she, Wyatt, and Mavis visited in the living room, Arch and I visited, in hushed tones, of course, in the kitchen.

"Why does Wyatt call your aunt Hildy if that isn't her name?"

"Hildy was my uncle's first wife. He didn't want to learn a new name. And she's been answering to Hildy for forty-seven years."

"I hate to tell you this, but I don't like him very much." I stirred the spaghetti sauce while Arch put lettuce in the salad bowls.

"He'll grow on you"

"So do warts, but I don't want that to happen either."

"He's a lot like Dad. You'll see."

"He's nothing like your dad. For one thing, he has his clothes on."

"Well, that's subject to change at any minute."

"Not in my house it won't."

Arch kissed me on the end of my nose and chuckled his way back to the living room. Maybe I was just a little out of sorts. Baby hormones could cause that. If I tried harder to get to know Uncle Wyatt, surely I would learn to like him. After all, I wasn't all that crazy about Arch's father when I first found him sleeping in the re-cliner Wyatt now sat in. But I'd grown to love Pete.

Full of determination, I rejoined the family in the living room.

"Hildy, take my boots off," Wyatt demanded.

She jumped to her feet, straddled his out-stretched leg, and pulled off the first boot. As she started to take off the next one, Wyatt smacked her on the backside. "Your butt gets wider every day."

Aunt Mavis' cheeks flushed a bright red, but she followed through with her chore. No matter how Arch felt about his uncle, I couldn't like him. The best I could hope for was to not tell him what I thought of him and possibly smack him upside his head for good measure. I went back to the kitchen and soon served dinner.

Afterward, while I put leftovers away, Arch gathered dishes and carried them to the sink. Mavis had excused herself to go to the bathroom and was just walking back into the kitchen.

"Well, looky here, Hildy," Wyatt grunted. "That's something *you* don't see every day. A man washing dishes."

"That's for sure." Mavis gathered the last of the things from the table and placed them on the counter.

"Come on, Arch. That's woman's work. Let's you and me watch the news."

Wyatt made a bee-line to the sofa. I scooted Arch along behind his uncle.

Later, after Mavis and Wyatt had been tucked into Petey's trundle bed, Arch gave me a long gentle hug. "Thank you for—"

"For not killing your uncle?" I interjected.

"I was going to say for welcoming them into our home. I know they're strangers, but they've been a big part of my life. Although I don't understand the horrible way Uncle Wyatt treats Aunt Mavis, I don't think it is our business to interfere in what has been working for forty-some-odd years. Let's simply make the most of it. Try to enjoy their stay and hope the next two weeks pass quickly. Okay?"

Sometimes I had too much family, but Arch had very little. Wyatt, Mavis, a couple of cousins and that was about it. "Of course,

I promise I'll behave."

Arch went to bed, and I waited in the living room for Petey finish her shower. I still didn't have any idea how to bring up the subject of Jessica the Hun, but surely I would think of something after I started talking to my daughter. After all, didn't her birth mother send word just that afternoon I was doing a good job with our little girl? I shook my head. Was being delusional a good thing or a bad thing? Whatever, it built my confidence.

As I tucked the blanket around Petey's small body, I cleared my throat at least twice.

"You want to talk to me about something?" she asked.

Surprised, I drew back. "Well, yes, but how did you know?"

"You always clear your throat just before you say something important."

"Oh, well, then let's get right into it." I sat beside her and pushed a stray, damp strand out of her face. "Is everything going good at school? Any problems?"

"You read my diary, didn't you?" Her eyes widened. I guess mine did, too.

"No, I didn't." That wasn't a lie. "Mary Lou read it."

"Oh, well, I knew someone had because it was tucked inside my clean pillow case." She pulled the blanket under her chin. "Did she read the whole thing?"

"No, she went to strip the bed for me and when I caught her reading it, I made her quit. She told me someone named Jessica was taking your snack money. Is there anything I can do to help defuse the situation?"

"Whatever does that mean?"

"It means to smooth out a problem."

"Well, it's been defused."

"Good. How did you do that?"

"Jessica said if I didn't give her my snack money every afternoon, she was going to tell Randy Carson I was in love with him."

I didn't know what was worse: Petey being threatened, or in love with Randy Carson. I shuddered.

"How did you take care of it?"

"I told Randy I love him myself. He told Jessica she was committing *stortion* which is punishable under the law and she would be arrested and maybe hung."

"I think you mean *extortion*," I said. Certainly, Donna's juvenile delinquent, Randy, would know about such things.

"So, Jessica isn't bullying you any more?"

"No, ma'am. Once I told Randy and he threatened her with the law, she and I been really good friends."

I was glad to hear that. "You know, Petey, you can always come to me with any problem you have." She nodded and lifted her arms around my neck. I gave her a quick peck on the cheek. "Good night, sweetheart."

"Mom? I was wondering if I could have a sleepover after our company leaves."

I wanted to meet Jessica, the extortionist. I needed to know the kids Petey considered her friends. "Of course, dear. We'll invite Jessica for a sleepover in a couple of weeks."

"Jessica? I want to have Randy come over and spend the night."

Oh, good Lord. "Sweetheart, you can't have a boy over to spend the night at your age."

"How old do I have to be?"

"No, that's not what I meant. It's just that boys and girls don't have sleepovers until after they are married. Understand?"

"No, but I have a list of things I don't understand written in the back of my diary. I'll put that right under *extortion*."

Just for an instant, I wondered if I should try to explain it all to her, but she closed her eyes and was already headed to sleepy town.

In our bedroom, Arch was in deep slumber. I lifted my gaze upward. "Thanks for the vote of confidence, Nola. I think we handled that pretty well."

With each passing day, I grew to like Aunt Mavis more and Wyatt less. He seemed to get ornerier as the time went by. Mavis reminded me a lot of my Nana Byrd. They had the same build, same hair color and a very quick wit. The major difference was Mavis remained oblivious to the unjust way Wyatt treated her. However, if old Wyatt had ever told Nana she was fat, she would have taken her daddy's hand gun, which she gave me on my sixteenth birthday, and changed old Wyatt from a dude to a dudette.

I don't remember Grandpa Byrd because he passed away when I was three, but Nana and I were inseparable until the day she died. Actually, she's still with me in so many ways.

Mind your own business, Roberta, and no one will have the right to mind it for you. Her words had been following me around since Arch's aunt and uncle arrived. So, as the perfect Southern lady I did exactly as told until . . .

About eighty-three hours and twenty-seven minutes before their stay was to end, we were just finishing up dinner.

"How's Jim doing?" Arch asked of his cousin and Wyatt's oldest son. "Haven't heard from him in several years."

"He's as good for nothing as he always was. Gets that from his mother's side." Wyatt jabbed a fork in Mavis' direction.

Just in case Arch had any thought of finding humor in his uncle's unflattering statement, I brandished my fork in his direction. His gaze quickly dropped to his plate, but I could tell he was struggling not to burst into laughter.

In the meantime, Nana's words shouted in my brain like they came from a ghetto blaster. *Mind your own business.* Do you think I listened? Of course not.

"Why on God's green earth would you talk about your own child like that?"

"Because it's true."

"It may be true he's a problem child, but I doubt it's Mavis' fault." I reached out and touched her arm.

"Thank you, dear," she said.

"Well, it sure ain't my fault," Wyatt scoffed.

"What's Jim done that's so bad?" I asked.

"He robbed a bank and has three more years to go on his sentence."

Jeeze, he really was a not-so-nice person.

"How old is he?" I asked.

"Thirty-seven," Mavis answered.

"I believe there comes a time in every person's life when they have to stop blaming their parents for their wrongdoings. At his age, he has to accept responsibility for his actions." I articulated my rationalization in a clear, concise voice.

Arch was steadily tapping me on my leg in a feeble attempt to get me to be quiet. Defiantly, I faced off with Wyatt. "How can Jim robbing a bank be Mavis' fault?"

Arch slumped back into his chair. "Oh, brother," he said under his breath.

"Why, don't you know? Mavis drove the get-away car." Wyatt heehawed like an ass.

"I tried to warn you." Arch placed his fingers under my chin and pushed upward to close my gaping mouth.

"You know I was acquitted of that," Mavis shouted at Wyatt, and turned to look at me.

"Jim needed cigarettes, and he asked me to drive him to the store. I parked in front of the Piggly Wiggly, and I thought he'd gone inside, but he went around the block to the bank. After he robbed it, he came back to the car and we drove off. I thought it was funny that he didn't have any cigarettes in the canvas bag he was carrying." Mavis' eye did its sticking thing, and she promptly straightened it out.

At that point, I wouldn't have been surprised if my own eyes spun around in their sockets. I couldn't believe my ears.

"I didn't know what had happened until the coppers blue-lighted me," Mavis continued. "I was doing thirty-five miles per hour in a forty-five zone. So, I knew I wasn't speeding. Jim dropped to the floorboard and used his hand to push on the accelerator. Next thing I knew we were in a high-speed chase. I finally got stopped. The police pulled me out, handcuffed me, and hauled my butt to jail."

"Well, why aren't you in prison, too?"

Wyatt quit laughing long enough to tell me, "For some reason the authorities believed her story. She was set free. I tell you, this woman is a nutcase."

"You don't have a right to talk to her like that. She was an innocent pawn of *your* son." I felt so sorry for poor Mavis.

"That's just one thing in a long string of goofy things she's gotten into in her life. Her whole family is like that. They're from Jones County where the gene pool is a little stagnated."

"Well, what about your other son?" I asked.

Arch choked on his sip of coffee. I slapped him on the back and trudged right through with my question.

"Surely your other son has brought you some happiness."

"Oh, yes," Mavis piped in. "For a short time, he was mayor of our small town."

That sounded impressive. I suppose that son got his good traits from his father, or at least in Wyatt's eyes.

"It was a really short time," Wyatt added. "But long enough to get away with half of the money in the city's benevolent fund."

Maybe not.

"So, is he in jail, too?' Inquiring minds and all that jazz.

"No, there was only one-hundred dollars in the benevolent fund. So, the fifty he got away with was a misdemeanor. Mavis paid it back to the city, and the charges were dropped."

"What's he doing now?" My head was starting to hurt, probably from that imaginary block Arch dropped on it.

"He's working on a hog farm where they raise prize piney-wood rooters."

"Well, at least that's an honest job."

"Yeah, we're thrilled with our two offsprings. They're both in pens."

Everybody laughed but me. Poor Mavis saddled with two worthless sons *and* Wyatt. She certainly had her lot in life.

Later that night, as Arch and I snuggled together in our bed, I asked him why he had never told me about his cousins.

"In case you didn't figure it out at dinner tonight, they aren't much to talk about. Your family is so different. All of you have the close relationship I never had, except for Mom and Dad, of course. Jim and Josh were always pains in the rump. I only had to contend with them on their two-week visit every year."

"Did you go visit them?"

"No, Mom said that my being around them once a year was enough."

"Did you like being around them?"

"No, they were so mean. Until I was about fourteen, I was afraid of them."

"What happened then?"

"Jim was tormenting my dog. I picked up a two-by-four; hit him in the head with it. His head then banged into Josh's. They both went out cold. Mom scolded me, but Dad took me aside and told me he was proud of me for taking a stand against those two bullies."

"So you gave your cousins a two-for-one special. Are there other stories like that I should know about you?"

"Eventually you'll hear them all, now that it's too late for you to back out of our marriage." He rubbed my tummy and the baby gave a soft kick. How could this man be related to Wyatt and his sons? Evidently he took after his mother's side, and for that I was very thankful.

Every layer of my husband held a pleasant surprise for me. Once in a while I learned he was not always the mild-mannered science teacher he pretended to be. He wasn't real froggy, but he could jump if the need arose. Feeling secure in his hug, I floated off to sleep on a cloud of happiness.

The next evening, when I returned from work, Arch and Wyatt were watching television and Petey was doing her homework.

"Is Mavis in the bathroom?" I hoped not because that was where I needed to go.

"She went for a walk." Arch glanced at his watch. "That was about an hour ago."

I hurried to the bathroom and then walked outside. Mavis stood under Barbie's infamous tree. I joined them.

"Are you two having a nice visit?" I asked.

"Oh, Bertie, Aunt Mavis is the most interesting person I've met in a long time." Barbie was beside herself with excitement. "Why haven't I met her before?"

"I just met her myself last week."

Mavis looked happier than I'd seen her since she arrived. Actually, I was happier than I'd been since she arrived. Watching Wyatt treat her the way he did was a real downer.

"What are you two talking about?"

"We've been talking about the miracle of childbirth. Did you know Barbie is going to have a baby?' Mavis covered her mouth and giggled.

"Yes, I did. Isn't it wonderful?"

"Bertie's having a baby, too," Barbie announced with pride.

Mavis gasped. "You are? How wonderful." She hugged me.

It never occurred to me Mavis and Wyatt didn't know I was pregnant. Their arrival had come so suddenly, I assumed Arch had told them. Even if he hadn't, I would think since I looked like I was smuggling a watermelon under my blouse they would have figured it out.

I pointed to my tummy. "You didn't notice this?"

"Wyatt and I thought you were just fat, but we're happy you're not." She rubbed her hands together rapidly.

"Look out," Barbie screeched from her perch.

While I was looking at her thinking my friend must be falling from her tree, Mavis latched onto my bare arm, sending a painful shock across my flesh.

"Ouch." I recoiled and rubbed my arm.

"I tried to warn you." Barbie swung down from her branch.

"You're going to have a girl." Mavis bounced up and down, pleased with her proclamation.

"For crying out loud, what was that all about?" My arm still tingled.

"I know that hurt." Barbie rubbed my arm. "She zapped me, too. I almost fell out of the tree."

"It's a gift. I rub my hands to cause friction and then I touch the expecting lady with both hands. If my right hand shocks, it's a girl. The left, it's a boy." Mavis giggled.

"Know what happens if they both shock?" she asked.

"It's twins?" Barbie and I said in unison.

"No, I get knocked on my butt because the charge is so hard." Mavis giggled. "I've told hundreds of women what they were going to have. I was right with all of them. I'll be with you, too. You'll see."

"I'm having a girl, too," Barbie announced, fully convinced of Mavis' powers.

I was a little skeptical. Okay, a lot skeptical.

Mavis said her good-byes and walked toward my house.

Barbie leaned closer. "She's a nutcase," she whispered.

I offered a weak smile to my friend. "You know what they say? It takes one to know one." I smiled widely, hoping it would take the edge off my statement.

"Just think," Barbie said, "you know *both* of us."

"Ouch." Only the truth hurts.

Chapter 11

The day before Mavis and Wyatt were to depart, I went to the garage early so I could catch up on paperwork and be able to leave earlier to spend the last evening with Mavis. She really was a sweet lady, but even after two weeks I still couldn't figure out why she put up with Wyatt.

After I paid bills and emptied the trash cans in the office, I took a yellow pad and made a list of his and her good traits. Mavis' outweighed Wyatt's ten to one. Which really meant I could only think of one good thing to say about him: He had a great nephew. Okay, two things. Tomorrow he'd be gone.

By eight-thirty, Carrie Sue arrived and was sweeping the floor. Linc was late. The only other time that had happened was the morning he was kidnapped and put in a tomb in the cemetery. Surely that wouldn't be the excuse he used again.

Out the front picture window, I saw my wrecker pull into the lot. A police car followed close behind. Carl Kelly opened the door and motioned for my driver to enter. Linc passed in front of me on his way to the bathroom. A dank odor followed him, and he had dark greenish mold or mildew smeared all over his uniform.

"Same vault?" I asked.

Linc grunted something and disappeared into the bathroom. Carl nodded. "Same vault, same grass cutter."

"Has Linc told you about being threatened by the Redneck Mafia?" I waddled around the counter and took a seat in the waiting area.

"We've checked out Mr. Craig, and he was at home last night." The deputy wiped the inside band of his cowboy hat. "Any other ideas?"

"No, that's all I can think of." As I got up from the chair, Carl took my hand and helped me stand. If I had that much trouble rising under my own steam, what would it be like during my last trimester, which was only two weeks away? I'd have to strap a tow truck winch to my back and hook it to something before I sat down.

Carl left, promising to report back if he learned anything new. I measured my baby's cocoon, holding my hands out in front of me so I could visualize the approximate size of my unborn child. I really had put on a lot of weight, and in three and one-half months I'd be twice my present size. Reality settled in every nook and cranny of my mind—the big baby I was carrying would grow even bigger and eventually would have to come out.

That one horrendous fact had been smoothed over by my excitement at being a mommy. Suddenly, every tidbit of chatter I'd heard between my mom and my sisters-in-law rushed through my thoughts and stopped me cold in my tracks.

"I felt like someone was driving a Buick through me," Bobby's wife had said.

"I tried to slap Billy into a new world, but I was too weak." That was Diane's take on the matter.

I plucked the phone from its cradle. When Mary Lou answered, I dove right in. "On a scale of one to ten, how much pain was there?"

"I wondered how long it would be before you got around to that question. Let's see, you are a little over five and a half months. Yep, that's about the same time it hit me that with this wonderful, blessed event would come pain."

"Well, how much? Tell me the truth. I have to know," I shouted.

"The truth is, on a one-to-ten scale, the pain was about fifty. During the process, you will look and sound like the little girl in the *Exorcist* except your head won't really spin. Pea soup is optional."

"Oh, Lord, my dear friend, couldn't you have lied to me?" I sank back into the chair and lowered my throbbing head to the cool table.

"Yes, but if you are expecting the worst, it won't be that bad." Mary Lou's voice carried a tone of understanding. "Bertie, it will be the most wonderful thing you'll ever experience. And when they place your baby in your arms and you look at the little human you and Arch have created, the pain will be the last thing on your mind. It's too amazing for words."

Her last words came from a constricted throat. She and I sniffed in unison.

"Thanks, I knew I could count on you to help me feel better."

"I got to run. Rex the second is crying. Oh, one more thing, since Arch has been through this before he probably already knows, but it's a good idea he keep all his vital parts out of your reach, especially during the final stages of labor." She hung up the phone.

I touched my tummy and made a promise to my baby. "I won't let my fear of the pain take away any of the pleasure of seeing you come into the world where I can hold you in my arms and tell you over and over again how much I love you." My heart did a flip. "Oh, yeah, and I promise not to injure your father in the process."

At home that evening, Wyatt continued to be just plain rude to Mavis, yet she never seemed to notice. While she and I cleaned the kitchen after dinner, and since they were leaving early the next morning, I felt obliged to offer some advice from one woman to another.

"He's kind of hard on you, don't you think?" I handed Mavis a plate to dry.

"Who? Wyatt?"

Who else would I be talking about? "Ah, yeah, Wyatt."

"He's always been like that since the day I met him."

"Where did you meet him?"

"I worked in a bathhouse outside of Hot Springs, Arkansas. He said I was the cutest towel girl he'd ever seen, and he wanted to take me home so I could take care of his terry cloth forever." She appeared to be reaching way back in her memory, perhaps to a happier time. "I found out real quick that handing him a towel was not all he had in mind."

Dark shadows shrouded her gaze. Evidently even their beginning wasn't all that happy.

"You know, Mavis, you don't have to put up with the way he treats you."

"I know, but I'm afraid to live alone."

"You could get a roommate. You know, someone who could help share expenses. You're very pretty and seem to have a lot of common sense. You don't need anyone telling you what to do all the time. You could get a job and be self-sufficient."

"Job? I never even thought about getting a job. Except for the two weeks at the bathhouse, I've never worked. Would I *have* to get a job, or could I just live off the one-hundred thousand dollars I get each year from the trust fund my dad left me?"

For cripe's sakes, maybe she didn't have as much common sense as I once thought.

"You mean to tell me you get that much money and you still put up with that nincompoop?" Maybe she should use some of that money for therapy. If they stayed at our house much longer, I would need a healthy dose of therapy myself.

It must have been at that precise moment when Mavis' switches all clicked to the working position because the next morning, after she'd carried the luggage to the car, she walked back into the house and faced Wyatt.

"This is where you and I part ways. I don't have to put up with you any more, you old nincompoop."

As my own words came back to bite me on the butt, I broke into a coughing fit. Neither Wyatt nor Mavis seemed to notice so I slinked out of the line of fire and went to hide out in my bedroom. There was a little bit of raised voices, mostly on Wyatt's part, but by and large the murmur of Mavis' whispered tones were all I could hear. So, I quietly cracked the door and pressed my ear to the opening.

"You've treated me like dirt everyday of our miserable lives together," Mavis said.

Great. I could hear much better.

"But—" Wyatt tried to speak.

"Put a sock in it, you old poot." I heard a noise that sounded a lot like a raspberry. I'm not sure who emitted the childish gesture, but my money was on Wyatt. He seemed to be at a loss for words.

"You can't—" he tried again.

"Your days of telling me what I can and cannot do are over. I have one thing to tell you. If you'd like to see the sunrise tomorrow, I suggest you march your arrogant behind out to the car and hightail it on back to that cold house you refer to as home. I'm not sure how you'll survive, but here's how the morning ritual starts out. You put your own socks on over your nasty, gnarled toes, get your own newspaper, and fix your own grits and eggs. Oh, yeah, one over easy and one scrambled, you know, like your brains."

The front door opened causing a draft to swirl around me. What had I done? Why couldn't I mind my own business? In less than two weeks, I'd destroyed a forty-seven-year marriage. And why? Because I didn't like the way Arch's uncle treated his wife even though she didn't seem to object until I pointed out the error of her ways.

The front door slammed, rattling the windows. Quickly it re-opened. "Hey," Mavis shouted.

I figured she had her say and now she'd changed her mind. Thank goodness. I didn't want to have the end of their marriage on my conscience.

"And one more thing, you old goat, my name is Mavis. M-A-V-I-S!"

As the front door slammed again, I slumped against my bedroom wall. I didn't know how all this would work out, but the one thing I knew for sure was that Arch was going to kill me.

I left Mavis camped out at my house and I headed to the garage. I felt lower than the bottom of the echo well located behind Pop's house. He filled it in many years ago because of an incident where two brothers put their baby sister into a large water bucket and lowered her to the water below. I'll never forget the way my screams echoed through that well. But I digress.

I felt terrible my big mouth convinced Mavis to put an end to her forty-seven-year marriage. Since we didn't have a blackboard at our house, I wondered where and how many times my husband, the teacher, would make me write "I will mind my own business."

A snicker rumbled in my throat. I'd give anything to have actually seen Wyatt take off with his tail tucked between his legs. Since I hid out in my bedroom, I didn't really know for sure how he looked. But it brought me pleasure to picture him that way.

Something else that always brought me pleasure was Elton Taylor's donuts. Since I was right in front of his shop, I whirled into the parking lot.

When I entered, Elton motioned for me to sit at the counter on a chrome stool with a blue vinyl-covered seat. The aroma of frying dough made my mouth water.

"What'll you have, my Little Queen of the Hubcap?" he asked.

"I'll have a cup of coffee and a cream-filled donut with chocolate glaze."

He nodded and turned.

"Oh, and how about a sprinkling of pecans?" I added.

"You got it." Again he turned.

"And maybe a dusting with powdered sugar."

He faced me. "Will that do it, my Pearl of the Oil Pan?"

I nodded. "I'll eat the donut here, but put my coffee in a to-go cup."

He stared at me for a moment to make sure I was through with my order. He took two steps.

"Lots of cream in the coffee, please." I couldn't help myself.

Elton set a plain, no glaze donut in front of me.

"This isn't what I ordered." I pushed the saucer back to him.

"I know, but you don't need all the sugar. I've noticed you're putting on weight." He shoved it back at me.

"Helllooo, Elton." I pointed to my protruding tummy. "Baby on board."

"Oh . . . well, then the baby doesn't need all that sugar either. It'll get the little dickens all hyped up and you'll feel like you're carrying the Atlanta Falcons in your tummy." He set my coffee down and pointed to my plain, very plain donut. "Eat up."

I did just that.

"Where's Linc this morning?" Elton used a bleach-soaked rag to wipe the counter.

"You mean you haven't seen him? I figured he'd been here and gone by now."

"He's a no-show today. That's not like him."

Good heavens. Could Linc have been kidnapped again? I, for

one, had had enough. Maybe he was afraid to rat on Bubba and his little buddy, but I wasn't. After all, every time Linc was abducted, he was in my wrecker. I had to put a stop to it.

I stuffed the last of my donut into my mouth, plopped down a few dollars, and grabbed my coffee. Ten minutes later, I screeched to a halt in front of the huge wrought iron gate at the entrance of Gilbert's Cemetery. It wasn't locked, but it was closed. I opened it and started cruising along the dirt road that wound through the hundred and seventy-five-plus-years-old graveyard.

Nana Byrd's plot was at the other entrance in a section called "Sermon on the Mount." Arch's father and mother were to the right of the mausoleum where all the Gilberts were at rest. When I arrived at the Garden of Serenity, it dawned on me that Linc never said which tomb he was put into. I had no idea where to look.

Since I didn't see the lawns keeper, I couldn't even ask where the kidnappee was found on previous occasions. I parked and started walking through the cemetery. "Linc," I called in as much of a whisper/yell as I could without disrupting the tranquility of the beautiful gardens. I must have walked a mile, calling, trying to see if any vault lid would slide easily.

"Linc!" My voice had gotten progressively louder. "Linc, where are you?"

I strolled up and down the paths, my eyes shifting left and right. On this bright sunny morning, not a soul visited their dearly departed. Only my calling for Linc interrupted the eerie quiet. As stealthily as my mommy-to-be body allowed, I moved between graves, careful not to tread on any of them.

I stopped near a huge magnolia tree which shaded the grave of

Leonard Dorsey, one of Sweet Meadow's founding fathers. He was credited with coming up with our town's motto: *There's no place as sweet as Sweet Meadow.* Legend has it he came up with that back in 1912 when he returned from serving time in the Army. Nana Byrd used to say he came up with it after serving time in prison. I never knew if that was true or not, but it made Nana laugh out loud each time she said it.

Suddenly, I felt I was being watched. I moved on and with each step I took the theme from *Jaws* played inside my head. I quickened my footsteps. "Linc, where are you?"

The feeling of dread grew thicker and thicker. "Linc." As I scurried past another mausoleum something touched my shoulder. I screamed and twirled around and screamed again.

An elderly lady tugged on the leash of her little white dog. She stopped to pick him up and clutched him to her chest. "I didn't mean to frighten you," she said in a high-pitched, definitely-startled voice. "I just thought I might be able to help you find your lost dog."

At first I was confused, but then I realized it must have sounded like I was calling a dog. I tried to smile to hide my embarrassment. "Thank you, but it's not my dog I've lost, it's my tow truck driver."

Her mouth formed a pitiful *O.* She placed her dog back on the ground. "I'm sorry. Was it a sudden death?"

"No, you don't understand. He's not dead, but I have to find the tomb he's in. You see?"

"Oh, yes, of course I do." She nodded and began running and dragging her puppy down the road.

When I recapped our conversation in my head, I agreed with her rapid departure. I would have done the same thing.

I spent at least two hours roaming among the graves whispering to every one adorned with some type of door or lid that could conceivably be opened and someone placed inside. I didn't find Linc, or the lawns keeper who could tell me where he might be stashed.

I decided the best thing to do was to get to my tow truck and call back to the office for them to dispatch the police to help me look for Linc. He could possibly be in serious trouble. Maybe hurt, maybe locked in a dark hole gasping for his last breath.

I had to hurry. I jumped back into my car and drove all around the outside of the cemetery, but I couldn't find my truck. It was just as I feared. Something bad happened to Linc, and now my tow truck was gone, too.

I needed to get help. I sped along the street and made rolling stops through two red lights. When I skidded into the parking lot of my garage, loose gravel flew all over my tow truck. The one I thought was stolen.

Linc and Carrie Sue came out of the office to meet me.

"Is something wrong?" she asked. "Are you in labor?"

"No." I raced past her and started looking Linc over for bullet holes. "Are you okay? I was so worried about you."

"I'm fine, Mrs. Bertie. Why were you worried?"

I collapsed against the side of the building. "Elton said you didn't go by to get your donuts this morning, and I assumed, just like the other two times you were late, you'd been kidnapped."

"I had a flat tire on the way in. I didn't want to be late, so I skipped my donuts and came straight to work."

I'd just about recovered from the whole ordeal when Chief Kramer drove up. He got out, put on his hat, and flipped open his ticket book.

"License, please." He looked right at me.

"You talking to me?"

"Yes, I need your license."

"What'd I do?" I knew, but I played the innocent part.

"You know exactly what you did." I guess my innocent look needed work. He furrowed his eyebrows. "You were speeding and you ran two red lights."

"What took you so long to get here?"

"I *stopped* at the lights, Missy."

"Come on, Chief, I thought Linc had been kidnapped again and I was hurrying to get to a phone. I spent all morning in the cemetery talking to the tombs and scaring the life out of an old woman and her dog. I deserve a break."

He stared at me. I think he was in shock. Flipping his book shut, he retreated to his car and climbed in.

"Whatever it was you just said you did, don't do it again." Chief Kramer slammed his door and drove away.

I'd only been away from my house for less than three hours, yet it felt like a week.

"I'm taking the day off. So far it's been more than I can handle," I told Linc and Carrie Sue. "Call Pop if you need help."

I was sure the type of stress I experienced that morning couldn't be good for my baby. I thought it best I go home and rest for at least twenty-four hours. I needed to take a hiatus from people and put an ice pack on my head.

As I pulled into my driveway, I remembered Mavis was at my house. I would need two ice packs.

That night, dinner was almost ready when Arch and Petey came in from school. After she dropped her books on the table, she hurried to the bathroom. I said a quick prayer and prepared to spill my guts about Aunt Mavis still being here, and the part I played in making that happen. From behind, Arch wrapped his arms around me. I leaned against him and savored the magic of the moment before it all disappeared. After he found out what I'd done, there was a chance he would never hold me again.

"I hear you had some excitement today," he whispered next to my ear.

His hot breath melted my insides. He already knew, and he didn't sound angry. Evidently, Wyatt had tattled on me. And here I hoped I'd get to explain how it all came about and how it really was best for Aunt Mavis. But that wasn't to be.

"Are you mad at me?" I asked.

"Of course not; I've done things like that before."

For some reason I didn't believe it. My husband never stuck his nose in where it didn't belong, but he was kind to try to spare my feelings. No wonder I loved him so much. He deserved a cup of coffee, which I handed to him along with a paper napkin. Just as he took a seat at the table, Petey came into the kitchen.

"I thought Aunt Mavis was leaving this morning. Why is she sleeping in my bed?"

I tucked a piece of her long blond hair behind her ear. "Well, you see, honey, she's going to stay here for a little while until she can move into her own place. I'm sure you noticed how Uncle Wyatt treated her. I helped her understand she didn't have to live with him if she didn't want to." I was feeling pretty good I'd been able to help set Mavis' world right. And Arch had understood.

"You did what?" my husband roared from behind me.

I spun to see his face turn red with the slightest tinge of purple near his temple. He rose, and I scrambled behind Petey. Using her as a shield, I asked Arch, "Didn't you just say you understood? You even said you had done things like that before. I didn't believe it, but you just said it two minutes ago."

Really loud, Arch counted to ten. Slowly, some of the flush drained from his face. "I had done things like *run a red light*. That I can understand. Imposing my own values on someone like Aunt Mavis and turning her world upside down, not to mention ours, I don't understand."

"Wait a minute, how did you know about the red light?"

I didn't know Arch was capable of glaring like he was at me. "I don't think that's relevant right now, do you?"

"No, not really. I was just mildly curious."

"Well, I'm strongly curious about how, in less than two weeks, you managed to rip apart two people who were married for forty-seven years." For emphasis, he ripped the paper napkin in two. Spittle formed at the corner of his mouth.

Petey twisted from my grasp. "You're on your own, Mommy." She went outside. Moments later I saw her speed past the window on her bicycle. I thought about running away with her, but Arch's glare pinned me to my spot.

"I'm sorry," I said. "I knew it was wrong of me, but Aunt Mavis deserves to be treated better than that old butthead treated her." His angry eyes softened.

"I know she did, but it wasn't our place to make it happen."

"I was shocked when she told him to take a hike without her. I was also proud of her."

Arch let down his defenses and I zoomed in. I put my arms around his neck and lightly grazed my lips across his. "You should have seen it. Wyatt was flabbergasted. It took him a full minute before he could comprehend what was going on and respond. Of course, it was then I took my leave and hid out in the bedroom until he was gone. I missed a lot of the verbal exchange, but her final words were worth it all."

"What were they?" By now my husband was back to his usual mellow self.

"My name is Mavis. M-A-V-I-S. Then she slammed the door. I wish I could have been a fly in that car. I bet Uncle Wyatt talked to himself non-stop all the way home."

"Yeah, me, too." Arch actually laughed, but it faded quickly. "Bertie, we're over-crowded already. Petey's sleeping on the couch. We don't have a room for the new baby who'll be along in a couple of months. So, Miss Fix-the-World, what are we going to do with Mavis?"

"I have it all planned out."

"I figured you would. What's the plan?"

"Mavis is going to rent a room from Millie Keats. She has that big house all to herself, and I think if she had a roommate she wouldn't be so lonely and she'd stay out of mischief."

"How will Mavis pay rent? I'm sure Uncle Wyatt won't willingly give her money, and it will take a long time to fight it out in the courts."

"Actually, it'll be Wyatt asking for alimony. It seems Mavis' father left her quite an inheritance. She's been getting one-hundred thousand dollars each year since her father passed away thirty-five years ago."

"You mean to tell me she's had access to that kind of money all these years, and she still put up with Uncle Wyatt's abuse?"

I nodded.

"I hate to admit it, but as long as it's what she really wants, I'm happy for her."

"Yeah and when Wyatt sues for his share of that money, you and I can be witnesses to the abuse he subjected her to."

His gaze narrowed. He placed his finger against my lips. "We will do no such thing."

"But—"

"Not a word."

"But—"

He tapped his finger against my lips.

To lock my words inside my mouth, I turned an imaginary key and pretended to drop it down the front of my blouse. Arch pulled it out and took a peek inside.

"Lose something?" Aunt Mavis' voice made us both turn with a start.

"Hi, Aunt Mavis. I just heard you're going to be with us a little while."

"Not too long, I'm moving in with someone named Millie Keats first thing in the morning. I talked to her on the phone earlier today and she said as long as I didn't mind cats or loud music, we'd get along just fine." Mavis lifted the lid on the simmering chili and inhaled the rising aroma.

I always prided myself on making pretty good chili. Today I made a really good batch.

"Needs more salt and a little less cumin." Mavis replaced the lid.

"You didn't even taste it. How do you know?"

"I can tell by the smell. I won fifty dollars in a smelling bee about two years ago."

Petey came back inside. "Wow. How cool is that?" Her eyes were big as saucers. Mine were rolled back in my head. She took a big sniff of the air. "Can you teach me to do that, Aunt Mavis?"

She pinched Petey's nose. "I might be able to. You have a strong beak."

"Well, that'll be fun." She winced and rubbed her nose. "I think."

"Come on." Mavis took Petey's hand. "I'll give you a quick lesson." They went into the living room.

I put my arms around Arch. "I'm really sorry I interfered."

"Well, Aunt Mavis seems to be doing okay. I would have expected her to be a little less . . . happy."

"I got home before noon today, and she was on the phone giggling like a school girl. She told me later she was talking to her sister. Apparently, she's been a champion for Mavis to leave Wyatt for years."

Arch shook his head. "Who knows, maybe your meddling was a good thing this time. Only time will tell." He lowered his mouth to mine. A moment into our kiss, his lips started vibrating. I stepped away from him. His whole body shook with laughter. Red-faced, breath-stealing, doubling-over laughter.

"What's so funny?" I didn't have a clue why, but I chuckled, too.

"I wonder if Sweet Meadow is ready for the dynamic duo of Millie and Mavis?"

My laughter stopped. That could mean only one thing—no matter what kind of trouble those two got in to, I'd be blamed because I stuck my nose in where it didn't belong. I created a monster with two heads.

Chapter 12

Mavis moved in with Millie. Two days later, I called to check on her.

"Hi, Millie, is Mavis there?"

"Yeah, but she's passed . . . asleep right now. May I take a message for her?"

"No, I just wanted to make sure things are going good with her being there."

"She is so smart, Bertie. She's promised to teach me how to do several things I've always wanted to do."

"Well, that's great, Millie. Has she heard from Wyatt yet?"

"Yeah, he called today."

"Have her call me when she gets up so she can tell me what he said. Okay?"

"I can tell you what was said."

"Oh . . . all right."

"Wyatt said he wanted to know if his wife was ready to straighten up and fly right home. Mavis told Wyatt she'd be home when cows fly."

"What'd he have to say about that?"

"Everything was quiet for a second. Suddenly, the name calling and foul language spewed forth. Boy, I tell you it was something." Millie laughed out loud. "Some of those words I've never even heard before let alone coming out of a woman's mouth. That's the first thing Mavis is going to teach me—how to talk like that. I can't wait."

"Good heavens, Millie. The last thing you need to add to your repertoire is foul language."

"Oh, lighten up, Bertie. You take life way too seriously. It might do you some good to use a few bad words now and then."

I thought of a few I'd like to say at that moment, but I let them slide. "Just tell Mavis I called. If she wants to call I'll be home all evening."

"I'm not sure she'll get up until tomorrow. After she talked to Wyatt, we cracked open a bottle of wine and celebrated the death of Mavis' marriage and the birth of her new life." Millie laughed in that ornery way she does when she's up to something. "She can't hold her liquor very well, but don't worry, that's what I'm going to teach *her*."

The next afternoon I paid bills and put them in the mailbox in front of the shop. I'd just walked back into the air-conditioned office and stood daydreaming out the front window when a monstrous, older red Cadillac pulled into the parking lot and nosed its way into a slot right in front of where I stood. I'm not sure what grabbed my attention first: Mavis driving and Millie riding shotgun, or they weren't stopping.

Years ago, Pop installed metal poles filled with concrete for this very reason. The pole in front of the Caddy did its job. A large crash ripped through my already frazzled nerves. Too startled to close my eyes, I saw the two elderly women lunge forward. Millie disappeared from view. I assumed she was now on the floorboards.

I ran out the door. Carrie Sue and Linc hurried from the garage bay and pulled open the car doors.

"Are you two okay?" we all asked at the same time.

Millie crawled back into her seat. "That was a much better stop than the one you made at the Pack and Sack this morning."

With the imprint of the steering wheel emblazoned on her forehead, Mavis agreed.

"You'll get the hang of it." Millie patted her new friend on the back. "I just hope I'm still alive to see it."

"Where did you get this car? Do you even have a license? Do both of you have a death wish?" I sputtered questions left and right.

"One question at a time, please," Millie said.

"Okay. Where did you get this car?"

"Ain't she a beauty?" The women got out, and Mavis ran her hand over the rusty, red fender of the Cadillac, circa early 1980s. "I stole it from Joe's House of Parts."

The thought that her history included an arrest for bank robbery caused my eye to twitch violently. "Please tell me this means you got a good deal and it's not a literal statement."

Mavis winked back at me. "I got my new sled for only two-hundred dollars."

"Sleazy Joe never knew what hit him," Millie added.

"You didn't run over him, too, did you?" My heart pounded.

"Bertie, you have to calm down." Millie grabbed my shoulder and shook me. "You're going to give yourself a heart attack."

I rolled my eyes, not that it left an impression on her.

"Do you have a license, Mavis?" I asked.

"Sure."

"Show me."

She dug in her purse and handed me her opened wallet.

"This is a hunting license." I nearly choked on my words.

"Yeah, me and that old poot used to go deer hunting every year."

"You have to have a *driver's* license to drive a car."

Millie stepped forward. "We know that and as soon as she learns to drive, she'll go get one."

My glare made her step back. "You two are going to drive me crazy."

"That'd be a short ride," Millie mumbled under her breath.

I expelled a huge puff of wind that fluttered her hair. "Here's the deal. You are going to leave this car here. Carrie Sue is going to take you home."

Millie stuck out her chest. "We are taking this fine specimen of a machine home with us."

I couldn't tackle them and tie them up. So I did what anyone in my condition would do. I planted my having-a-baby sized body behind the vehicle. Millie summed up the situation and leaned into the front seat and pulled out a bottle of drinking water. She opened it and let the liquid trickle slowly onto the ground. I watched, mystified by the fruitcake's action. In my stomach, butterflies tickled my baby causing the sweet thing to do the Tango on my bladder.

That and the dribbling water sent me racing inside to the bathroom. When I returned, the two terrors of Sweet Meadow were gone.

I was in the process of deciding if I should call Chief Kramer to get those two off the streets, but he called me.

"Afternoon, Bertie. I understand Millie's new roommate is your aunt. Is that right?"

"Oh, no, what's happened to them?"

"They're fine, but can you send a wrecker to Jasper and Search?"

"You're sure they are okay?"

"Oh, yeah, wish I could say the same for old man Yunkoffer."

I didn't even say good bye. I slammed down the phone and hollered for Linc to bring the wrecker around. "I'm going with you."

When we arrived on the scene, a big crowd had gathered. It was hard to tell what was going on and who was involved. Since Mavis' car was already a hunk of junk, I couldn't tell where it had been damaged. Yunk Yunkoffer was in the back seat of the squad car. Shoving my way to the front, I found Mavis first. Millie was in a deep conversation with the Chief.

"Are you hurt?" I hugged Mavis. "Did you run over Yunk?

"What's a Yunk?"

"That's him over there." I pointed to the police car. "Yunk Yunkoffer. Why isn't he in an ambulance? What's going on?"

"You know, sweetheart," Mavis took my arm and led me to a bus-stop bench, "Millie's right. You're going to give yourself a heart attack."

I took several deep breaths to stave off hyperventilation. I put my head between my knees which was crowded with my baby belly.

"Are you okay, Mrs. Fortney?"

With my head down, I recognized Chief Kramer's uniform pants and boots. I raised my head. "I'll be fine. I've had a lot of excitement today."

"Bertie, I wasn't talking to you." He turned to Mavis. "Are you okay? Do you need the paramedics to take a look at you?"

"No, I'm fine."

"Will some one please tell me what's going on? I'm scheduled for a nervous breakdown this afternoon and I don't want to be late." I stood on shaky knees.

"Millie and your aunt—"

I held up my hand. "Just for the record, Mavis is Arch's aunt. We're only related by marriage. Although I may be responsible for her being here, I'm not accountable for her actions. Are we straight on that?"

"Got it."

"Very good. Now, what's going on?"

"Mavis and Millie spotted Yunk driving erratically down the street."

"He was zipping from one side to the other, up on the sidewalk for a ways and then back into the street." Mavis did a wiggle motion with her hand.

"A kid with a cell phone to his ear stopped beside us a few blocks back," Millie carried on with the story. "I hollered for him to call 911, and Mavis and I tailed Yunk."

I glanced over at Yunk, who was yelling obscenities in our direction. He didn't appear to be hurt. Evidently Mavis hadn't run over him or injured him in any way.

"So, what happened?"

"Yunk pulled over between two cars parked next to the curb. These two blocked him in," Kramer explained.

"He was trapped like the rat that he is." Millie squealed with delight. "The city should give us a Citation of Merit for thwarting what could have been a major pile-up."

Something wasn't jiving. "Wait a minute," I said. "Yunk can't walk. What was he doing driving a car?"

"He wasn't." Chief Kramer removed his hat and scratched his head. "He got a snoot full down at the Dew Drop Inn and was racing his motorized wheelchair in and out of traffic. I'm hauling him in on DUI charges and I need you to impound his ride."

"Well, that certainly is a perfect ending to a perfect day." I rubbed the twitch in my eye which had moved to the other side.

"We're all through. Ya'll can go on your way." Kramer dispersed the crowd.

Millie and Mavis loaded back into their red "sled" and drove away, barely missing the police car. I prayed they made it home without incident.

"Mrs. Bertie," Linc interrupted me. "I don't know how to tow that motorized wheelchair."

I didn't either. For a moment, I scratched my head. Silently, I strolled over to the contraption, climbed on, and drove away from the scene. Linc followed along behind me with beacons flashing. At the top of my lungs I sang a song I'd made up years ago. It's to the tune of Gilligan's Island.

Sing it with me. "For new folks to move to Sweet Meadow, they must have a lot of guts, to live among the long-time citizens, 'cause all of them are nuts."

Normally after school, Petey waited for forty-five minutes with other children in the cafeteria until her father picked her up on his way home from the middle school. Millie's house was located two blocks from Sweet Meadow Elementary. Petey asked to be allowed to walk to the short distance after school and stay with her Aunt Mavis and Mrs. Keats until Arch arrived.

"I don't know if that's such a good idea." I passed meatloaf to my husband. He handed Petey the carrots.

"I think she's old enough to walk two blocks unchaperoned. There's a crossing guard and I'm sure Aunt Marvis will watch for her."

"Therein lies the problem. Do you think it wise for her to spend that much time with two not-so-stable older women? What kind of things will they teach her?"

Petey jumped in her seat and waved her arm in the air. "I know. I know."

Her father and I looked at her.

"They'll teach me about being a woman and surviving good-for-nothing men," she said.

I glanced back at Arch. "See what I mean? I don't think they'd be positive role models."

"I promise not to learn bad stuff. Just the good stuff."

"How will you know the difference?"

"I ask myself if you'd do what they say. If the answer's no, then I'll pretend like I didn't even hear them."

Her words banded my heart and tightened with a loving squeeze.

For a moment I lost my voice.

"I think what Petey is trying to say, sweetheart, is that she's old enough to know right from wrong." Arch laid his hand on my arm and Petey's smile melted my resolve. Maybe her idea was a good one after all.

"Okay, we'll try it for a little while, but at the first sign of trouble it will have to stop without an argument. Agreed?"

"Agreed." Petey nodded. "May I be excused? I want to call Aunt Mavis and tell her we can start my training for the smelling bee in Albany next month. Woohoo!" she shrilled, and ran from the room.

"Are you sure about this?" I asked my poor naïve husband. "Did you forget Aunt Mavis was arrested for driving a get-away car for her own son."

Arch chuckled aloud. "You are such a worry wart. She'll be fine."

If only I had that much faith. But not only was Mavis a worrisome part of the whole scenario, there was also Millie Keats to take into consideration. I shuddered.

Two weeks later, I returned to the garage from my monthly check-up with Dr. Johns. The baby was doing great, and everything was right on schedule. I danced around my waiting area, singing an unidentified tune, and feeling pretty happy with my life.

I didn't notice a car pulling into the parking lot, so I started when the office door opened. I came to an abrupt stop standing belly-to-belly with Gertrude Yunkoffer. I was with child. She wasn't. Yet we both had about the same size tummy.

"I'm so sorry. I was just exercising a little. Please, come on in." I scurried behind the counter and pulled out the paperwork for her husband's motorized wheelchair.

"Chief Kramer called a little while ago and told me you'd be coming by to pick up Yunk's chair."

"He said I would owe you one-hundred forty-eight dollars and ninety-eight cents. Is that right?" Her voice was soft and pleasant.

"That's right."

She plopped a brown paper bag on the counter. "There you go. Knock yourself out."

I turned the bag upside down. Dollar bills and pennies tumbled out. "Jeeze, didn't you have any bigger bills? They're gonna hate me at the bank."

"No one deserves that more than you." The words rolled off Gertrude's tongue like a raw egg rolls off a roof onto a small girl's head. In both cases, I was hit with something vile and didn't even see it coming.

I shivered. "Why do you feel that way?" I knew, but I stupidly asked anyway.

"You took an old, disabled man's wheelchair from him, and now we have to pay all the money we have saved to get it back. Isn't that blackmailing or kidnapping? Or, something like that?

"Maybe it should be chairnapping. How does that sound?" I asked.

"Sounds to me like you have a smart mouth."

"That can't be right, because if I had a smart mouth, I'd keep it shut."

"There should be laws about things like this," Gertrude gasped.

"There are. You break the law, you get arrested, your mode of transportation is impounded, and you pay to get it back. That's the law." I counted out the dollars and pennies while Gertrude huffed and puffed. After marking the receipt paid, I handed it to her.

Linc brought the wheelchair around and helped load it onto the bracket attached to the back of the Yunkoffer's car. As she pulled away, I waved to Gertrude. She thumbed her nose at me.

The sign above my garage caught my eye. *Bertie's Garage and Towing.* Pride filled my heart and pushed aside the doubts Gertrude's behavior evoked. Long before Pop turned the business over to me, he told me something he wanted me to always remember: For every unhappy customer who darkens the door of our office, ten happy ones will come along and appreciate what we do. That has proven to be true over and over again. I had my bad apple for the day. The next ten should be smooth sailing.

I decided not to tempt the fates. "Carrie Sue," I called. She peeked out from under a car hood where she was helping Linc.

"I'm going to the bank. Will you catch the phone while I'm gone?"

"Sure thing, boss." We were the same age, but she said it made her feel younger to call me that.

I smiled and gave her a friendly nod. She worked hard and deserved a little boost of ego now and then. I was glad to oblige.

When I walked into the bank, my favorite teller, Perrine Backus, had a major line of people waiting for her. Her life was better than a soap opera. When last Perrine and I met, she'd ridded herself of a parasitic husband and found a new love while hiding in the bushes, spying on the aforementioned wretch. Today she'd promised to fill me in on the next chapter of *The Life and Times of Perrine Backus.*

As much as I wanted to hear all the sordid details, I didn't want to stand in her long line, and I opted for the shorter one. The teller there was a trainee. Shirley Cameron, the bank manager, looked over his shoulder, monitoring the young man's moves.

For every one customer he waited on, Perrine did three. The wait seemed endless, but finally, my turn came. After he unzipped the bag and dumped out the deposit, he gave me an odd glance. Quickly, he counted the money.

"Sure are a lot of ones here." He placed a stack of money to his forehead with the flair of a clairvoyant. "Bet I can tell you what you do for a living."

Before I could point out the name of my business was written on the deposit slip, he spewed forth his best guess, loud and clear. "With all these one-dollar bills, my telepathic mind tells me you are a stripper."

The room erupted into whistles and laughter. I placed my hands on my protruding tummy to protect my unborn child from ridicule, then realized how useless it was. This baby was coming into *my* world, and he or she needed to accept everything that entailed.

Someone started humming *The Stripper.* On a whim, I raised my hands in the air and gyrated my hips.

"Go, Bertie. Go, Bertie," someone in the crowd yelled.

Hooking my leg around the lane-dividing pole, my tummy and

I slid up and down. Several people stuffed dollar bills into my maternity top pocket. When everyone applauded, I bowed and fanned my flaming face with my tip money.

Back at the teller's window, the young man blushed a vibrant red. "Boy, was I wrong. You couldn't possibly be a stripper."

I nodded in agreement.

"You don't have any rhythm," he added.

Shirley threw her body between me and the little twerp. By the time the desire to put my hands around his neck subsided, Shirley thrust my receipt at me.

"There you are, Bertie. Have a nice day. Next person in line, please."

A tall, burly man stepped up to the window and as I walked away, I heard him say to the teller, "Want to guess what I do for a living, Nostradamus?"

Amid several snickers, my anger died and I smiled all the way to my car.

As soon as they came through the door, Arch kissed me. Petey hugged me, burying her face against my belly. She inhaled deeply and then slowly released the breath. Without a word, she disappeared down the hallway.

"What was that all about?" I asked Arch.

"I'm not sure, but she smelled everything in the car."

"Did you ask her?"

"She said she's in training for a Smelling Bee and that Aunt

Mavis is coaching her every day after school," he said.

"Do *we* think this is an okay extra-curriculum?"

Arch snitched a hot French fry. "I can't see where it will do any harm. She appears to be putting her all into it. Besides, by the time she graduates from college she might be a pioneer in the smell-a-vision industry."

While I put dinner on the table, Arch went to wash up. My back ached a little, so I pressed it against the wide, varnished door casing. A whiff of furniture polish caught my attention. I dusted all the woodwork the day before and the pine scent still lingered. I turned and looked at it for several long moments.

"Why not?" I stuck my nose against the wood and sucked in so hard it was a wonder I didn't take in a few splinters.

"I would think the question would be *why?*" From behind me Arch spoke and Petey giggled. The baby gave me a sharp kick. I don't think I even turned red. Was it possible we were only given so many blushes in our lifetime, and I had used up all mine?

"Jeeze, I was just curious. That's all." As fast as possible, I set the food on the table. "Let's eat. It's getting cold."

After we sat, Arch had Petey said the blessing.

"Dear Lord, we thank you for the food we are ready to eat and thank you for Mommy who fixed it. Oh, and one more thing, please don't let my teacher, Mrs. J., want to talk to Mommy or Daddy about what I think she wants to talk to them about. Amen."

Her father and I exchange glances.

"Does Mrs. J. want to talk to your father and me?"

Petey handed over a folded piece of paper. I read it aloud. "Dear Mr. and Mrs. Fortney, I would like to have a conference with one or both of you around three-thirty tomorrow afternoon. If that isn't convenient, please call the school so we can reschedule. Thank you, Ida Mae Josevedo."

Petey stared into her plate.

"What does Mrs. J. want to talk to us about?" Arch asked.

"It could be a number of things. I'm really not sure." She smiled uneasily.

"Well, why don't you tell us a few of the things it might be?" her father urged.

"I'd really rather wait to see what she has on her mind." Petey filled her mouth with meatloaf. "Yummy. This is really good, Mommy."

I decided to let the subject drop for now. "Thank you, sweetheart."

Later, after Petey had gone to bed, her father and I decided I would go see Ida Mae and Arch would pick up Petey from Millie's. He and I tried to figure out what the problem could be, but since Petey gave us no trouble, we couldn't begin to imagine why we were being called to school.

I arrived at the school right on time. In Ida Mae's classroom, I found Randy Carson cleaning blackboards.

"Come on in, Bertie," she said. "Randy, you can go on home now. I hope we'll have a better day tomorrow."

"What do you mean *we*? *You* didn't have to clean the blackboards." Randy had his mother's attitude problem.

"Maybe we should just go ahead and schedule you for tomorrow afternoon right here and now." Ida Mae raised a menacing eyebrow at Donna's offspring.

"No, thank you. I'm gone." Randy grabbed his books and sailed out of the room.

"A long time ago, I had a chance to marry that boy's grandfather." Ida shook her head. "I shiver every time I realize he could be my grandson."

She was in her early fifties and had been married one time and it only lasted about two weeks. She was a handsome woman. Not beautiful, but definitely not ugly. She was a member of the city council for many years, volunteered at the hospital during her summer vacations, and all her students loved her. I never understood why she didn't remarry and have a family of her own.

"Donna's kids all need a positive role model in their lives. Maybe you could have been one for them and made a big difference."

"Maybe." Ida Mae stared off into the distance and appeared lost in a different time. She was only gone a few moments.

"Well, have a seat." She motioned to a chair next to her desk.

"Is Petey causing you a problem?" I asked.

"Well, not really. It's just that she smells."

Smells. I wasn't expecting that. "What does she smell like?"

Ida Mae cracked up laughing. "I don't mean she stinks. I mean she sniffs everything she comes in contact with."

"Oh, is that all?" Relief flowed though my anxious nerves. "Her great-aunt is training her for a Smelling Bee. It's just a phase. I'm sure she'll lose interest soon."

"I was going to suggest she may need something to distract her unusual interest. I'm really not sure how healthy it is for her to be sniffing so many strange substances. I've caught her with her nose in the chalk tray, a paste jar, pencil sharpener shavings, and Randy Carson's ear." She clicked her tongue. "I don't think that's natural, do you?"

"I felt that way in the beginning, but her father thinks it's an imagination stimuli and it might be a skill she can use later in life. I don't know about that, but I don't think it will hurt anything."

"Okay, I wanted to be sure you're aware of it."

"Petey's father and I appreciate it. I will talk to her about disrupting your class with her snorting."

"I'd appreciate it."

When I pulled into the driveway, Arch rushed out of the house. He dragged Petey behind him. They climbed into the car with me.

"Hurry. We've got to get Petey to the emergency room." He pushed her hair out of her eyes. "You doing okay, sweetheart?" he asked.

She nodded.

"What happened?" My heart pounded loudly.

"She wanted to smell my feet, and I wouldn't let her, so she stuck her nose in my fur-lined moccasin and took a big sniff." Arch sounded near hysteria.

My poor husband was losing it. "When has shoe smelling constituted a trip to the ER?"

"When a large hunk of fur lint goes up your nose and out of sight."

"Oh, my God." Now I was hysterical. I rubbed Petey's back. "Hang on, honey. We're almost there. They'll help you."

A few minutes later, Arch carried Petey through the hospital doors. I hurried to the desk and gave them all the information they needed. Shortly after she was placed on a bed and the nurse pulled the curtain shut. Dr. Johns' voice zinged its way to my throbbing heart.

"What's Bertie done now?"

Dr. Johns removed the fur from Petey's nose, and she seemed to come out of her ordeal with little to no mental anguish. Her father and I weren't so lucky. The incident scared the bejeezus out of us.

We spent the whole ride home explaining to her why she wasn't allowed to smell anything ever again. As a matter of fact, even smelling the roses along life's path was banned until she was eighteen years old.

After I helped Petey finish her homework and put her to bed, I found Arch sitting on the steps of the front porch. I sat beside him and slipped my arm through his. The stars twinkled in the dark sky and I felt truly happy. I hoped Arch felt the same.

"A penny for your thoughts," I whispered in his ear.

"I was reflecting on the day I've had." He sighed heavily.

"It wasn't all that bad. Petey's a child and will do things like that. Dr. Johns said there was no permanent damage. She's fine." I nudged him in a joking gesture.

"I know. It's just that it isn't every day my daughter sucks fur lint up her nose because she's in training for a smelling bee, or I get the strange news from a co-worker who recently returned from the bank that my wife was pole dancing in the lobby of our fair town's bank."

I was horrified. I buried my face against his arm. What could I say? It was all true and I had no words to ease the humiliation Arch must feel.

"I'm so sorry. It's all my fault. I'll stop Petey from going to Mavis' after school. And the dancing was a spur of the moment thing that won't happen again."

Suddenly his whole body shook. He was laughing uncontrollably.

"Please don't stop doing those kinds of things. They are what make me love you the most."

Chapter 13

When my brothers and I were mere children at our father's knee, we all shared his enthusiasm for animals. Our family vacations always included at least one trip to a zoo. We loved watching shows on television which told how the different species met, fell in love, mated, and had babies. Of course, that was how I thought of the process. My brothers just wanted to get to the mating part.

For some reason the ritual of flamingos fascinated me the most. The male strutted around with his chest puffed, wings spread out, head sticking up high. During mating, the male tucked his legs under the female's wings. Afterward, the male stood on the female's back and then jumped over her head.

Years later I was reminded of those pretty-in-pink males when I first met my ex-boyfriend Lee Dew. He waltzed into our local tavern in an outdated pink disco suit. I was blinded by the glint of the yards of fake gold chains wrapped around his neck and huge glass-laden rings on almost every finger. I hadn't thought about that in a long time, but as I always did when I thought of Lee, I said a silent prayer of thanks I hadn't ended up with him as a life mate. I had done so much better.

One morning when I arrived at the garage, the sun shone brightly from a clear blue sky. In a couple of days, I would have a sonogram and learn if I was delivering a girl or a boy.

When I got inside the office, Linc was already working on a vehicle in one of the bays. Carrie Sue showed up a few minutes later. As she came through the door, my memory of the flamingos vividly reappeared.

The female part of my drivers' team wore flamboyant pink coveralls. She'd pulled her shoulder-length, now pink hair back from her face with a feathered pink scarf. Her tennis shoes had been dyed . . . pink.

"Are you trying out for the re-make of the movie *Pretty In Pink?*" I almost had to shade my eyes merely to look at her.

"Naw, I'm trying to get Linc to kick our relationship up a notch. All he does is hold my hand. I want more. You understand?" Carrie Sue pulled lipstick from her pocket and applied another coat over her already bright lips.

"So you think if you glow in the dark, Linc will be better able to find you?"

"Very funny." She stuck out her tongue and crinkled her nose.

Linc chose that moment to enter the room. He appeared to stop breathing. When he regained his composure, he circled her. "Carrie Sue. You look beautiful."

He looked her up and down, all the while straightening his posture and thrusting out his chest. I tried to look away from what resembled the flamingo mating ritual, but it was like watching a train wreck. Besides, I certainly didn't want to miss it if Linc ran up Carrie Sue's back and jumped over her head.

Thankfully, the phone rang.

"Bertie's Garage and Towing." I turned my back on Linc and Pinkie.

"I'd like to talk to Lincoln," a deep voice demanded.

"Just a moment." I turned around to find my two drivers in a lip lock that would rival Scarlett and Rhett. Linc had Carrie Sue leaning backward, and she had her pink-covered leg wrapped around his. I hated to interrupt, but there was only so much my empty stomach could take so early in the morning.

I cleared my throat. No response. "Excuse me," I said with a little edge in my voice.

Slowly they melted apart and looked at me. I held out the phone to Linc. "A man wants to talk to you."

I think he looked puzzled. With Linc, it's hard to tell.

"Hello?" Linc said. He put his hand over the mouthpiece of the phone. "It's not a man. It's Judy."

Carrie Sue took a step forward. I stopped her. "Let him handle this, Cotton Candy."

I pulled her by her sleeve to the door. "Hook up to that black car over there and take it to Mrs. Everett. She won't be home, so back it into her carport."

Carrie Sue took one more glance in Linc's direction and stormed away.

I thought about leaving him alone so he could talk in privacy, but couldn't force myself to do it. I grabbed the checkbook and a handful of mail. Standing at the counter, I could pay bills and listen, too.

"I've told you over and over again. I never asked you to marry me. You are the one that did the asking. I never said yes, you just insisted it was the best thing for us to do. I don't now, and never have, loved you. I'm sorry to be so blunt, but it seems to be the only way you'll hear what I'm saying."

He paused. Apparently, Judy was giving him an earful, because, out of the corner of my eye, I saw him move the phone a short distance from his ear.

"What do you mean 'who is she?' Who is who?"

Another pause.

"Will that make you accept the fact there is no you and me?"

Pause.

"Okay, her name is Carrie Sue MacMillan, and I'm going to do everything I can to make her my girl. And by the way, you can remove my home phone number from your speed dial because I've changed it to an unlisted number. And don't call here again. This is a place of business, and we aren't allowed to get personal calls."

He hung up.

"Do you think it was wise to tell the Redneck Mafia daughter your girlfriend's full name?"

"I didn't think of that. I was just so mad." Linc went out into the garage and back to work.

As soon as Carrie Sue got back, I'd be sure to warn her to against taking late night calls to the cemetery, and to be suspicious of shoe strings.

"Randy Carson gave me the best idea today," Petey announced. We had finished dinner, and I was pigging out on caramel fudge ice cream Arch picked up on his way home from work. Just another reason why I loved him.

"Oh, yeah?" her dad said.

"Yes, sir. He said to make me feel more like a big sister I should get to pick the baby's name." Petey had a smile that could melt an iceberg.

Arch and I exchanged glances. I nodded.

"Okay, you can name the baby. There is only one condition." Her father held up a thoughtful finger. "You must name it after a smart person. So give that some thought and see what you can come up."

"Like who?" Petey looked puzzled.

"Well, I think Benjamin Franklin was one of the smartest people who ever lived." Arch took a sip of his iced tea. "So, we could possibly name the baby Benjamin Frank and call him Bennie or Ben for short. You see?"

"I think so."

I took a stab at it. "The smartest person I've ever known was my fourth grade teacher, Beth Anne Britton. Beth Anne is a pretty name. Don't you think?"

Petey nodded. "Yes, ma'am. Now I get it. That will take some thought. I want to make sure it's a really good name, because, if my sister doesn't like her name, she'll hate me."

"We don't know if you're going to have a brother or a sister. Keep that in mind when you're deciding."

"I will. May I go now? I want to call Randy and tell him he had a wonderful idea." She carried her plate to the sink and then went to the living room to the phone.

"I'm not sure it's such a good idea for Petey to have so much contact with Randy Carson." I gathered the rest of the plates from the table while Arch finished his tea.

"She's only ten. She's too young to think of boys in any capacity other than a friend."

"First of all, she's going to be eleven next week. Second, aren't you a teacher? Aren't you exposed to young people every day?"

"They are all teenagers. It's only natural they have raging hormones, but my little girl is just that, my little girl."

Poor Arch. How could he be so knowledgeable about anything and everything pertaining to science, and have no clue about the mindset of pre-teens? Maybe it had something to do with putting everything into categories. Flora equals plants life. Fauna, animal life. Pre-teens, no sex life. Teens, sex life.

I tried to think of a way to explain it to him without scarring my dear husband for life. With the quietness that had befallen our tiny kitchen, it was easier to hear Petey giggling into the phone in the next room.

"I'll see you tomorrow," she said a little louder than a whisper. "I love you, too, Randy. Night."

The problem of trying to explain it all to Arch was taken out of my hands. As he choked on his sweet tea, I knew he understood the bitter truth.

216

A little later that night, Petey bathed and put on her pajamas. Arch and I were watching television.

"Oh, no." I jumped to me feet. "I forgot to pick up a blank video tape. The nurse said if we brought one to the sonogram tomorrow, they'd tape it for us."

"I'll go get one," Arch said.

"No, I need a couple of other things from the pharmacy. I'll go."

"Let's all go." He stood and pulled his keys from his pocket.

"I can't go," Petey said. "I'm in my jammies, and I have to finish this homework." She pointed to her book and paper spread on the table. "You go on. I can stay by myself."

"I don't think that's a good idea," her father contended.

"I'm almost eleven, Father dear. You're only going ten minutes away. I'll be fine." Petey had a point.

"Okay," I said. "Call Barbie if you get scared."

"Oh, Mother, I won't get scared."

Arch and I drove the few miles to Fox's Pharmacy. Brody Fox started the establishment back in the forties, and his son took it over in the late seventies. It still had a soda fountain where handmade milkshakes were served daily. If forced to admit it, Fox's chocolate shakes were responsible for those pesky ten pounds I carried around all through my teen years.

When we arrived, the parking lot was empty except for one car on the side of the building. I glanced at the dash clock. Five after nine. Did they close at nine? They used to close at ten. The front lights were off, but the inside lights were still on.

Arch pulled close to the entrance.

"I'll go check it out." I opened my door.

"Do you want me to go in with you?"

"No, I'll just be a few minutes." I got out. Arch listened to audio books every chance he got. Sitting in the car, waiting for me to shop would be an audio opportunity for him.

He waited to see if Fox's was still opened. There were two doors. One marked *enter* and one marked *exit.* I pushed on the *in* door, and it opened easily. Arch waved and then drove a short distance to a parking slot. Once inside, I couldn't believe how quiet it was. Mr. Fox usually stayed behind the counter at the back of the store, but surely there should be a few customers, maybe someone stocking shelves, or a clerk.

"Yoohoo," I called out. No one answered. "Oh, well." I hurried to the camera aisle to get the video tape. When I picked it up, an alarm went off. A strobe light flashed and a siren screamed. I ran to the front door. I'm not sure if my feet touched the floor.

With the alarm blaring, I put my hands over my ears and shoved my body against the exit door. The only thing I succeeded in doing was knocking the wind out of myself. The next time I tried using my hands to push with all my might.

The %&$* door was locked. The *enter* door had no handle on the inside to pull on.

I'm slow, but sure. It finally dawned on me whoever closed up neglected to secure the entrance door. The police would arrive any minute, and I would be arrested for burglary. With the enthusiasm of an unfaithful husband trying to escape out the back door of his mistress' home, while his wife pounded loudly on the front door, and with almost as much guilt, I tried everything I could to get a grasp on the unlocked door and pull it toward me. No luck.

I could see Arch in the car, his head back, and his eyes closed. He was either really into his audio book, or he was sleeping. Either way, I couldn't get his attention. I yelled. I waved my arms wildly, but he never saw me.

With blue lights flashing, Carl Kelly pulled to a stop in front of the pharmacy. He exited his car and immediately pulled his gun. Racing for cover against the brick wall to the right of the entrance, firearm point skyward, he took a quick peek around the corner. As he stepped into my line of sight, he pointed his gun at me.

I looked down the barrel of a police service pistol. Not that I hadn't done it before, but this time I was in a precarious position. I was inside a closed establishment and in possession of merchandise. I threw the video tape to the ground and raised both hands.

Just as Carl opened the door for me, Mr. Fox arrived. Near the front door, he disabled the alarm. Even though it was off, my ears still vibrated, and I couldn't hear very well. I explained what happened. Mr. Fox grumbled something about the irresponsible boy that worked for him, but then corrected himself and said *used to* work for him. I felt bad someone would be out of work in the morning.

I picked up the tape I threw onto the floor and handed it to Mr. Fox. "This is what I came to buy. Tomorrow, I'm having a sonogram, and I wanted to tape it to show to the baby when he or she gets older."

He handed it back to me. "Take it. It's the least I can do for what you've been through. Another person might have taken advantage of the situation and hauled off a lot of stuff out of here."

If they could figure out how to get the door open.

"Are you sure?" I asked.

"Consider it a gift for your baby." Mr. Fox closed my hands around the tape.

"Thank you."

While he reset the alarm and locked the door, Carl and I waited outside. Arch still had his head back. Definitely sleeping. Carl and Mr. Fox got in their cars and by the time I got to mine, they were gone from the parking lot. I opened the door, and Arch came to attention.

"That was quick. I see you got it okay." He started the car.

"Oh, yeah, no problem." Deciding to leave him oblivious, we drove home in complete silence.

Around four in the afternoon, I arrived at hospital where my sonogram would be done. Arch waited there for me. With the anticipation of finding out if we were having a boy or a girl, I'd been giddy all day. Even Linc and Carrie Sue smooching and pawing each other *ad nauseam* hadn't dampened my spirits. But by the time the nurse called my name, my nerves were dancing all through my body. I was shaking, and I had tears in my eyes.

You would think I was delivering in the next few minutes instead of simply having a thing resembling a telephone receiver rolled over my very large tummy. By the time I climbed onto the table, I was blubbering so hard Arch had to put his arms around me. That was like an open invitation to break into uncontrollable sobs.

"Oh, my goodness," a man's voice sounded from the door. "What have you done now, Bertie?"

Through blurred vision, I looked at Dr. Johns. "Do I always have to have done something? Can't these be happy tears?" I swiped away my liquid happiness.

He rubbed my back. "Well, of course they can. It's just that with you . . . well, you know what I mean."

Unfortunately, he didn't speak with a forked tongue. I did have more than my share of mishaps and had to seek professional help for various injuries. Luckily, Dr. Johns had only known me for about fifteen years. Since my brothers left home, my accident rate decreased considerably.

"Are you going to do the sonogram?" Arch asked.

"No, I finished a delivery and saw Bertie's chart outside. Then I heard the waterworks going and thought I'd better check it out."

"Are you ready to get started?" The nurse came back into the room.

"We are." Arch eased me back onto the table and handed me a tissue.

"I've got to get back to the office. Hope your sonogram grants you your wish for either a boy or a girl." Dr. Johns smiled and left.

"He always says that as if there's a third choice, like a puppy maybe." The nurse laughed out loud.

"I only want it to be healthy. And preferably a boy or a girl. Although my daughter would be happy with a puppy."

Jeeze, my nerves really were shot to pieces. Arch took my hand and squeezed it gently.

The nurse raised my blouse and shoved my slacks and underwear down below my tummy. She squirted warm gel onto my skin and held up a piece of equipment.

"It looks like a microphone," I said.

The nurse rubbed the mic over my stomach. "In case the baby is singing, that way we can hear it." She smiled down at me.

I cast a surprised glance at Arch, who immediately shook his head to reassure me she was joking. I emitted a nervous giggle.

"Relax." The woman did her job and magically our baby appeared on the monitor. She pointed out things like its head and feet. I plainly saw its spine and hands. My little darling appeared to be thumbing his or her nose. How sweet. That would come from my side of the family.

"Can you tell its sex yet?" My tears were flowing again.

"Come on, little one. Cooperate. Turn around so we can see." She pushed harder on my lower stomach. "No, I'm not getting a clear shot to determine the sex positively."

Water sloshed in my tummy. The baby kicked hard.

"That was quick, but I think I caught a glimpse of something there. " The nurse tried one more time. "Yeah, I can't say for absolute sure, but it looks like a boy."

"A boy." Arch planted a kiss on my forehead. "That's wonderful."

"It is, isn't it?" I really didn't have a preference. I simply wanted it to be healthy. I heard my sisters-in-law say that so many times, and I thought it was something they just said. But now I knew it was true. My heart was ready for a son *or* a daughter. Of course, Petey wasn't going to be happy. She requested a sister and not a "stinkin' brother."

Arch and I picked Petey up from Millie's. On the ride home, we broke the news she was going to have a brother.

"I guess that'll be okay. Aunt Mavis said if it's a boy, he'll be younger than me, and I can train him like I want him."

I turned in my seat to face her as much as I could. "He's a baby, Petey, not a puppy."

She giggled out loud. "That's what I told Aunt Mavis, and she said someday I'd understand there wasn't much difference. They both grow up to be old dogs."

Jeeze. I didn't want my daughter growing up thinking all men where . . . dogs.

"Aunt Mavis is judging men by your Uncle Wyatt. Yes, he wasn't very nice to her, but it doesn't mean all men are like that." I wasn't sure I cleared it up for her. I looked to her dad hoping he could add something.

"Of all the men you know," Arch prompted, "besides Uncle Wyatt, can you think of any you would refer to as a dog?"

Petey sat quietly for a few minutes. "Only one," she admitted.

Curious, I asked, "Who would that be?"

"The janitor at school."

Her dad and I choked in unison. I couldn't imagine why she thought of Mr. Sharp, who had been the school custodian since I was student, as a dog.

"Why is that?" Arch asked.

Before she answered, my think-light-bulb went on. I knew the answer.

Together Petey and I said, "His name is Mutt. Mutt Sharp."

I collapsed into the kind of hysterical laughter that robs your breath, makes you cry, and, unfortunately, makes you wet your pants. We pulled into the driveway, and I raced into the house.

When I came out of the bathroom and joined Arch and Petey in the living room, she announced she finally came up with a name for the baby.

"Great." While her father and I sat on the couch, I urged her to take a seat on the coffee table so she faced us. "What is it?"

"Lois Jamie," she announced with so much pride I hesitated a few moments before I spoke.

"That's a girl's name, Petey. I'm having a little boy, and he needs a boy's name."

"But you said I could name the baby whatever I wanted, and I should name it after the smartest person I know. That would be Lois Jamie."

"Who is Lois Jamie?" her dad asked.

"She's a girl in my class, and she makes straight A's."

"Well, you see. She's a girl. We need a boy's name."

"I put a lot of thought into it, and it took me a long time, but that's the name I want. Lois Jamie."

Oh, no. She had tears in her eyes. We'd hurt her feelings. Probably not as much as it would hurt our son's feelings to be named Lois Jamie, but we promised Petey something, and now we were backing out.

It occurred to me this didn't have to be decided right now. We had several months before our son arrived, and maybe during that time Arch and I could diplomatically convince her to pick another name.

"Okay, sweetie. For now, it's Lois Jamie." As I gave Petey a hug, I felt Arch's gaze boring through me.

She went to her room to start her homework.

"Are you crazy?" Arch rose to his feet and towered over me.

I gave him my hand, and he helped me up. "If you don't know the answer to that question by now, I'm certainly not going to tell you."

"How wise is it to let her think we are going to give our son a girl's name?"

"We have a while before that happens. I think I can persuade her to pick another name. In the meantime, we haven't hurt her feelings or disappointed her."

He turned to walk away, and I swatted him on his backside. "Now don't be such a . . ." What was the word I was looking for?

"Dog?" Arch turned to face me.

"Well, maybe." I planted a kiss on his lips.

He barked.

The next day Arch and Petey weren't home when I arrived. It felt like a grilled cheese and soup night because I certainly wasn't up to cooking. Through my kitchen window, I saw my neighbor Barbie walking the perimeter of her yard.

She had the prettiest landscaping on the whole block. Most of it she took care of herself. As she strolled along, she deadheaded flowers, broke off twigs, and picked up a few leaves here and there. She appeared to be very distracted.

I decided to go see what was wrong and if I could help. Lost in thought, she didn't see me coming.

"Hi, Barbie," I said.

When she looked at me, she was crying.

"What's wrong, honey?" I put my arm around her and led her back to her house.

"Rick is divorcing me," she sobbed.

I couldn't believe my ears. Rick worshipped Barbie. I had no doubt of that.

"What brought this on? Are you sure? Why? When did he tell you?" I didn't know what to ask first. Evidently, she didn't know what to answer. She cried harder, and I started to cry with her. It was sad watching someone with delicate emotions struggle with heartache.

We sat at her kitchen table. While I floundered for what to do or say, I looked around her house. The place was immaculate. Not a thing out of place and as perfect as her well-manicured lawn. I'd only been in her home a couple of times. Usually we met in the huge oak tree on the property line between our houses. But now I thought about it, her house was always clean and tidy.

I looked at Barbie. Except for her red-rimmed eyes, she was beautiful. Every hair in place and arranged in a becoming style. Her normally trim body was just starting to show her pregnancy. I knew for sure the baby was conceived in love. Well, I wasn't actually there at the time, but I was around them enough to see how much in love they were. Rick couldn't ask for a better wife.

"Shouldn't he be home by now?" I asked.

"He called a little while ago. He isn't coming home." Barbie cupped her face in her hands.

"Listen, this has to be some kind of mistake. I'll make some tea and you tell me what happened." I sat the kettle on the stove and pulled cups from the cabinet.

"Before he left for work this morning, my mother called and said she'd like to come for a visit."

I handed her a paper towel, and she wiped her face. I lived next door to Barbie for almost two years, and her mother never visited. She and her daughter had a strange relationship. Barbie was born into money, and her mother demanded every move her daughter made was socially acceptable. Rick was not part of that package.

In a stroke of brilliance, Barbie faked being a little off balance to the point of embarrassing her mother. Suddenly, Rick became a real deal for Barbie because he would move her away from her mother's country club scene and take care of her for the rest of her life. Sounded like a real peach of a mom, didn't she? She made me think of nominating mine for Mother of the Year.

"All right, so how does that warrant a divorce?" I asked.

"I'm not sure. I said I didn't want her to come, and he argued that, like it or not, she was our baby's grandmother, and we had to let her be a part of our lives."

I set a cup of tea in front of Barbie.

"I agree with Rick. Despite the way she treated you, she is your mother. Surely, you learned some good things from her. You're going to be a great mother, and you'll be able to emphasize her good traits and deflect the bad ones."

"That's what Rick said."

"Well, then, where did this idea about a divorce come in?"

"Before he left, he said that next to Bertie, I was the nuttiest woman he knew."

Ouch. I want my tombstone to read, *I was just trying to help, when bam! I was blind-sided.*

"Although that may be a reason for me to slug Rick, I still don't understand why you think he wants a divorce. He loves you, and he's really excited about the baby. He told Arch that the other night when they were both taking the trash to the curb."

"He called from his cell phone a little while ago and said he was going to city hall to get a divorce after he ate and have it recorded. He said we're broken and can't be fixed."

That sounded pretty definite. "Did you ask why?"

"He didn't give me a chance. He hung up."

"Have you tried to call him back?"

"Yes, but it went to his voice mail."

I looked at the clock. Six forty-five. Rick always arrived home promptly at five-thirty. Since I didn't understand any of it, I couldn't console her. I hugged her and let her cry on my shoulder. Surely she would run out of tears soon.

Car lights slashed across the kitchen window. "I'll bet that's Rick now." I handed her another paper towel. "Here. Wipe your face."

Rick came into the kitchen through the door leading from the garage. Shock registered on his face.

"What's wrong?" He hurried to Barbie and knelt to face her. "Something wrong with the baby?"

He had a lot of nerve causing so much heartache and then acting like he didn't have a clue why his wonderfully sweet wife was crying. Plus, there was the being nuttier than Bertie comment he made. I balled up my fist and slugged him on his upper arm. He grabbed it and winced. I said a silent thanks to my brothers who taught me how to inflict pain.

"What'd you do that for?" Rick whined.

"How could you call your dear wife just hours ago and tell her you want a divorce, and now act so innocent?"

His mouth flew open. "Divorce?" He looked back at Barbie. "I never said anything about a divorce."

Barbie stood and shook her finger in Rick's face. "You said you were going to city hall to get a divorce after you ate and have it recorded. You said we were broken and couldn't be fixed. And you can't deny it."

Rick, still in a kneeling position, rocked backward and rolled onto the floor. At first, I thought he was having a spell, but soon realized he was laughing so hard he was snorting.

While Barbie stared at him, I toed him in the backside. "What's so funny?"

He got up from the floor and pulled Barbie into his embrace. "You are so cute when you are nutty. I love you."

"Apparently, you think I'm nutty, too, but I'll ignore that for the moment. Why did you tell her you were going to get a divorce?"

"I said I'm going by the Circuit City Mall to return my voice-activated recorder. It's broken and can't be fixed. I was in a bad area, and I guess the phone was cutting in and out. Then the battery died completely."

Relief visibly flooded through my dear friend. I was happy, too.

"Oh, Rick, I should have known better than to jump to conclusions. I'm so sorry."

Rick looked at me. "Aren't you going to apologize for hitting me?" he asked.

"Did you say I was nuttier than Barbie?"

He chewed on his bottom lip. "I guess I did."

"Consider the hit payment for that." I walked out into the dark night and headed across the yard to the safe haven of my home where I intended to give my husband lessons on speaking clearly and concisely into his cellular phone.

Chapter 14

Linc evidently kicked up his and Carrie Sue's relationship. The two were definitely in love. Just watching them smile at each other melted my heart and added to the giddiness I felt since I met and married my soulmate. I truly believed my two drivers had found theirs, too.

On the way back from the bank, I stopped by the diner and picked up lunch for the three of us. Linc and Carrie Sue set theirs up on the table in the waiting area, and I took mine to the counter where I usually ate.

We were engrossed in our burgers, fries, and cherry pies when a tall, thin woman entered the office. With Linc's back to the door, he and Carrie Sue were oblivious to anyone even being in the room with them. While I waited for the woman to approach the counter, Linc stuck a ketchup covered French fry into Carrie Sue's mouth. She was in the process of returning the favor.

"What is going on here?" The woman bellowed so loud she startled my baby, who kicked me in return.

Linc jumped to his feet, sending his chair over backward, and spun around. The French fry Carrie Sue had aimed for his mouth stuck out of his nose.

"Lincoln Johnson." The woman sprinted in his direction. "I figured something like this was going on. That's why you won't return my calls. Isn't it?"

Dumbstruck and white as a northern tourist's legs on his first day on a Florida beach, Linc turned to face her. She didn't need to be introduced. She could only be the Redneck Mafia boss' daughter, Judy Craig. Or, as Linc called her, Broomhilda.

She reached toward his face, and he ducked away, but not before Judy removed the French fry from his nose. After she tossed it onto the table, she glared at Carrie Sue.

"So, you're the hussy Lincoln's been sniffing around. I knew you'd be short and skinny since that's the type Casanova over there," Judy nodded at Linc, "always gets his shorts in a knot over."

Carrie Sue rose and looked up at the six-foot-plus hulk of a woman.

"I don't know who you think you're talking to, but next to you, any woman would be short and skinny. And don't even get me started on your nose."

"You have a lot of nerve talking about my nose. One more word out of you, you man-stealer, and I'll rub you back and forth between my hands and make that pink fluff on top of your head stand up like a troll's."

"That's enough, Judy." Linc took her arm and turned her to face him. "Carrie Sue is my steady girl now, and I want you to leave here and never come back. I never told you I loved you, and you know it. It isn't fair for you to fool others and yourself into believing we ever had anything going. We didn't, and you and I both know that."

Judy clenched her teeth, making her jawline harden like a man's. She started to speak, but Linc stopped her.

"Where'd you park your broom? I mean your motorcycle?"

She clenched her fists at her side. "It's around the side of the building, but I'm not going anywhere without you."

Carrie Sue got between Linc and Judy. An uglier scene was about to erupt, and I had to put a stop to it before blood started to fly. I almost made it around the counter when I halted. What was I thinking? I was big with child, and before Carrie Sue had married her now ex-husband, she had been one of the famous Barrow sisters. Any one of those three could take down a pit bull and have it whimper all the way home.

Before that thought finished forming, Carrie Sue had Judy backed against the wall and was glaring up at her.

"No wonder Linc refers to you as Broomhilda. You are a witch, but you don't scare me none. Linc is my man, and I don't intend to step aside for the likes of you. You're nothing more than an overgrown bully. Now, I suggest you get on your hog and haul it all the way back to Atlanta and never darken this section of Georgia again."

Somehow Judy managed to pull away from the wall and move into the center of the room. The two women stood about two feet a part and hurled insult after insult back and forth. I moved behind Judy and was in the process of trying to figure a way to ease her out the door.

Suddenly, I felt a sharp pain against the side of my head. I remember seeing the prettiest display of bright exploding lights right before it all went dark.

233

"What has Bertie done now?"

I awoke to the all-too-familiar catch phrase of Dr. Johns. If my mouth had worked correctly, I would have chastised him for always assuming the worst of me. Since my brain appeared to be scrambled, however, I couldn't assume I hadn't done something stupid.

Instinctively, my hands went to my stomach. It was still there, and the baby was kicking gently. "Is the baby okay?" I managed to ask.

"The baby's fine. I wish I could say the same for your eye." Dr. Johns looked into one ear, then the other. He pressed on my cheekbone, and I winced. "You're going to have a real shiner."

"What happened?"

For the first time, I noticed Carrie Sue sitting in a chair in the small, curtained cubical. She placed her hand on my arm.

"You were standing behind Judy Craig when she aimed a roundhouse at me. You took the hit instead."

I touched the side of my face. "Are we perfectly sure she's really a woman? She has a lot of manly features, including a punch that could rival Mohammad Ali." I worked my jaw and found it to be very sore.

"Well, Chief Kramer carted her off to the jail. I'm sure they'll find out if she isn't." Carrie Sue and Dr. Johns laughed.

I tried, too, but it hurt too much.

"Where to from here, doctor?" I asked.

"I don't think there's any reason to keep you overnight. You have a hard head, and it doesn't appear to have suffered more than the black eye. Go home, put your feet up." He slid the curtain aside. "See if you can stay out of trouble until after the baby gets here. Okay?"

"I don't look for it. It just finds me." I tried to defend myself.

"Yeah. Yeah. Whatever." He disappeared behind the curtain.

"Chief Kramer asked me to bring you to the station so you could press charges against that . . . Paula Bunyon." Carrie Sue helped me climb down from the examining table.

"Has anyone called Arch?"

"Your mom tried, but he's on a field trip."

"Oh, that's right. They went to the catfish farm in Shafer." Carrie Sue helped me through the door and into the parking lot.

"What are you driving?" I asked.

"I brought your car. I didn't think you needed to try to climb up into a tow truck."

"Actually, I feel like I've been hit by one." I spotted my car across the lot.

"Can you walk, or do you want me to go get it?"

"I'll walk. I need to clear my head a little."

She slipped her arm through mine to help steady me. "Thanks for taking that punch for me," she said.

I leaned on her slightly. "Believe me, it wasn't a conscious thought. I just happened to get in the way of her long arms."

"They were really long, weren't they?" Carrie Sue helped me into the car.

I waited until she slid into the driver's seat. "I think they hung to her knees."

We laughed all the way to the police station. I knew Judy didn't

235

have excessively long arms, but it made me and Carrie Sue feel better to laugh. I touched my swollen eye. Long or not, those arms were powerful weapons.

Inside the police station, we found Judy locked up in a small cell, the only one Sweet Meadow had. It sat in the corner of a big open room with a long counter that divided the public from the officers, all three of them. A woman doubled as the receptionist and dispatcher.

Chief Kramer saw me enter and motioned for me to come to his desk in the rear of the room. Carrie Sue went with me.

"You took a hard hit there, kiddo." The chief motioned for us to sit down across from him. "Are you going to be okay?"

"I hope so." I glanced over at Judy, who sat on the edge of a cot watching me. "What's going to happen to her?"

"That depends on you. I can charge her with assault. Since there were witnesses, she'd probably plead guilty and be given a few days confinement, plus pay a fine." He pulled a paper from a cubby hole beside his desk. "Do you want to press charges?"

I was about to say *yes*, when a thought came to me. "I'd like to talk to her first, if that's allowed."

Chief Kramer rose and led me to the cell. "Miss Craig, the lady you cold conked would like to speak with you."

Judy walked to the bars, her arms hanging at her sides. It was all I could do to keep from laughing. They did hang to her knees.

Before I spoke, she did. "I'm sorry I hit you. I would never hit a mother-to-be. I was aiming for pinky over there." I didn't have to follow her finger to know she was pointing at Carrie Sue who grunted behind me.

"Well, I'm afraid you're going to have to face the fact that Pinky and Linc are in the present, and you and he are a thing of the past. If there ever was a *you and he*. Now, I'll tell you what. I'm willing to not press charges against you for assault, if you go back to Atlanta and leave Linc and Carrie Sue alone. If you don't agree to it, I'm filling out the papers right now."

She thought about it for a moment. "Okay, I agree to leave them alone."

Chief Kramer unlocked the door and set her free. Carrie Sue and I thanked him, and we walked out into the later afternoon sunshine. We just reached the car when someone called my name.

"Mrs. Fortney."

I turned to find Judy waving and running toward me.

"Yes?"

"My motorcycle is back at your shop. How about giving me a ride?"

"You have a lot of nerve," I said, and motioned for her to get into the back seat. I took the keys from Carrie Sue. "I'll feel safer driving myself with you two in the car. Get in."

The ride back to the garage was quiet except for the buzzing in my ears. I wondered how long that would be with me. Once there, we all got out of the car. Judy straddled her hog, revved up the engine, and yelled to me. "I'll leave them alone, but I can't guarantee my father will." With that she sped away, sending gravel into the air and raining onto Carrie Sue and me.

"You're welcome," I screamed at the top of my lungs.

She saluted me with one finger and disappeared down the road. I had the headache from Hades and although it wasn't quite quitting time, I went home where Arch was probably going to make me stay until I safely gave birth to his son.

Arch was understandably concerned with the damage Judy had done to my face. The fact I had not pressed charges against the "Neanderthal" went way over his head.

"It was a perfect opportunity to gain Linc his freedom with as little bloodshed as possible," I explained.

My husband pointed to the blood stains decorating the front of my shirt. "What do you call that? Ketchup?"

"I said *as little bloodshed as possible.*"

"You and the baby could have been seriously hurt." He had a point.

"Okay, I'll admit I probably should have had her butt thrown in jail, and if she comes back to town, I'll do just that." I put my arms around Arch and kissed him on the lips.

Gently, he backed out of my hug and traced the side of my face.

"The bruise is spreading. Does it hurt much?"

"Only when I laugh."

"Come on." Arch led me to the kitchen. "I brought Chinese home for dinner. We're going to have a celebration. "Petey, Mom's home."

Before I could ask if we were celebrating my injury, she raced from her room. "Did you tell—" My darling daughter hurried to me. "What happened to you?"

She pushed a strand of hair away from my face and examined my black eye very closely.

"Linc's old girlfriend took a swing at Carrie Sue, and my face jumped in line with her punch. Ain't it a beauty?" I asked.

Petey whistled. "It sure is. I can't wait to tell Randy you got a shiner while saving his Aunt Carrie Sue's life."

"Well, it wasn't that impressive, my little Drama Queen. I just happened to be in the wrong place at the right time."

"He doesn't need to know that. A little embellishment never hurt anyone."

Arch and I looked at each other. Quickly, we summed up our daughter's attitude.

"Millie and Mavis," we said in unison.

"You know lying is wrong, don't you sweetheart?" I asked.

"Sure. Aunt Mavis and Mrs. Keats explained it to me." Petey used chopsticks to lift lo mien to her mouth.

"So what, exactly, is the difference between lying and embellishing the truth?" Arch asked.

"People would rather hear embellished facts than the standard, run-of-the-mill truth. That's what Aunt Mavis said."

Fearing I would stab myself in my good eye if I tried to use chopsticks, I chose a fork to eat with. "How did you and the elderly advice-givers come to talk about this subject in the first place?"

"Uncle Wyatt called, and Mrs. Keats told him Aunt Mavis wasn't home. She also told him that Brody Fox had called Aunt Mavis, and she might be over at his place."

"Was that the truth, or had she made it up?"

"She embellished. When she looked at the caller ID and saw who was on the phone, Aunt Mavis ran out onto the front porch and stayed there until the call ended. Mr. Fox called earlier from the pharmacy to let her know her pills were ready to pick up. Mrs. Keats told me since she couldn't see Aunt Mavis out on the porch, she very well could have gone to the pharmacy to get her pills. She said it was just a little trimming on reality to make it sound more important than it really was. You know, like me saying you saved Carrie Sue's life sounds better than saying you got clobbered by a runaway fist."

I knew I should set Petey straight, but for the life of me, I couldn't think of a way to do it. Her way of saying it was definitely more pleasing to my ears. Maybe my brains had been a little scrambled while I was saving Carrie Sue's life.

Arch took over for me. "Your mother and I prefer you not embellish, trim, or decorate the truth in any way. Do you understand?"

Petey twisted her lip into a mock pout. "Sure. I'll make a note." She pretended to write on the table. "When relating a story, be sure to stick to the facts. Have no fun whatsoever." She looked up at her dad. "Got it."

Arch took his seat at the table. "Exactly."

Petey had an answer for everything. I twisted my lips, too, to keep from smiling. I knew from experience a quick wit would bring her a lot of trouble. Could she have inherited that from me even though I wasn't her biological mother? For the time being, I chose to blame it on Millie and Mavis.

"I seem to remember you said we were celebrating something, and Petey wanted to know if you'd told me something. What is it?"

Petey bounced in her seat. "Can I tell her?"

Arch nodded.

"Dad's going to be the principal of Sweet Meadow High School. Isn't that cool?"

My gaze snapped to Arch whose smile confirmed the happy news, but his eyes told a different story.

Even though I was confused, I didn't question what I saw in his gaze. "That is exceptionally cool. When and how did all this come about?"

"The superintendent asked me to stop by his office on my way home this afternoon. He said the board had met and wanted to offer me the position. I have to let him know before the next meeting."

"When is that?"

"Tomorrow night."

"That quick?"

"The answer has to be *yes*. For my dad to be the principal of the school I'll be attending in a few years would make me really popular." Petey was through eating, but stayed to join in the conversation.

"You know your dad would not give you or your friends preferential treatment." I smiled in a way I hoped said *I'm not admonishing; I'm only guiding you to be a better person.*

"Oh, I know that. Just so he treats us more special than the others. That's all any daughter could ask of her perfect father."

"If I decide to take the job, you know that would never happen." Arch raised his I-mean-what-I-say eyebrow.

"Yeah, I know, but you can't blame me for trying." Petey giggled and went to her room to do her homework.

"Why do I get the feeling you're struggling with the offer for your new position?" I sipped the last of my coffee.

"I'm not sure if I should take it. It will mean longer hours. I'll have to be there earlier and stay later. With the baby coming soon, I don't want to abandon you when you'll need me more than ever."

"I wouldn't feel abandoned. Mom is going to keep the baby. He'll be right next door where I can visit him during the day."

"Yes, but right now, Petey only stays with Millie and Mavis for thirty minutes. She would need to stay with them for at least two more hours. Are we sure we want that to happen?"

"No," I answered abruptly. "I'm sure we can work it out to have her ride the bus to the garage. She can wait at Mom's until I get off work. She can do her homework there. Or, help Mom with the baby." I rose and went behind his chair. Wrapping my arms around him, I leaned my cheek on top of his head. "This is an honor, and I think you should take it. We will all adjust."

The baby chose that moment to kick him in the back of his head. "See? Even our son agrees." I kissed Arch on his ear. "Now, take the job before I kick you a little lower."

He stood and took me in his arms. "It will mean a nice raise. Maybe we can move to a bigger house."

Sadness flowed through me and swelled my heart. I loved our little house. I couldn't picture us living anywhere else. "Would you want to move to a new house?" I asked.

"Not really, but we need another bedroom for the baby, and I thought you'd like a more modern home."

I shook my head. "This is the only home I ever want. Yes, we do need another bedroom and maybe a bathroom, but we have plenty of room for expansion. I knew we didn't have the extra funds to do that, but with your new job, now we can add on. What do you think?"

"I think it took me a long time to find the most perfect woman to be my wife and mother to my children, but you were worth the wait."

"Thank you. I love you," I managed to say before he kissed me.

My heart was light, but my head ached. It might have been brought on by trying to decide the precise way to straighten out Petey's attitude without doing irreparable harm to the poor child. Or, it could have been the excitement of Arch's great news. Then again, it might simply be a result of the major hit I'd taken earlier in the day.

Arch escorted me to the recliner, and I'd just kicked back when Mary Lou called.

"Hi, Bertie. I haven't talked to you in several days. What've you been up to?" she asked.

"Well, today I hope I explained the difference between telling and embellishing the truth to my daughter. My husband was promoted to the position of principal of Sweet Meadow High. As for me, today I saved Carrie Sue's life."

My black eye adorned my face for over a week. On Sunday morning, I dug through my closet to find something to wear to church that wouldn't clash with the putrid green and repulsive yellow coloring my cheek and brow. I decided a denim jumper, which Novalee gave me when I started showing, would do the trick.

Novalee lived down the street from my house, and she's Carrie

Sue and Donna's cousin. Novalee's a hit-and-miss parishioner, so she wasn't in church that morning. When the service ended, her mother asked if I'd take a small box of glasses to her daughter. I wanted her to see how cute I looked in her old jumper with its pink and blue baby lambs romping near the hem which hung mid-calf on me. I agreed to save Mrs. Barrow a trip just to make the delivery.

I told Arch and Petey I was going for a walk to Novalee's, and I'd be back soon. When I passed Helen Weidemeyer's home, I saw several bags and boxes of trash stacked at the curb. Evidently, she'd been spring cleaning and, by the mountain of stuff piled along the street, it was for more than one spring. That was something I'd have to do soon because Arch started drawing plans for the bedroom and bathroom addition we'd make to our house very soon.

We had a large closet at the end of the hall, too small to be a bedroom, but big enough to hold tons of boxes containing things Petey, Arch, and I packed in there following our wedding. We were hard pressed to even name what the boxes contained, but we knew we couldn't live without it.

I happily strolled along and, in my mind, I decorated the nursery for our baby who would make his entrance into the world in less than two months. I pictured wallpaper with all sorts of sport equipment, a hat rack with ball caps of various teams, and a cozy rocking chair snuggled into the corner. Deep in my own world, a commotion snapped me from my reverie.

Novalee's son Ralphie and Donna's two darlings, Pam and Jude, materialized from behind Helen's mound of trash. Pam jumped in front of me, pointing a super-sized water gun.

"Halt," she demanded. "Put you hands up."

Thinking quickly, I pulled the box of drinking glasses to my chest with one hand and used the other to make a grab for the gun, but I failed. Something held me back. I twisted as best I could in my condition and saw Jude sitting in the middle of the road, his legs stretched out on each side of my feet. The twerp held tight to the back hem of my jumper. I couldn't reach him, I couldn't de-arm Pam, and to make matters worse, Ralphie rode a tricycle around and around us like an Indian circling the wagons.

"Jude Carson, you let go of my dress right this instant."

He tugged harder, causing me to leaner further back. Pam squirted me with a blast of water. "No talking."

I glared at the hellgrammite and wiped at the water dripping from my chin. "If you do that again—"

Squirt.

"Pam, stop that. I'm going to tell your mother and, boy, will you ever get it." *Jeeze, Bertie, can you sound any more like a child?*

"Let go of my dress, you doo-doo head." *I guess that answered my question.*

Jude swung harder on my hem. "Ralphie, that's a nice trike you have there. How about riding it over to your house and telling your mom to come here really fast? Okay? Can you do that?"

"I can do that," he said, but continued to ride around us.

"Well, go, Ralphie," I prompted. "I need your mother to corral these two holy terrors."

He started toward his house. Pam swung the gun around with the precision of Annie Oakley and shot a stream of water into Ralphie's ear. Before his scream finished piercing the air, Pam whirled back and squirted me again. He halted.

"If you don't go now, Ralphie, I'm going to beat your bottom." He took off again. Somehow I managed to grab the barrel of the water blaster, but Pam held tight with two hands. Being at a disadvantage, what with my body being cumbersome, one hand full of breakables, and a small child hanging from my dress tail, I was forced to let go.

She let me have it again. The cold water startled me. She blasted me once more. Right in my mouth. I spewed the plastic-flavored water onto the ground.

"Hey, you spit on me," Jude yelled.

"If I could get a hold of you, I'd do worse than that. You're going to make me drop these glasses your grandmother sent for you aunt." I clutched the box to my chest. With all the turmoil, it was a wonder I hadn't already broken the fragile contents. If I threw it to the ground, I'd be able to use both hands to combat my captors, but I didn't have the heart to destroy what wasn't mine.

With great effort, I finally connected with Jude's hand, knocking his grasp free. I could step forward. I set the box down and lunged at Pam. A struggle ensued, but I got the water gun away from her as her butt landed on the hard asphalt.

Just then Novalee and Donna raced my way.

"What's going on here?" Donna bellowed like a wounded bull moose.

"Your little darlings—" That was as far as I got before the three kids started blubbering, almost incoherently.

"Bertie yelled at me." Ralphie pointed an accusing finger my way.

"She took my toy gun away from me and shoved me down."

Pam cried real tears.

I couldn't believe my ears. Those future criminals where making me the bad guy. I wanted to throttle them and their mothers, but all the excitement had brought on a condition which plagued me constantly since I became pregnant. I had to go to the bathroom.

I glared at Donna and Novalee. "You know that's not what happened." I pointed at Jude, who was still seated in the middle of the road. "He had a hold of my dress tail and wouldn't let me move."

We all stared down at him. He looked at us through misty blue eyes. "She hit me and spit on me."

Oh, that was all I could take. I started to stalk away when I almost tripped over the box at my feet. I bent, picked it up, and in one quick motion, with gusto, I tossed it to Novalee. "Here, your mother sent you this." I spun around so fast I didn't see what happened next, but I heard it. The box thudded to the ground, and the sound of shattering glass mixed with Novalee's yelp.

I didn't turn around, but called over my shoulder, "My bad."

Chapter 15

In a few weeks, our little home on Marblehead Drive would have a new bedroom and bathroom. Permits were obtained, the contractor paid a hearty advance, and the foundation was being formed that very day. All in time for our baby boy's arrival.

Arch and I were still faced with the problem of going back on our word that Petey could name the baby. Lois Jamie was not a good name for a boy, but for some reason Petey insisted it would be the name with which the poor child was saddled. Each time we broached the subject, she reminded us we promised. So, for the time being, we put it on the back burner.

After weeks of fretting, Barbie's big day arrived. That afternoon her mother would make a grand appearance for her first visit to her daughter's and son-in-law's home. I tried not to form a negative opinion of anyone, at least until after I met them, but I already knew I wouldn't like Barbie's mother. From the things my neighbor said, her mom had preconceived ideas of who and what her daughter should be. None of which Barbie was, or ever could be.

Her father owned a prosperous nuts and bolts manufacturing company. She could have had anything she wanted if only she conformed to the mold her mother tried to place her in. A marriage to J.R. Throckmorton III had been talked about for years. Talked about by their parents, but never by Barbie and Throcky.

Before the wedding of the century could take place, something got in the way. Barbie fell in love with Rick, the accountant. When her mother forbade her daughter to see Rick, Barbie started acting like a flawed debutante. That's the way I chose to think of her, but the truth is, she's a bubble off plumb.

Whether Barbie was acting or not, her mother couldn't marry her daughter off to Rick the accountant fast enough, especially when he made plans to move far away from Atlanta to the podunk town of Sweet Meadow. Barbie is such a treasured friend, and I felt Atlanta's loss was my gain.

On the momentous morning, Barbie asked me to ride with her to pick up her mother at Shafer Express Airport. She had never been to the airport before, but more importantly she appeared to need the moral support. Even as she gripped the steering wheel of her VW Bug, her hands shook.

"You really are a nervous Nellie, aren't you?" I massaged her shoulder. "Relax. It's only your mother. She'll come, see how happy you are, and go on her merry way back to her bridge partners and country club friends. You'll see, it won't be too bad."

Reluctantly, she nodded in agreement.

"Okay, now we're going to take a right." I pointed a short distance ahead. Barbie made a sharp turn into the very next driveway and skidded off the end of a concrete pad, miraculously coming to an abrupt stop just short of a beautiful flowerbed of petunias and marigolds surrounding a family of plastic flamingos.

When the hair standing straight up on the top of my head re-laxed a little, and I could loosen my grip on the dashboard, I looked at her. "What'cha do that for?"

"You said turn," she explained.

See, that's my point exactly. You can't be sure if her nuttiness is an act or a fact of life. Act or fact, she made life interesting.

"Okay, sweetie, back out of here before the homeowner comes out with guns a blazing," I jested.

A loud boom rang out. Before I dove for the cramped floor-boards, I saw Manny Ortega standing on his front stoop with a shotgun pointing skyward, the butt resting on his hip. I tried to scream for Barbie to get us out of there, but before the words could squeak past my heart, which was lodged in my throat, she slammed the car into reverse and stomped on the gas pedal. She laid rubber all the way out of the driveway and backed onto the highway with-out even slowing down.

Just as fast, Barbie found first gear, and we sped away. I didn't hear any horns blaring, or tires squealing, or metal crashing, so I as-sumed we had not pulled into oncoming traffic. I assure you, it was only by the grace of God.

Mario held the steering wheel tight with one hand and helped me struggle back into my seat with the other. My baby kicked the daylights out of me as if asking what was going on in the outside world. "Trust me, sweetheart," I whispered and rubbed my stom-ach. "You don't want to know."

Barbie turned right at the appropriate intersection, and we were again underway to the airport to pick up her mother. I figured after that ordeal, the rest of the experience would be anti-climatic. Oh, silly me.

We arrived in time to watch a small plane bump along the tarmac and nose its way into the terminal. Through the huge plate-glass window, we saw a tractor pull baggage carts to the belly of the plane, and a truck begin refueling. The ground crew scrambled to push the stairway to the door. It swung open and a few business-men emerged.

Then a statuesque, bleached blonde materialized in the opening of the plane.

"Mama." The word slipped past Barbie's lips on a wispy vapor of melancholy.

I stole a glance at her. Tears trembled on her lashes, and she appeared to be battling for restraint.

I took her elbow and led her toward the door where the passengers were coming into the terminal. "Come on, kiddo. It's going to be just fine. You're going to be a mommy. Your mother's going to be a grandma. That puts both of you on different playing fields."

Barbie swiped away her tears and forced a smile. Just then, her mother came into the building. Meticulously dressed in white slacks and a royal blue silk blouse, she had not one hair out of place. The perfect shade of red glistened on her perfectly-shaped lips, and when she removed her large designer sunglasses, assessing, almond-shaped eyes were revealed, perfectly made up, of course. Barbie looked a lot like her. Just not so . . . perfect.

The woman saw Barbie and motioned for her to come closer.

"Smile," I whispered to my friend.

She beamed and nearly ran to her mother. Instead of welcoming her daughter with open arms, the woman grabbed Barbie's shoulders, keeping her at a distance, and air kissed each cheek. By that time, I waddled next to them.

"Mother, this is my friend, Bertie Fortney. This is my mother, Maxine Dunn." We cordially shook hands, but the vibes that buzzed through my fingers were not happy ones. For Barbie's sake, I smiled at the woman.

We gathered Maxine's bags and made our way to the yellow Volkswagen waiting in the parking lot. Barbie opened the luggage compartment, loaded what would fit into it, and forced it shut. The rest of her mother's things were stacked in the back seat, leaving barely enough room for Her Highness. For a moment, she looked like she expected me to crawl back there, but one look at my pregnant body, and she was smart enough to know that wasn't going to happen. Silently, she gave up and climbed in.

As we pulled out of the parking lot, Maxine sniffed loudly and declared, "I smell rubber burning. Barbara, do you have your emergency brake on?"

"Barbara?" I snickered.

"No, Mother."

"We had a little mishap on the way to the airport," I said. Barbie glared at me and shook her head without even moving her head. Just her features quivered in a comedic way. I almost chuckled, but instead I proceeded to tell her mother how Barbie made a wrong turn into Manny Ortega's yard and drove onto his grass and almost ran into his flowers, which were his pride and joy. I was about to relay the details of the shotgun blast when Barbie dug her nails into my thigh in a way that told me if I continued I might die.

Finally, I got the hint and said we may have spun our tires a little when we pulled back onto the highway, and I quickly changed the subject to the fact Maxine was going to be a grandmother.

Quick as a flash, Barbie sank her talons into my flesh again. "Yow!!" I hollered.

"You're going to have a baby, Barbara?" a shocked voice came from the back seat.

Ah, nuts. "I'm sorry. I didn't know you hadn't told her." I thought she was over the fear of her mother knowing she had sex with her husband. I assumed she told her parents about the baby a long time ago. Evidently, that wasn't the case.

"I was waiting for the right time to tell you, but, yes, you're going to be a grandmother." Barbie smiled widely, but the corners of her mouth quivered.

My heart ached for her. This should be happy news she wanted to share with her mother. Now I really didn't like the harpy crammed in the back seat. I hoped her Guccis were being squashed.

Barbie pulled into my driveway to drop me off.

"Is that where you live?" a panic-stricken voice whispered behind me.

I would have spun around to glare at her, but, being in such cramped quarters, it was physically impossible.

"No, Mother, Rick and I live next door." Barbie motioned to her neat home with the beautifully manicured yard. "This is Bertie's house."

"I'm certainly glad to hear that."

What was wrong with my little piece of heaven? "My husband was raised in that house, and we find it very comfortable. We're even adding a bedroom and bathroom for when our son makes his entrance into the world."

"Very quaint," she said.

I didn't feel hospitable enough to say I was glad to meet her, so I did the next best thing. "I'm glad you're here to visit Barbie."

I'm not sure what her response was because I slammed the car door hard enough to rattle the window glass.

I didn't wait for them to back out of my driveway. I just stared at my little house Arch's father built many years before any of the others on the street. Barbie's home was less than ten years old. It was made of concrete and stucco and naturally looked more dignified than my unassuming, wood-framed home with white vinyl siding.

Arch spiffed up the flowerbeds his father planted a long time ago, and the grass managed to get cut in a timely manner. True, it didn't have that golf-course manicured facade like Barbie's, because I wasn't home all day like she was. I had to work for a living.

I'm not sure if the baby kicked me harder than usual, or if I was merely struck with a sick feeling in the pit of my stomach. Maxine's remarks disappointed me, and instead of aiming my anger at her, I took it out on my undeserving friend. Although I hadn't said it, I only thought it, I still felt the sting of the unfairness on my part. I realized right then I'd have to take a deep breath and be a little more considerate in my opinion of Barbie's mother.

After all, you should never judge anyone until you've walked a mile in their shoes, or in Maxine's case, her seven-hundred-dollar Guccis.

254

I managed to stay away from Barbie for three days. She and her mom needed to bond, and I wasn't sure I could contain myself if she made any more snide remarks about my little house which now had an addition sprouting off its backside. But my luck ran out. I'd just slipped into my granny gown and curled up in front of the television to watch Dateline.

Barbie called. "Hi, Bertie, I have a favor to ask you."

"As long as it doesn't have anything to do with your mother, you're on." I forced a giggle to relieve the harshness of my statement.

"Well, she wants to take Rick and me out for dinner tomorrow night, but he has to work, and I really need a buffer between Mother and me."

I really didn't want to go, but I could hear the desperation in my friend's voice, so I agreed.

"Where are we going? To the Bull's Tail Bar-b-que?"

"One of the ladies she plays bridge with told her about a place in Shafer. A French place where we can eat things we can't pronounce. Wear your best bib and tucker. We have to make Mother Dearest proud. We'll leave at seven."

"Yeah, seven," I mumbled. What could I possibly have in my mommy-to-be wardrobe to wear to a fancy French restaurant with a judgmental woman? I looked in the closet and found two dresses. My denim jumper with lambs playing, and a flowered shift I bought on a day when my hormones played games with my ability to make rational decisions.

I chose the bright shift because, despite its loudness, it had a lace collar. That was about as dressy as I could get. I'd simply have to be careful not to sit on any flower-covered sofas. The color explosion could possibly cause blindness.

The next evening I dressed and waited on the front stoop. When I saw Barbie and her mom come out of the house, I walked across the lawn and got into the car, determined to be nice to Maxine.

"Thanks for inviting me. I looked forward to this all day," I tried to make nice.

"Yes, so have I," she said, then belched. "I'm so sorry. Please excuse me."

I wasn't shocked at hearing a burp. Lord knows, I've heard many. I have brothers. But what shocked me was hearing it come from a high society lady, and one who was on her way to have dinner and shouldn't be full enough to burp.

I stole a sideways glance at Barbie who stared straight ahead and appeared to be fighting a smile.

As we drove along, I realized we were not going to Shafer.

"Did you change your mind about where we were going to eat?" I asked.

"Yeah," Barbie said. Again the corner of her mouth twitched.

Something strange was going on and with the way my life goes, that could be very scary. Not wanting to give her mother the impression I thought her daughter wasn't capable of getting us where we were going, I turned slightly in my seat to ask Maxine if she had enjoyed her visit, but she had her head back and her eyes closed. I decided to do the same thing.

In a few minutes, we stopped in Millie and Mavis' driveway.

There was a slew of cars parked on their street and down the block.

"Are Millie and Mavis going with us?" I asked.

"No, come on in. They have something they want to show you."

I offered Maxine my hand and pulled her from the back seat. As we walked up the steps, the lights in the house went out. I heard a lot of shushing coming from inside. It was then my own light bulb of realization clicked loudly in my head.

Before I could react, the door flew open, the lights came on, I was shoved over the portal, and loud screams of "surprise" jarred me so hard my eye teeth shook. For a moment, I was speechless. All around me were friends and family. Streamers and balloons hung everywhere. The room was filled with the aroma of fresh coffee brewing and I could almost taste the spinach dip, salami stuffed with potato salad, chicken salad sandwiches, and Millie's famous shower cake, which would be covered with shortening and powdered sugar frosting.

All the feel-good women in my life greeted me with hugs, smiling faces, and laughter. Dear Millie and Mavis. My best friend, Mary Lou. My tow truck driver, Carrie Sue, her sister, Donna, and their cousin and my neighbor, Novalee. Mom was there and, of course, Barbie and her mother.

Shortly after we arrived, Arch dropped Petey off so she could join the party. Everyone circled the food table like vultures going in for the kill. We balanced our paper plates loaded with food and small plastic cups with orange sherbet punch sloshing over the top. From my seat of honor, I saw everyone engaged in conversation and having a good time.

Everyone, that is, except Maxine. Barbie's mother sat on the edge of her seat in an over-stuffed chair, her ankles crossed demure-ly, and her hands cupped in her lap. If she sat any straighter, we could bend her over and use her for an ironing board. Worse yet, she was vittleless.

I believe there is a law in the South all shower attendees must pig out on pigs-in-a-blanket and sausage balls. And if there isn't a law, there should be.

I leaned nearer to Barbie, who sat at on my left. "Maybe you should get your mom a plate. She isn't eating."

With her mouth shielded by her hand, Barbie whispered, "She ate before she came. Earlier today, I made the mistake of telling her that when I went to your wedding shower, I ate venison sausage and mini-venison burgers."

I smiled as if Barbie relayed a humorous antidote, and tried not to look at Maxine the Ramrod. How could she hold her posture like that for so long? Surely the rigidness cut off the oxygen going to her brain.

I promised myself I'd be nice to Maxine outwardly, and inside my sometimes mean-spirited mind. So, every time I had a not-so-nice thought about her, I added *bless her heart.*

"Millie," I said gently. "Maxine doesn't have anything to eat."

"That's okay, dear, I'm on a diet," she protested.

"Nonsense." Millie was already piling a plate with a sampling of delicious goodies, none of which had any deer meat in them. The fact we had some at my wedding shower was a fluke. It was during hunting season and my dad shot a deer. It pleased him to no end to furnish some meat for my shower. So Mom cooked it, and we all ate it. Even Barbie. Although the rest of us had not given it much thought, evidently Barbie had.

Millie handed Maxine the plate. "Be sure you try the pigs-in-a-blanket, honey. The sausage is great."

I swear she looked a little green around the gills. I got the feeling although she was a snob, she wasn't rude. So she graciously smiled and took a bite of the little sausage link wrapped in canned crescent rolls. Since she was being courteous, I suggested Barbie go whisper in her mom's ear there was no deer meat in any of the food.

Barbie did just that. Maxine's frown lines softened instantly. She finished almost everything she was given, and when Barbie took her plate I heard Maxine comment that she really enjoyed the baby pizzas on rye bread.

"They're called Hanky Pankies," I told her.

"Oh." Her mouth formed a perfect *O.*

Barbie's mother was served a plastic cup full of sweet punch. I knew for a fact it had been dipped from a special bowl Millie kept separate from the regular sherbet one. The regular one was for children and pregnant women. The special one was laced with a hefty dousing of Kentucky's finest.

I started to mention it to Maxine, but decided it might help her relax. Instead, I sat back and watched her belt down three cups in succession. Shortly thereafter, her eyes twinkled and her mouth sported a smile which seemed painted on. It was about that time she decided to help herself to some more drink. I steered her to the regular punch, but after one swallow she realized the other bowl sitting on a back counter must contain the good stuff, and made a beeline to it.

"Time for games." Mavis came into the room carrying a straw

Dolores J. Wilson

basket lined with a blue baby blanket and various baby items. Everyone took a seat and quieted so Millie could explain what was going
to transpire. I should say everyone but Maxine. She hovered around
the watering hole, drinking her fill of bourbon-laced punch.

"Maxine has to play, too," I said, hoping to get her to her seat
before she fell over.

Barbie encouraged her mother to sit by her. Maxine obliged, but
brought a full cup of libation with her. She sat a little too close to the
edge, nearly missing the seat completely. Somehow she recovered
and never spilled a drop of punch. Barbie looked away and dabbed a
napkin to her mouth. No one else appeared to notice, but I could tell
she was hiding a smile. When our gazes met, I smiled, too.

Millie led the group of ladies in a game of Pin the Diaper on the
Baby. We took turns being blindfolded and trying to stick the paper
diaper onto the baby's bare bottom on a poster hanging on a wall.
When it was Maxine's turn, Barbie stood on one side of her and I on
the other. We held her elbows and led her to the board. She promptly
stuck the diaper on the baby's head. The crowd erupted into laughter. Maxine removed her blindfold and started laughing, too.

Suddenly, she stopped, became stone silent for a moment, and
then announced, "I have to pee." She made a rapid escape to the
bathroom.

Barbie and I stepped out of the way of the next player. "I've
never seen my mother drunk before. Come to think of it, I've never
seen her laugh out loud either, especially in public." Barbie was truly
enjoying herself. "I may be prejudiced, but I think she's beautiful."

"She is, especially when she smiles," I said.

Barbie nodded, and I saw a longing in her eyes. "Penny for your thoughts."

"When I was younger, Mother and I had good times together. It wasn't until I became a teenager and had to attend the affairs she thought were important for me to become a lady. Then our time together was always strained because to Mother it was her job to groom me for society. She took her job way too seriously, and I didn't take it seriously enough. Tonight's the first time I've seen her look happy in a long time."

"You do know it's alcohol induced, don't you?"

"Yes, but I'll take it any way I can get it."

Maxine came back into the room. The time to open gifts had arrived, but first I needed a hug from Petey. I squeezed her to me and whispered, "I love you, my dear daughter, and I always will. You bring so much happiness to my heart."

"I love you, too," she said and backed away from me.

Through misty eyes, I saw her smile and shake her head.

"Something wrong?" Barbie had seen my tears.

"I think her hormones are acting up again." Petey announced. "It's going to be okay. Randy promised this would all go away after my little brother gets here." She rubbed my shoulder in a consoling way.

"Of course it will be okay." I didn't want to tell them I was saddened by the possibility some day there could be wedge between me and my daughter like there was between Maxine and Barbie. I wanted my and Petey's bond to last forever, and I would work hard to make sure nothing ever broke it apart.

Opening the gifts of soft blankets, bibs with cute animals on them, rattles, and pacifiers made it all seem real. I was having a baby, and he would be here soon. Mom and Pop's only daughter would give them a grandchild. As I unwrapped each present, Mom took it and gently touched each item. At one point, when Mom looked at me, I knew she was remembering a time when I was a baby.

A reassuring calmness came over me. Instinctively I knew Petey and I would always be close, that breaking a mother-daughter bond was not inevitable. My own mother and I had already proved that. We never had problems too big to overcome. This small town Georgia gal had hit it pretty lucky, and I knew it.

While I opened presents, Maxine had another cup of punch. Granted, they were small, but I knew from past experience they were powerful.

Petey handed me a box. Inside, a necklace lay on a square of white cotton. The gold cursive letters read *World's Greatest Mom.*

"Thank you, sweetheart." I gave Petey a hug. "You are the world's greatest daughter. I couldn't ask for any better." I spoke with a heavy catch in my throat and deep love in my heart.

I gave the necklace to Barbie for her pass around for everyone to see. When she handed it to her mom, Maxine began to sob.

"What's wrong?" Barbie asked.

"This is just so sweet." Maxine swiped the back of her hand across her nose. A tear dropped from her eye onto the cotton in the box. "Oh, no, I've gotten it all wet." She cried harder.

Barbie pried the box from her mom's hand and passed it on. She put her arms around Maxine and held her quietly while she composed herself.

Millie handed her a napkin. "Could I get you something, Maxine?"

"Yes." She blew her nose. "I'd love some more of those Hanky Pankies." Her words slurred. "They were quite *detectable*."

"You mean delectable?" I asked.

"Yes, they were, weren't they?" She leaned back in her chair and passed out cold.

The ladies were busy filling their plates with leftovers to take home with them, so most didn't notice Maxine snoring loudly in the chair.

Luckily, Arch came to collect me, Petey, and our bounty. After loading all my wonderful presents into the trunk, we put Maxine in our car, too, because it was easier to get her in and out. Petey rode home with Barbie, and we followed along behind them.

At the house, Arch pulled into the neighbor's drive. Rick was home waiting for us. He and Arch pulled Maxine out of the car and then were forced to carry her the rest of the way. Barbie ran ahead and turned back the covers on the bed. The men had Maxine's arms around their necks, and they each held a leg. Her head was hanging back, and she continued to snore uninterrupted. Once in bed, I took off her expensive shoes, and Barbie pulled the covers up.

In the living room, our husbands waited to hear what had happened to Barbie's mother.

"I didn't know your mom had a drinking problem," Rick said with a slight smirk.

"She never drinks. That's the problem. Millie and Mavis had a plain and a spiked punch. Mother really liked the spiked one. Do you think she'll be all right?"

"She'll be hung over in the morning, but I'm sure she'll be fine." From my own personal experience, the words *hung over* and *fine* did not belong in the same sentence. They were bitter opposites. But they were the only ones I could come up with to reassure Barbie.

"I've never seen my mom like that before, but I'm sure she had a good time. Don't you think she did, Bertie?"

"Yes, indeedy, I do. When she wakes up in the morning, I hope she'll think it was all worth it." I took Arch's arm and started out the door.

"I just hope she remembers she had a good time," Barbie said with a note of wistfulness her voice.

The next morning, Saturday, Petey went with Arch to run a few errands, and I got to sleep late. Unfortunately, the baby had different ideas, so I was up and showered shortly after they left. I dressed and went into the kitchen. The message light was blinking on the phone. It must have rung while I was in the shower. I listened to Barbie's message.

At least for the time being, she was happy having her mother there with her, and the party the night before had evidently prompted her revelation. Maxine was still sleeping it off, and Barbie had to run into town to get something special for her. She thanked me for being her friend and hung up with a *tootles.*

She made me feel like singing, *if you're happy and you know it, clap your hands.* Someone knocked at the front door, and I clapped all the way there.

Standing on the stoop, not looking too bad after the night she had, Maxine offered a lopsided smile.

"Good morning, Bertie. I hate to impose, but could you possibly give me a ride to the airport?"

"I thought you were staying for at least another week." I motioned for her to come inside.

"I'm afraid I owe you an apology for my deplorable actions last night. I don't know what came over me."

I felt sorry for her. She appeared devastated.

"Good heavens, Maxine. You have nothing to apologize for. Millie is notorious for her spiked punch, and you should have been warned. You appeared to have a good time. And there is nothing wrong with that. You didn't insult anyone or barf, so you've done better than some of the others who where there last night. Barbie is—"

"I know." Maxine held up her hand to stop me. "Barbie must be completely humiliated. She left the house before I got up this morning so she wouldn't have to face me. I can't say that I blame her."

I put my arm around Maxine's shoulder and walked her into the kitchen. "You have it all wrong. Barbie is thrilled to have you here. Listen to this." I pushed the button to replay the message I just listened to.

"Hi, Bertie." Barbie's voice filled the room. "I had the best time at your shower last night. Of course I always have a good time when I'm with you and your friends and family. Thanks for allowing me into your life the way you have, and for making Mom feel welcome, too. I cherish your friendship." She faltered slightly, but then continued. "Mom is still sleeping, but I have an errand to run. There's something special I want to give her when she wakes up. She's going to be here for another week, and I'm looking forward to spending time with her. I feel I've learned a lot about family interaction from you. And I hope Mom and I can experience some of that same relationship. I really want that. Talk to you later. Tootles."

I turned to Maxine who looked a little stunned.

"Does that sound like she's humiliated and wants you to leave?"

"I had no idea she felt that way. My mother died when I was very young, and I was raised by a grandfather who showed no emotion at all. I've always known something was missing from my life, but I wasn't sure what." She took a seat at the table, and I poured her a cup of coffee.

"When Barbara . . . I mean Barbie . . . was born, I was so happy." Maxine's face brightened. "Until she became a teenager, we had wonderful times together laughing and talking. But then it came time to introduce her to going to parties and special dinners and fundraisers."

Her smile faded. "Suddenly everything was work, work, work. No more fun. The more I tried to make her fit in, the more she seemed like the square peg in a round hole. I came to believe she had no social skills or the ability to learn them. Actually, I blamed myself. I surely must be a terrible teacher.

"Whatever the reason, Barbie hated going to big dress-up affairs, and finally I gave up trying to make her. Once she met Rick, things really went downhill. She began acting out in ways that were totally unacceptable in our social circle. I don't believe she realizes I know she did it on purpose. At first I thought she did it simply to embarrass me, but after a while I understood she would settle for nothing less than marrying Rick. Although I felt she was making the biggest mistake, her father and I agreed to let the wedding take place."

"Had you ever allowed Barbie to make decisions on her own

before?"

"Maybe not."

"Then you really had nothing on which to base your opinion she couldn't make a decision like who she wanted to marry. Right?"

"No, I couldn't say for sure it was wrong, but Rick had no means of giving her the things she was accustomed to in her life. I thought she'd miss them. After visiting for these few days, I realize how wrong I was.

"Barbie and Rick were made for each other. You can't be in their presence and not see it. She doesn't have the material things she had with her father and me, but she has what was missing there. She shines with Rick's love, and it makes me very happy to see it." Maxine took a big gulp of coffee and pressed her fingers to her forehead.

"Have you taken anything for that headache?" I asked.

"No, I was in a hurry to pack and get out before I had to face my daughter."

I went to the cabinet and gave her an over-the-counter pain-killer. "I hope you change your mind about leaving. Barbie wants you here, and I think the two of you need to have a long talk. You need to tell her all you just told me. Although I'm glad you told me because I can see things more clearly now, I think Barbie is the one who really needs to hear it from you. There are things she has to say you need to hear, too."

I took her cup from her and pulled her to her feet. "Come on. I'll go with you and help you unpack before Barbie gets back. She never needs to know you planned to leave." I placed my finger over my lips. "Mum's the word."

We hurried across the yard and into the house. We barely started when we heard Barbie's Bug driving up. We scurried around, throwing things back into drawers and into the closet. Maxine slid the last suitcase under the bed, and we were almost to the kitchen when her daughter opened the door.

"Hi." She looked puzzled.

"I just came over to check on your mom. Make sure she was okay," I said.

"Oh, I'm glad you're here." She took her mom's hand and led her to the kitchen table. We all sat.

Barbie handed her mom a small box. I didn't have to see the content to know what it was. Even before Maxine opened it, I had a knot the size of Texas stuck in my throat. I made a sound that could have passed as a dog whimper.

Maxine opened the box, and I was right about my assumption. With shaking fingers, she pulled out a gold necklace with cursive writing which read *World's Greatest Mom.*

It turned out stand-offish, uptight Maxine was sappier than me. She cried her heart out, and I was right there with her. Poor Barbie looked dumbstruck. She didn't know who to console first. So, she just sort of pulled us into a group hug.

We then proceeded to do our imitation of the *Waltons,* but instead of *good night, John Boy,* there was a lot of *I love you* going on. I couldn't take any more. I backed out of the hug.

"You two have so much to talk about. Talk. Talk a lot. Bye." I blubbered my way out the door.

When I got back to my house, Arch and Petey were home. I was still bawling like a baby.

"What's wrong, honey?" Arch asked.

I couldn't say anything. I rushed into his arms and cried against his shoulder. He whispered to Petey, "Go call Randy and see what we do now."

Chapter 16

By the time Monday rolled around, I thought I had come to grips with my over-active emotions and regained my ability to think fast on my feet. Apparently, the theory would be put to a test quicker than I would have liked.

I was at work for less than two hours. I hadn't even had my second cup of coffee and was only half through with my new copy of a parenting magazine. I subscribed to it shortly after I found out I was pregnant because I figured I needed all the help I could get.

While reading an article about what to do when your child talked incessantly, I made a mental note to anonymously send a copy to Booger Bailey. He certainly could benefit from the advice in that department. His son Art talks a mile a—

"Hey, little lady." Booger's voice boomed through the office.

I jumped to attention. Good heavens. Where had he come from? He came into the office, dragging his goat behind him. The one that barks and chases cars like he thinks he's a dog or something.

"Mr. Bailey? I was just thinking about you."

"Well, for crying out loud, don't let my wife hear you say that. One time Mildred Locke called our house to tell me I left my wallet at the Chow Pal Diner, and Icie went ballistic." Booger pulled a blue bandana from his bib-overalls pocket and wiped his brow. "I mean ballistic with capital balls."

Lord, whatever I've done to deserve this, I promise I'll never do it again. Please make Booger go away.

"May I help you with something . . . like maybe leading your goat back outside?" I took the leash from him and walked through the door.

He followed. "Did you ever notice how Mildred walks funny?"

I wanted to ask if he meant the way she lumbers along like Dufus the Saint Bernard from Perkins Park in south Florida, but I thought better of the idea. I certainly didn't want to discuss something of that nature with a man I barely knew. Especially a man with a name like Booger.

Out in the bright sunlight, I tried to hand him the rope back, but he didn't take it. He just continued on talking about his wife.

"Yes, sir. Icie went over there and kicked Mildred in the shin and told her she'd better leave me alone." At that point, Booger cracked himself up. "I tell you that were so funny."

"Yeah, I bet Mildred dies laughing every time she thinks about it." I shoved his goat leash back at him. "I've really got to get back inside."

"Well, wait a minute," Booger said. "I need you to take care of my goat while I go out of town."

I felt like someone had boxed my ears. They rang like someone was playing the Bells of St. Mary in my head.

"What planet did you drop in here from that makes you think I'd do something like that?" My voice literally squeaked. "I don't know you. I don't know anything about taking care of a goat. And if I'm being absolutely honest, I don't even like you or your goat." I think I sprained my vocal cords.

"Well, you have to either goatsit for me or babysit with my boys. Which will it be?"

I had to keep calm for my own baby's sake. I was feeling a little trapped, like I usually do when someone asks me to do something for them, like take them to a doctor's appointment or pick up their dry cleaning. No matter how hard I objected, I always relented. But wait a minute; those were my friends and family. Booger didn't fall in either category. I owed him nothing.

"I won't be a sitter for your goat or your two boys," I said so matter-of-factly it scared me.

"I have three boys. Art, Bart, and Fargo."

"Fargo?" I cringed so hard my eyebrows hurt. "I didn't know about him."

"I didn't either until a few years ago when his mom dropped him on our doorstep. Sure was a good thing she didn't wait around for Icie to get home from the grocery store, because she probably would have kicked her in the shin, too."

I raised my hand. "Stop! Stop this instant. I don't want to know any more about your business. I'm not going to watch your kids or your goat. You have a good day." I turned to run into the office. When I got there, I intended to lock the door and put out the *Closed* sign, but Booger stopped me.

"You certainly can't expect me to take them and the goat with me to the big town of Atlanta. It takes a lot to keep them all corralled."

"I don't mean to seem insensitive, but I . . . don't . . . care . . . about . . . your . . . problem."

"Oh boy, I was hoping to get this settled without Icie's help, but I don't guess I can."

I felt trapped. I couldn't even see my shins for my protruding belly, but I knew they were there, and I didn't want them to be kicked. I don't know what made me do it, but I snatched the rope from Booger's hand. "Give me the freaking goat. What do I feed it?"

From the bed of his pickup, he pulled a big bag of dog food. What else would you feed a goat who thought he was a dog?

"He gets two cups of this each morning and all the garbage he can eat." Booger climbed into his truck.

"What's his name?" I yelled.

"Goat," he called.

"Goat? Why not Dog?"

"I didn't want him to lose all his identity."

I just stood there, watching him drive away, and wondering if my brothers paid Booger to play a joke on me. Naw. Billy and Bobby didn't have the ability to come up with something of that caliber. It had to be the real deal. After all, wasn't I holding a goat on a leash and watching his owner drive away?

But wait. Booger was turning around. The joke was over. He pulled up beside me.

"By the way, don't let him eat any newspaper. The ink gives him the runs."

Booger and his family stopped on their way out of town to drop off the goat's medicine. By then I had my mental faculties back in working order enough to ask how long I would be a goatsitter.

"We'll be back on Tuesday afternoon." Booger handed me a plastic sandwich bag with several very large, brown pills. "Give Goat one of these every morning with his food."

"What are they for?" Curious minds, etc.

He stepped closer to me. "It's for a little condition we don't like to talk about in front of the boys."

All three boys took a step closer, too. My mind ran the gamut of what the condition could be, but with little pitchers having big ears waiting with bated breath, I didn't ask. I probably didn't need to know anyway. I'd give Goat the pill every morning and everything would be fine.

"Okay," I said.

"Be sure you don't forget because Bart and I think what will happen is his nose will grow like Pinocchio's. Huh, Bart?" Art elbowed his brother who shrugged.

"On second thought, don't give it to him. Compile a report on what happens, and I'll read it when I get back." The little twerp gave me a thumbs-up.

I gave him one, too, although I had a different hand motion I thought about using. "Yeah, sure, kid. I'll jump right on that."

Booger herded his little tribe to the truck, and they were off. From my way of thinking, it was none too soon.

Goat and I got along pretty good considering he was a goat. He had a tendency to nibble on the hem of my blouse, but a few whacks on his nose with a newspaper and it wasn't a problem any more. Of course, I had to be careful not to leave the paper lying around where he might eat it. Evidently, he had an allergy to the ink.

I was afraid to let Goat have free run of the storage yard. There were too many places he could slip through the fence, and the last thing I needed was to have to form a posse to go in search of a goat. Or, worse yet, I feared he would chase cars on the busy highway in front of the garage.

Linc and Carrie Sue used some old chain-link fencing Pop had to fix the goat a dog-run. He had plenty of space and a patch of green grass to nibble on. I put Linc in charge of making sure Goat had his meds every morning. I didn't warn Linc by doing so he would be doing his part to keep a mysterious condition at bay, because not only didn't I want to talk about it, I didn't even want to think about it.

Several times a day, I hooked the leash to Goat. He and I went for a walk through the storage yard. Walking was good for me and the baby. It also gave me a chance to examine the fence lines and inventory the cars.

It was hard not to like Goat. He was cute and playful, but every once in a while he stopped and stared at me. He tilted his head from side to side and then give his head a hard shake. His little goatee (oh, that's where that word came from) gave him an air of being highly intelligent. My ability to analyze a goat and come up with these results showed that I wasn't.

After a morning stroll with Goat, I put him back into his pen and removed the leash. When I closed the makeshift gate, I saw a piece of paper skewered to a sharp piece of the fence. I picked it up and read it.

Your boss lady can't protect you forever. Your days as a single man are numbered. Wedding plans are being made right now.

It was signed *Budda*.

I knew that note was not there when I took Goat out. Someone put it there while I was only a few hundred feet from it. I hadn't seen anyone. I looked around, but still saw no one.

Inside the garage, I gave Linc the note. "This came for you. Special delivery."

He took it. While he read it, I slid a chair up behind him because I knew he was going to need it. Linc turned as white as the inside of a turnip and slumped into the awaiting chair.

"What am I going to do, Mrs. Bertie? They're never going to leave me alone."

"I have a feeling you're right. I'm going to call Carl Kelly and see what he advises. I don't like the idea they came on to my property in broad daylight, and I didn't even see them. They're a sneaky bunch."

"They're scary, too." Poor Linc was beside himself with fear. Maybe he had a right to be. The Redneck Mafia had given him and me both things to think about.

We told Carl all the details about the latest invasion by *Budda* and his Redneck Mafia.

"Since he signed his name to that note, it gives us proof he was here, or at the very least is threatening Linc. We're pretty sure those two are the ones who kidnapped Linc those times. I'm going back to the station and get things underway. It's time to put a stop to this."

He went to his car, pulled a package from the back seat, and brought it back to me. "This is from Karen and me. She was coming to your shower the other night, but our little girl was sick."

"Oh, thank you. That's so sweet." I took the beautiful gift wrapped in paper covered with lambs. "I hope your daughter is okay."

"She only had a cold, but Karen was afraid she'd bring the germs to you."

"That's very thoughtful. I'll be sure to send her a thank you note. And thanks to you, too, for anything you can do to give Linc relief from Budda/Bubba."

That afternoon, when it was time for Goat's walk, I insisted Linc go with me. I always heard there was safety in numbers. We hooked the goat to his leash and walked halfway around the perimeter of the yard. Linc held the rope, and I walked ahead right beside Goat. I scratched his back, and he seemed to enjoy it.

We had a building located at the back of the storage yard where we locked up towed vehicles connected to some sort of crime. Since Sweet Meadow was relatively crime free, we seldom had to use the lock-up building for its intended purpose. Pop stored his bass boat in there.

Linc, Goat, and I had walked past the building when Bubba and his little buddy stepped into our path.

"Sorry, ma'am, but Linc has to come with us," the overgrown warthog said.

"No, he doesn't. Do you, Linc?" As I waited for Linc to respond, I heard a grunt and turned in time to see Linc throw down the leash and run for all his worth out of the yard.

"Yeah, that's a good idea," I hollered. "You go call 911, and I'll hold 'em here." Linc had no intention of making a phone call, and I knew it. He was hauling his sorry carcass to the office to lock the doors. I'd probably find him hiding behind a desk. But maybe I could hold off the two men until he got there so they wouldn't catch him.

Suddenly, Goat made a noise that sounded very much like a growl. It grew into a bark, followed by several more. The hair on the ridge of his back bristled. The goat's actions startled Bubba.

He shoved his partner. "Go get Linc, you fool."

The skinny man shook his head and backed away, never taking his eyes off the agitated animal.

"You go get him. I'm leaving," he said.

"I have to do everything myself." Bubba took one step forward.

Goat lunged at him. Somehow I managed to scoop up the end of leash and bring the charging goat to an abrupt halt. Bubba took off at a dead run, following in his partner's footsteps. Goat followed suit. He pulled me behind him, and there was nothing I could do to stop him.

There I was, a couple of weeks from my due date, being pulled at a full run by a goat who thought he was a dog, chasing the Godfather of the Redneck Mafia. The words *Story at eleven* screamed in my head.

Miraculously, Bubba caught up with his assistant. They both headed for a topless car. It had been a hardtop until it went under a semi. The men shinnied over the trunk and jumped into the seats.

Bubba was surprisingly agile for a man his size, but then again fear-induced adrenaline probably had something to do with it.

I dropped the leash, and Bubba turned to watch Goat race at him. The animal climbed onto the trunk a lot faster than the heavy man got up there. The goat placed his paws on Bubba's chest, knocking him down into the seat.

"Help," he screamed like a girl. "How could that beast climb up here that fast?"

By that time, I arrived. I grabbed the leash, but didn't pull Goat back. I needed him to keep Bubba right where he was.

"What do you mean how did he get up there so fast? He's a goat, as in *sure footed as a goat*," I explained.

"Well, get him off me," he bellowed.

"Not until the police get here." I hoped they were on their way. Even if Linc hid under a desk, he'd come to his senses and call Carl eventually. At least I hoped he would. I heard the siren in the distance and knew help was on its way.

Carl, my own personal cavalry, arrived with trumpets blaring. Another deputy arrested Bubba Craig and his partner, whose name turned out to be Scooter Conner. If I were him, I think I'd stick with the name I gave him—Little Buddy.

Despite my objections, Carl insisted the EMTs check my vitals to make sure I was okay. The baby and I were fine. I thanked God I didn't have to go see Dr. Johns because even *he* would not believe this one.

"Bertie, if I was your husband, I'd hogtie you in a closet until after you delivered that baby. What is wrong with you, out here chasing bad guys? Are you nuts?" He held up his hand. "Never mind; I know the answer to that."

"I'm going to look on the bright side. They say walking helps bring on labor; surely running is even better." I rubbed my tummy. All quiet on my western front.

Carl pointed at my very big stomach. "That kid is probably terrified to come out of there. It wonders how it will ever survive with a mother who runs around like she has a death-wish. Go home. Go to bed and wait for the big event before I take you into protective custody."

"Yeah. Yeah. Whatever." Goat and I scurried back to his pen.

When I got home that night, Arch and I decided I should stay home until after the baby was born. Since school was out and would start again in a couple of weeks, we thought it would be a good idea for me to spend the rest of Petey's vacation at home with her. She rotated her time between Mavis and Millie's and sometimes at Mom's. For a few days, Petey stayed with Barbie before her mother came. I said she could spend her days at the shop with me, but the other ladies clamored for her, and Petey loved the attention they showed her.

"They're old, and they need me to help them out. Plus, they're so funny I laugh all day long," was her argument.

"Barbie's not old," I said. "What intrigues you about her?"

"I think I want to be a doctor some day. A psychiatrist maybe. Barbie is a great subject to study. You wouldn't believe some of the things she says and does."

Unfortunately, I knew first hand the things Barbie was capable of saying and doing. Petey had been exposed to enough nuttiness for the summer. Maybe it was a good idea for her to stay home with me until school started again. I felt there was something out of kilter with the rationalization, but I voted against trying to figure it out. Arch agreed. He said it was bigger than both of us.

So, for the next two weeks, Petey and I sat around the house listening to me groan and the carpenters nail and saw our new rooms together. I hoped they finished before the baby came so Arch could paint, and Petey and I could get everything set up. But so far, that hadn't happened.

We had, however, ordered from catalogs things to decorate the nursery whenever it was finished. I picked out borders, sheets, blankets, a lamp and pictures, all in a sports theme. Perfect for a little boy's room.

Petey picked out lambs romping. What was it with the romping lambs? Since I realized I was going to have a baby, I was plagued by those silly things. Granted, they were cute for a baby girl, but we were having a boy, and playful lambs were not going to cut it.

In the end, I vetoed the lambs and went for the baseballs and footballs. Everything arrived, but since the room wasn't ready yet, I left it all in the boxes it came in, stacked neatly in a corner.

School started. I was left alone all through the day, except for the workmen. I cleaned every inch of the house, including all the drawers, closets, and cabinets. Mom said I was nesting and labor shouldn't be too far away.

The baby was three days late, and I was beginning to believe Carl might be right. My son wasn't coming out because he knew

281

the crazy mother he would have. I couldn't take it any more, and had Arch drop me off at the garage. I could pay bills and do things to keep my mind busy. Mom and Pop were next door in case labor should ever decide to come. I wasn't holding my breath. I was sure I would carry the baby for the rest of my natural life.

It was a little after two when Mom and Pop stuck their heads in the door.

"Hi, sweetheart. How ya doing?" my dad asked.

"I'm still here. Still miserable. Still pregnant."

"It'll be over soon," my mother assured me. "We wanted to check on you before we went to the grocery store. You don't think you'll be going into labor before we get back, do you?"

"You could probably cruise to Hawaii and come back and still be safe." I really didn't mean to be sarcastic. "I'm sorry. I'm a little irritable."

Mom came on into the office, gave me a hug and kissed my forehead. "It's all going to be okay. You'll see. Just be patient."

They left and I walked out into the bright, hot sunshine. The heat felt good against my skin, cooled by the air-conditioning. I strolled around the parking lot for a few minutes. Although my back ached with each step, I wanted to stay outside. Trying to ignore the twinge of pain and hoping to simply get comfortable, I walked out into the storage yard.

Linc marked our ID number in the windshield of a red Altima he recently towed. I was only a few yards from him when I felt the gush of water run down my legs. Stunned, I stood there for a moment, but then an excruciating pain shot through my midsection, knocking my breath away. Before I could catch it, the pain came again, stabbing through my back bone. Again through my stomach. It was all happening too fast. I couldn't take a step or scream. The baby was going to be born. Now!

I held tight to my stomach and tried not to slump onto the sand.

"Linc," I yelled. But he couldn't hear me above the chugging of the wrecker's diesel engine.

I had a few seconds of pain-free calm. I started toward him, but was soon stopped by another round of dueling pains. First, my stomach felt like a wrecker was winching my baby out of me. Then my back felt like the bumper of the truck was trying to push it back in.

I let go of the death grip I had on my stomach long enough to wave my arms above my head, hoping to attract Linc's attention. It worked. He saw me.

He climbed into the tow truck and rapidly backed it next to me. He raced around and opened the passenger door. Bless his heart; he was as scared as I was. He tried to lift me into the seat, but couldn't. He got behind me and used his shoulder to shove me upward. I was no help to him at all. There was no way I could climb into the seat.

"Wait a minute," he said. Linc took off in the direction of the garage, leaving me standing there, soaking wet, in horrendous pain, and crying like the baby I was about to have.

"I'm coming," I heard Linc calling to me, but the pain stole my sight. My eyes were squeezed shut and I couldn't open them.

"Help me," I cried.

When he touched me, I managed to get my eyes pried open enough to see the golf cart. Linc helped me onto it. Once I was seated, I slid forward and placed both my feet on the dash.

"Hang on, Mrs. Bertie." He stomped on the pedal. The gas engine revved, my head snapped back, and I screamed at the top of my lungs, "Hurry."

As we neared the gate, Linc laid on the golf cart horn. By the time we got to the parking lot, Carrie Sue was standing at the garage door.

"We're having a baby," Linc told her on our way past.

"Don't let Millie hear you say that, for crying out loud," Carrie Sue managed to say before we hit the highway.

I twisted in my seat as best I could with my feet on the dash, my legs spread, trying to keep the baby from being born on a speeding golf cart. I looked back at Carrie Sue.

"Call Arch," I yelled, and immediately started panting like a dog on a hot summer day. "Please hurry, Linc. I don't think I'm going to make it."

"You have to. I don't know anything about delivering babies unless it has four legs." Linc tried rocking in his seat as if he thought the momentum would help us go faster.

We took the same route to the hospital we had when he knocked me off the golf cart and ran over my foot. The difference this time was I really didn't care about the horns blowing or the people who yelled for us to get off the road as they sped past us. All I cared about was the fact I didn't want to have my baby on the side of the road. I was sure Arch would frown upon that.

We made it to the emergency room entrance with the baby still inside me. From that point, things happened so fast I can barely remember them. I know I was placed on a stretcher and wheeled at a high rate of speed past the reception area. My clothes were taken off me and I was shoved into a hospital gown. It didn't take long to realize it didn't matter if I had one on or not.

Several people snapped on gloves and checked me to see how many centimeters I dilated.

"Eight," one of them announced.

"You have two more to go," another peppy nurse declared.

"What do you mean two more? This baby is coming out now. I can feel it."

The woman smiled and wiped my brow with a damp cloth. "Don't you worry. It's not quite ready, but it won't be long. You're having good, hard contractions, and that's a good sign."

"I need something for the pain. Please."

"We'll give you something to take the edge off as soon as Dr. Johns gets here. He's on his way." She swabbed my mouth with something that looked like a cotton lollipop. It had a pleasant lemon flavor, so I let her do it all she wanted.

More people snapped on gloves and checked me again. Where were all those people coming from? Surely there weren't that many maternity ward personnel. I think the last one might have been the hospital janitor.

The contractions were coming faster and faster with almost no relief between them.

"How much longer before the baby comes?"

"Not much longer now," someone said.

Once I heard someone say having a baby was like having a Buick drive through you. They were so wrong. It was more like a big Hummer.

I was tired and I didn't want to play their game any more. "I've changed my mind. I want to go home. Please get my clothes for me?" I pleaded.

"Too late for that, honey. Just relax."

I tried to get out of bed and pulled a monitor line loose, causing it to beep loudly.

"What have you done now, Bertie?" Dr. Johns came to my bed-side.

While the nurse readjusted the machine and got it to stop its infernal beeping, I grabbed the good doctor by the front of his jacket and pulled him to me. "You know what I've done. Now what are you going to do to get it out of me?"

"You are a trip, Bertie." He freed himself from my clenched fists. "I meant what had you done to cause the machine to sound off?" He turned to a nurse. "How's she doing?"

Just then a major pain hit and at the same time the nurse checked me. "She's ready. The baby is crowning."

I felt like a turkey whose little red thing had popped out to tell the cook it was done roasting. As they wheeled me to the delivery room, I was so happy it was almost over. In a few minutes, the baby would make its entrance into the world. The only thing that would have made it a happier time would have been if Arch was with me.

"Arch, oh my God," I screamed. "Where's my husband? The baby can't be born without him here. Make it stay in there until its daddy gets here." They were running down the corridor pushing my gurney. Sheets flapped in the breeze. "Is anyone listening to me? I can't have this baby until my husband gets here."

They laughed at me. I was not in control of the situation or, for that matter, my body. They rushed me into another room, slid me onto another table, stuck my legs into some kind of straps which held them up and apart. Someone else injected something into an IV line which I didn't even remember getting.

"This'll take the edge off, honey."

Within seconds, I was very relaxed. Things sort of squiggled in front of my eyes.

"Where has that stuff been all my life and can I buy it by the quart?" I asked the lady beside me.

She snickered and rubbed my arm. Dr. Johns came in looking like Zorro behind his mask. Behind was another masked man. I'd know those eyes anywhere.

"Arch," I whispered, and held out my hand.

Chapter 17

*A*rch's beautiful brown eyes sparkled above his mask.

"How ya doing, sweetheart?" His voice sounded like heaven to me.

"Better now you're here." Actually, I was better when they gave me the stuff that made me woozy, but he made me feel pretty darn good, too.

Suddenly, my few moments of tranquility erupted into more chaos. The team on the right was yelling for me to "Push." The team on the left was telling me to "Breathe."

Breathe. Push. Breathe. Push. I couldn't do both at the same time. What was wrong with those people?

My wonderful husband let me squeeze his hand as hard as I could without wincing. What a trooper. He kept his lips close to my ear and whispered, "You're doing good, baby. You're doing good," over and over again. From somewhere under the sheet covering my spread legs, I heard Dr. Johns say, "Almost there."

Before I could ask almost where, a baby screamed at the top of his lungs.

"It's a girl, Bertie," Dr. Johns announced.

I thought I was hearing things. I was supposed to have a boy.

"We got a girl. Isn't that wonderful?" Arch sounded genuinely happy.

A girl? What had they done with my boy the sonogram had said I was supposed to have? "A girl." It sounded really nice.

Petey would be very happy about it. She never wanted a "stinking brother." I would have been happy with either one. As long as it was healthy. By the sound of my new daughter's cries, she at least had a good set of lungs.

Besides the fact the ordeal was over, the best part was our daughter could wear the name Lois Jamie with pride. There was no other way to explain it except . . . Divine Intervention.

Arch cut the umbilical cord, and I got to hold our baby for the first time. As I looked her over, I couldn't believe that, with Arch's help, of course, I had made this tiny, perfect person. She was beautiful.

Daddy rubbed her cheek and then let her cling to his finger. Hers were so tiny wrapped around his. I watched the expression on Arch's face as he stared down at his brand new daughter. He'd given me more happiness than I ever thought possible. I loved him deeply in a way I could never describe.

His gaze shifted to mine, and I thought my heart might stop beating. It was all so overwhelming. As he looked at me, I wondered aloud, "How can I ever repay you for bringing so much happiness into my life?"

His mouth formed the softest, gentlest smile I ever saw. "Just promise you'll always look at me with that light in your eyes."

289

For the rest of the evening and the whole next day, I felt like a queen, especially when I looked at my little princess. Petey was so proud of her little sister she dragged several strangers from the hallway in to take a look at Lois Jamie.

"I picked her name. Mommy was sure it was going to be a boy, but I knew I was going to have a sister," Petey told a grandmotherly lady who made a big fuss over the baby and her big sister. The kindly woman asked if she could hold the baby, and I agreed. Her cooing and gentle tones were repaid by Lois Jamie's ear-splitting cries.

"She has good lungs," the lady said. "Maybe she'll be a singer."

"That's it." Petey started jumping up and down and clapping her hands. "We'll call her LoJ. Almost like a very good singer's name. Maybe she'll be famous someday, too."

An elderly man came to the door. "Are you ready to go, Patty?"

She handed LoJ back to me. "She's beautiful," the woman said, then turned to Petey. "So are you, little lady."

My oldest daughter beamed.

Before Petey invited her in to see the baby, the woman and her husband had been standing in the hallway with several other people. As the woman re-joined her husband, who was evidently hard of hearing, I easily heard her tell him, "Would you believe they are naming that sweet little baby after that hussy who used to live next door to us?"

"Which hussy?" he asked.

"The one who used to leave her bathroom curtains and window

opened while she sang in the shower."

"I remember her. Lorna Jackson."

"That's her. She was such a hussy."

"Yeah." He had a longing in his seventy-plus-year-old voice. "She was good. I liked watching her sing."

They were so cute together. I tried to picture Arch and me at that age.

By then, his hair would have fallen off his head and started growing out of his ears. I would have gray hair and carry a purse that would have to match my purple coveralls because I was sure I'd still be working at my garage. By then the name would be changed to *Bertie and Daughters*.

Millie and Mavis stopped by to check on us. Each took turns holding little LoJ. They were as giddy as school girls. Mavis had adjusted well to life without Wyatt. Neither cared about having papers that said they were divorced, so Mavis gave him an allowance. He lived in a different city and promised not to darken her door again. She once told me she'd have paid him twice what he asked just to be free of him.

Millie appeared to have faired well, too. She wasn't alone in her big house any more, and with Mavis she constantly had irons in the fire. Some of which, I was sure, would eventually give me a heart condition since I was responsible for putting Sweet Meadow's dynamic duo together in the first place. They appeared to be having the time of their lives. Maybe that was what I should concentrate on.

There in my hospital room, the two women examined LoJ and tried to decide who she looked like. It was when Millie said my baby looked a lot like Yunk Yunkoffer that I feigned being tired so they would go on their way. As they hugged me goodbye, I noticed specks of pink paint in Millie's blue-gray hair and green in Mavis'.

"Have you two been painting?" I asked.

"Us?" Millie looked a little shocked. "Oh no, we haven't been painting, have we, Mav?"

"Nope. We gotta go." They ran into each other trying to make their get-away.

I couldn't imagine what they were up to, but one thing for certain, having just given birth, I couldn't stop them. I said a silent prayer that whatever it was, it wouldn't get them, or anyone else, maimed or killed.

Early the next morning, LoJ and I were packed and ready for her daddy to pick us up from the hospital.

"Where's Petey? I thought she'd come with you." I was a little disappointed she hadn't come with Arch.

"She's waiting at home. She said she is a big sister now, and she could surely stay by herself for less than an hour." Arch helped the nurse load a cart with the many bouquets I received, and our other belongings.

The baby and I were wheeled outside. After a little juggling to get everything into the car, we were on our way to our little house on Marblehead Drive. I wished Petey was with us as her sister took her first car trip, but proving she was a responsible young lady was also important.

Our street was lined with cars. Pink helium balloons flew from our mailbox. Sticks with huge mint green, pink, and white bows lined the path leading to the house. A large plastic stork was plastered to the door. People peeked out every window.

"Wake up, LoJ, all your friends and family are here to welcome you home," I said as Arch helped us out of the car.

Inside were more people than I could count.

"We're not going to stay and wear you out," Mom said. "We just had to be here for the big surprise."

"Surprise?" I wobbled a little. "What surprise?"

Petey put her arm around my waist and led me down the hallway to the closed door of our new addition to the house.

"This is why I didn't go to the hospital with Dad," she said. "I had to stay and help them get everything set up." She opened the door and waved her hand like a model showing off a refrigerator on a game show. "What do you think?"

I couldn't believe my eyes. The nursery was completely done. The carpentry finished. The walls painted pale shades of pink and green, just like Millie and Mavis had in their hair. Even though we picked out the furniture with a boy in mind, I was pleased to see how well it worked for our daughter, too.

A brand new rocking chair with a big pink bow sat in the corner.

"Your mom and I got you the rocker." Pop gave me a big hug. "Just think—our little baby has a baby." While Mom hugged me, Pop pulled out his handkerchief and blew his nose. "Must be allergic to all this new baby stuff," he said, and made his way through the crowd.

"Thanks, Mom. I love you. Maybe you better go check on Pop.

She nodded and followed after him.

"Who did all this?" I was awestruck.

"Everyone here did something." Mary Lou took the baby from my arms and Barbie walked me to the rocker.

I sat and took LoJ back.

"It's all so beautiful. I don't know what to say." I choked on my words and tears rolled freely down my face. "Thank you. You're all so special."

Millie held out her hand, and Mavis slapped a twenty-dollar bill in her palm. "Told you she'd cry." Millie giggled and stuck the money in her pocket.

Novalee worked her way into the room. She clicked on the lamp on the chest of drawers next to the rocker. "I got you this."

"Thank you," I said.

"We've got to go," Carrie Sue and Linc called over Arch's head. "Deputy Kelly needs us on Highway 440. He said to tell you and Arch congratulations." She waved and they disappeared. I heard the diesel engine of my tow truck start up and disappear into the distance.

Petey pulled back the blanket from LoJ's face. "Hi, sis. Mavis and Millie took me to Ivey's Department Store so I could return some of the old boys' clothes Mommy got at her shower. I got you some pretty cool baby girl outfits."

She slid the closet door open. Several beautiful dresses hung on tiny hangers.

"They're beautiful, sweetheart. Some day when LoJ is old enough to understand, I'll tell her what a wonderful thing you did the day she came home from the hospital." I looked up at the many faces staring at me. "I'll tell her what all of you did. Thank you so much."

Arch started herding the group down the hallway. After a chorus of *goodbyes,* they all disappeared. Evidently, Petey and Arch walked outside with them because the house was quiet. I could hear the gentle breathing of the prettiest baby girl in the world. Looking around the perfect room, I had to admit I couldn't have done a better job myself.

Warmth covered me. I could feel Pete's presence.

"Your son and I did a good job, didn't we?" I whispered.

The light beside me dimmed slightly. "I think so, too." I hugged LoJ closer.

I looked at all the details so many wonderful people put into my daughter's nursery. The border, the lamp, the coverlet, the sheets, and the pictures were covered with romping lambs. They were the sweetest things I'd ever seen. They made me feel warm and fuzzy, but most of all they let me know that I was loved.

Be sure not to miss Bertie's next adventure:

Dolores J. Wilson

Jail Bertie
and the
Peanut Ladies

Bertie is at it again.

It starts when she wants a traffic light at a dangerous intersection. But because the purchase of an automatic traffic counter would cut into the city council's Christmas party fund, Bertie is forced to count each car personally and present a report. Then Bertie, in her inimitable fashion, gets into it with one of the council members. When he dies of a heart attack, she's accused of causing it. Goaded into running for the now-open position, an unlikely political career is launched.

That's not all.

She finds herself running against Booger Bailey, he of barking goat fame. That's going to be interesting. Who, for instance, is the mysterious donor financing his campaign?

And then there's the two octogenarians who talk Bertie into backing them in a business venture: street vending their boiled peanuts. But what are they really up to?

Seemingly insignificant events once again twist Bertie's life into a series of improbable, and hilarious, misadventures. Because Bertie is off . . . and running.

ISBN# 1-933836-11-3
ISBN# 978-1-933836-11-9
Platinum Imprint
US $24.95 / CDN $33.95
May 2007

Dolores J. Wilson

Dolores J. Wilson's real life is known to be as full of mishaps as her characters'. When she's not writing, she's likely to be cooking up a southern barbeque or creating a theme party for friends and family. She and her husband Richard love to travel in their motor home, where Dolores enjoys one of her favorite past times, visiting and researching historical sites, but she says it's always nice to come back home where she can spend time with her grown children and grandchildren. She is an avid reader, but also enjoys bluegrass music and a multitude of crafts.

Since she and her husband own a body shop and towing service, it was only a matter of time before Bertie Byrd was created. They make their home in Florida, where she's hard at work on the next adventures of Bertie and her gaggle of misfits.

www.doloresjwilson.com

For more information

about other great titles from

Medallion Press, visit

www.medallionpress.com